THE GHOST HUNTER'S DAUGHTER

CAROLINE
FLARITY

This is a work of fiction, and the views expressed herein are the sole responsibility of the author. Likewise, certain characters, places, and incidents are the product of the author's imagination, and any resemblance to actual persons, living or dead, or actual events or locales, is entirely coincidental.

The Ghost Hunter's Daughter
Copyright © 2019 by East Side Press
carolineflarity.com

First paperback edition April 2019

Cover design and interior by ebooklaunch.com

ISBN: 978-0-9968450-0-7

PART ONE

GOBLIN GIRL

CHAPTER ONE

THE KINGDOM OF CRAP

A nna Fagan's mattress shook so lightly it was almost imperceptible. She opened her eyes and groaned. The only thing worse than getting up for school on a Monday was waking up to a Trickster an hour before the alarm went off. Invisible and mischievous, Tricksters were the least dangerous kind of spirit attachment, but annoying as hell.

The spirit board. She forgot to seal it last night after trying to contact her mother's soul. A waste of time as always, but at least she tried, unlike her father. Tomorrow was September 15, the eighth anniversary of her mother's death, an occasion he'd yet to acknowledge.

Anna could get up and perform a closing ritual on the board, recapture the pesky spirit attachment, but her warm bed and grogginess kept her put. Besides, the mattress had quieted down, hopefully for good. But the moment she faded back into her pillow's embrace, the shaking began anew.

"Rock-a-bye baby, on the treetop," she sang, hoping to irritate it, then allowed the faint movement to lull her back to sleep.

Soon the Trickster struck again. A prickling chill pulled Anna back from the crest of slumber. A draft from her bedroom window hit newly exposed skin on her arms. Her comforter was being slowly pulled down, perhaps only a few millimeters per minute. Or had she just shifted slightly? Anna sighed.

Tricksters were masters of subtle manipulation and had endless patience.

Most people had no idea that Tricksters existed, attributing their restless nights, lost keys or missing socks to simple bad luck. Anna was all too familiar with Tricksters and their shenanigans, but they could still make her doubt herself. She yanked the comforter up, kicking her feet in frustration.

"Knock it the frig off," she said.

But acknowledging its presence only encouraged it, and for the next half an hour it fiddled with her hair so gingerly that it felt like a fly walking across her scalp. Finally, Anna snapped her lamp on in a gesture of surrender.

Her bedroom was a bright oasis amid the larger chaos of her father's cluttered house. Calling it *his* house made her feel less responsible for the embarrassing condition of the modest colonial on Eden Street. Her room, however, she took full ownership of, keeping it tidy and organized. The walls were splashed with photo collages of her two best friends, Doreen and Freddy, and her dog, Penelope. A framed picture of Anna's mother, Helen Fagan, sat perfectly centered on the bureau.

Sitting cross-legged in front of her full-length mirror, Anna ran a flat iron through her frizzy brown hair. She did what she could to mask the inch-long section of waxy pink skin extending from her right temple in a jagged line, dabbing on layers of concealer. The scar turned eight years old tomorrow, born the day her mother died.

Anna reached under her bed and pulled out the Ouija Queen spirit board, surely the source of the bratty Trickster. She arranged the board and pointer as she'd found them the night before, cursing herself for not salting them before going to bed. Her father, Jack, would have a conniption if he knew she'd borrowed one of his client's haunted objects, especially one he hadn't cleared.

Jack didn't like spirit board jobs. It was *insane*, he said, that people who'd never sit on a bench next to a creepy stranger had no problem inviting spirits directly into their homes. Spirit attachments were hard to get rid of, as were the boards themselves. The boards often refused to burn and were known to find their way back into homes perfectly intact after being thrown away, buried, tossed over bridges, chopped up or any combination thereof. But the real reason Jack disliked spirit boards was that they occasionally had more than a Trickster or earthbound spirit attached to them. Dumb teenagers or jealous lovers sometimes took ill-advised dips into the deep end of the *dark arts*, invoking something with a board that they'd live (barely) to regret: a demon.

Even Jack Fagan, a veteran paranormal investigator, wasn't sure where demons came from or even what they were—fallen angels, some said, or embittered lesser gods. According to the less religious, they were supernatural creatures borne from hateful human emotions: evil and deadly *thought forms*. Most could agree that demons were powerful, vicious, intelligent and often telepathic entities of nonhuman origin who seek, simply, to destroy.

Anna's father didn't take on demonic cases, referring them out to demonologists. One demon per lifetime was more than enough for him—the demon that had, quite literally, driven his wife to her death.

The Ouija Queen in hand, Anna stepped into the hallway and was assailed by the stagnant smell of dust and mold. With each passing day, the cardboard boxes and broken furniture stacked against the walls swallowed more of the wood floor. Soon the narrow walkway would disappear altogether, and she'd have to clamber over her father's crap to get to the stairs.

Anna lifted a canister of salt from a cup holder nailed to the wall and poured a line of salt on the floor along the perimeter of her bedroom door. She didn't want any other intruders traipsing about in there. After shaking salt on the Ouija Queen, she brought the box close to her mouth.

"I revoke your invitation to enter my private space and bind you to yours."

That should keep the little sucker in check. Standing on her toes, Anna slipped the Ouija Queen back on top of the cluttered shelf that ran the length of the hallway, accidentally nudging a stack of magazines that cascaded over her head along with a cloud of dust. Her fingers found something soft and sticky in her hair. *A freakin' spider web!* Hadn't the Trickster been enough for a Monday? Spider webs in her hair would be just what the kids at school needed to confirm her status as Goblin Girl, the ghost hunter's daughter.

Anna made her way through the ever-narrowing hallway toward the stairs. After tripping over a book last year and bruising her coccyx bone, she now made a point of kicking any riffraff on the steps down to the hoard below.

She stepped off the bottom stair and straight into another path, which had become more of a tunnel as Jack's Crap grew higher on either side. The path made a sharp right at the Mountain of Mail beside the front door and burrowed past the unlivable living room, where towers of dust formed a tenuous skyline in unreachable corners, and mounds of thrift store clothing covered the floor and furniture.

The path led into the kitchen where her father sat hunched in a chair at the kitchen table, holding a piece of mail. It was a bill. She could tell by the protruding vein on his forehead.

Jack was only forty-two, but the gray in his salt-and-pepper hair was clearly winning the spice war. Well over six feet tall, he tended to duck his head even when sitting, as if afraid he'd bang into something. With his hopelessly out-of-date jeans and stained T-shirts, Jack still looked like a plumber, even though he'd changed professions years ago.

"We have to start turning off the lights around here," he said.

"But then it would be too dark." They'd had this conversation before.

"Open the curtains then."

"They are open, Dad. Your *things* are blocking the sunlight."

That's what Anna called Jack's Crap to his face. He didn't like the words *junk*, *clutter*, *hoard*, *pile* or *crap* and especially objected to the term *recyclables*. They were his *things*.

Ignoring her dig, Jack placed the bill back into the envelope. It would be tossed atop the Mountain of Mail in no time.

The kitchen was, aside from Anna's bedroom, the only room not entirely cluttered with Jack's things. He used the kitchen table as his workstation and two of the four chairs were still usable. The floor space in front of the basement door was remarkably clear as well, but the door was padlocked. Jack kept the *dormant objects* down there and had the only key.

Jack became a big deal within the world of paranormal investigators due to his theory that haunted houses were actually homes containing haunted *objects*. Therefore, houses could be free of unwanted supernatural activity by identifying the object and cleansing it of its spirit attachment. He went on to prove this premise in a series of investigations that led to paying clients and, unfortunately for Anna, the attention of the scornful local media. As a kid, she begged her father to let her tag along on his investigations, but now wanted nothing to do with them. Jack had given up on trying to contact her mother's spirit, so she didn't see the point in helping him communicate with randoms.

Someone knocked on the front door.

"Who's here this early?" Jack said. "Take a peek, please."

Freakin' Christ.... Anna made her way back into the foyer and peered through the sliver of window still accessible over the Mountain of Mail.

"It's a blue SUV."

Jack mumbled something obscene under his breath about the BHA.

He no longer opened letters from the Bloomtown Homeowners Association. They were tossed unmolested atop the Mountain of Mail. The blue envelopes stood out due to the blood-red text stamped on each one: "Final Notice!!" The exclamation points were handwritten with a red marker as if someone at the BHA was on the verge of popping a vessel. In the past, Jack always mowed the lawn after a threatening letter or two. But now that the front yard was a full-blown extension of his Kingdom of Crap, mowing the lawn was no longer an option.

Anna had no interest in dealing with whomever Jack was clearly dreading from the BHA. She pushed her way inside the cramped bathroom just off the kitchen to do a last hair check. The tiny bathroom was stuffed with winter coats and boots of varying sizes, the result of the manic "bargain" shopping her father couldn't resist.

Leaning in toward the dusty mirror, something hard poked into her ribs, an old set of skis protruding from a pile of coats stacked on the toilet. Anna elbowed the skis out of the way and refocused on the mirror.

The tip of her nose immediately went numb as her breath hit the glass in an icy fog. A black figure, featureless and human-shaped but impossibly tall and skinny, sprouted from the stack of coats like a mutant weed. It loomed over Anna for a moment, hunched and no-faced, before shooting out of the bathroom, taking the arctic air with it. She stuck her head out the door and watched it lurch up the steps and turn right toward her dad's bedroom. Shadow people popped up occasionally in the Fagan house. Despite their name, they weren't thought to be *human* spirits. They were, however, attracted to spirit activity, and there was plenty of that in Jack's house. Maybe she should warn her dad about his new roomie.

"Dad! There's a shadow person upstairs!"

"Enough with the yelling!" Jack yelled from the kitchen. "We have company. Come say hello!"

Anna made her way, rather begrudgingly, back into the kitchen.

Jack stood by the kitchen table, fake smiling, too wide, too much gum.

"Remember Saul?" he said. "From Bloomtown Realty?"

"Yep. Hi."

If Bloomtown had a town mascot, it was Saul Gleason, a popular real estate broker who looked like he'd jumped out of a Gap ad. Saul had the whitest teeth she'd ever seen. He sat in her chair at the table, wearing a blue blazer atop a polo shirt the color of withered grass.

"Well, look at you," Saul said. "Growing up to be a lovely young woman."

Anna had to squeeze by Saul to get to the refrigerator. He smelled like cologne and toothpaste, pleasant but overly sweet. She searched the fridge for the half-empty can of dog food she'd left there yesterday.

"You two have a visitor upstairs?" Saul asked.

"No biggie," Jack said. "The house may need to be cleansed."

Anna opened the produce drawer, now occupied by a package of tube socks. Damn. Jack made a Costco run. Never a good thing.

"Now that you mention it," Saul said, "this place *could* use some sprucing up."

Someone was confronting Jack about his hoarding? Anna strained to hear every word.

"Not cleaned," Jack said, "*cleansed.* A clearing out of any wayward entities. It's a casualty of the trade. They tend to... collect."

Saul shifted in his chair. "Ghosts?"

"Earthbound spirits, yes, but other things, too." Jack said. "We don't know what some of them are, exactly. It's possible they might bleed through from other dimensions."

Saul cleared his throat. "You know that spooky stuff isn't my thing. But, hey, everyone's gotta make a living. But Jack... the state of *this* property, now that concerns me."

Anna lifted the package of tube socks. Bingo. The dog food. Her beloved beagle wasn't allowed inside these days due to Jack's worsening dog allergies. Further complicating things, Peeps recently birthed a litter. The puppies would be given away once they were old enough. Anna already dreaded it.

"Things may look unorganized," Jack said, "but everything has a purpose, and if I need something I know where to find it."

Like you found Mom? She didn't say it. It was a low blow.

Saul raised an eyebrow. "Moldy newspapers have a purpose?"

"There are articles I may need to reference."

Anna took a jug of water from the fridge. "There's this thing, Dad, a research tool you may not have heard of. It's called the Internet."

Jack pointed a finger at her. "Tone."

"It's a joke, sheesh," she said, grabbing a glass from the cupboard.

Saul cleared his throat again. "I was telling your dad that with new staff he's going to need an office, and a nice little ranch just opened up on Washington Street."

Any appreciation of Saul evaporated in a flash.

"In Bloomtown?" she asked. New staff? New office? It was bad enough having the town weirdo for a father, but now he was *expanding*?

"Saul's getting us the first couple months rent-free," Jack said.

Anna tensed. What did he mean *us?* Her father needed an office because *he'd* crammed the house with junk and was too embarrassed to have clients over. But instead of saying anything, she occupied her mouth by pouring a glass of water and taking a swig. The walls of her throat constricted.

Anna tried to force a swallow just as the shadow person entered the kitchen with a loping stride. It stopped short, crouching behind Saul, who was clueless to its presence. *Oh no.* She couldn't get the water down. The need to breathe took over and Anna spit the water out, spraying both the shadow person and Saul. The shadow person instantly evaporated.

Saul jumped up and closed his blazer, hiding the wet spots.

"I am so sorry!" Anna said, mortified.

"Accidents happen," Saul said evenly, his fingers working the buttons on his blazer.

Anna examined the jug of water, noticing for the first time its telltale green lid. "Why is there *holy water* in the fridge?" She wiped her tongue down with a napkin. "It tastes *weird.*"

Jack used holy water to pry unwilling spirits from the objects they attached themselves to. If a spirit refused to budge, he used it to *bind* them to their object, inhibiting their ability to cause trouble. But even bound spirits were always free to cross into the great mystery of Source. Jack's connection with Source had dwindled considerably, so he could no longer make holy water himself. He now bought it pre-blessed, which was expensive given the volumes he used.

Saul was in a sudden rush to leave. "You two can think about the extra office space. Good to see you, Ms. Fagan."

"Sorry again about the spitting."

Saul flashed his Chiclets at her. "Not a prob."

Jack followed Saul to the front door. Their voices carried from the entranceway.

"Look, I bought you some time from the bank," Saul said. "But we're gonna have to get an inspector in here to get that new office loan approved. Which means you're gonna have to—"

"Clean up," Jack said. "I know. Consider it done." The front door opened and closed.

"Don't start," Jack said, returning to the kitchen.

"This freak show cannot duplicate itself anywhere else in town," Anna said. "It will be the end of me. A social death, and believe me, I'm already in a coma. Don't pull the plug, Dad. I'm begging you."

"With extra office space and another pair of hands, I can take on new clients. So, dial back the drama. And by the way," Jack said, changing subjects, "if you use a client's spirit board again, you're grounded, no phone, no laptop."

How did he know about the Ouija Queen? Did he check every inch of his hoard on a nightly basis? From outside came the toot of a horn. Freddy was there to drive her to school, and he had good timing.

"Got it and gotta go," Anna said, almost tripping over a box of empty mason jars on her way out the back door.

CHAPTER TWO

TWO BLOOMTOWNS

P enelope's doghouse sat in the center of the gated backyard, the roof painted cobalt blue and adorned with a large *P* made of glued yellow rhinestones. Was it cheesy to bedazzle a doghouse? Probably. But why should Peeps have to live in a dump, too? Anna emptied the can of dog food into Penelope's dish and brushed fallen leaves from the doghouse roof before peeking inside.

Penelope lay listless while her two tiny puppies suckled. The beagle had droopy ears and wide-set watery brown eyes that made her look perpetually sad. Anna reached in, making sure the dog saw her hand coming. Penelope had been unpredictable since giving birth. The beagle responded to Anna's ear scratch with lackluster wags of her white-tipped tail.

Only two of the four pups in the litter survived, and from the looks of them, the yappy terrier down the block was the puppy-daddy. Jack planned to get Penelope spayed years ago but never got around to it, too busy growing his hoard and chasing down haunted toasters. But that wasn't entirely fair. Anna could have, *should* have, pushed the issue. They'd both failed Penelope.

Anna got to her feet, suddenly feeling old and tired in her strong sixteen-year-old body. She said good-bye to Penelope and the pups, wincing as a faint throbbing kicked in behind her eyes.

There wasn't time to track down a Tylenol; Freddy waited out front.

Anna picked her way through the side yard. She'd made it outside but had not escaped Jack's hoard. Winding around from the backyard along the side of the house was a massive pile of old newspapers. The papers sat corroding atop an old stack of kindling for the unusable fireplace in the unlivable living room. Along the base of this Great Wall of Crap, scattered in the grass, lay Jack's collection of pipes from his plumbing days.

In the front yard, the claustrophobic din of Jack's Crap gave way to the boring suburban landscape of Bloomtown, New Jersey. The early-fall air was thick with the sounds of sprinklers *whick-whicking* over the neighbors' well-manicured, uppity middle-class lawns. Freddy was parked across the street in Major Tom, the name he'd given to his dad's old Jeep. He spotted Anna and smoothed down his mop of curly brown hair—or as he called it, his jewfro.

"Your dad's car is hemorrhaging again," Freddy said, as Anna got in the passenger seat.

Jack's aging sedan, green except for one rusted beige door, sat in the driveway crammed so full of papers, boxes and trash that only a few swaths of the pleather interior were visible. On either side of the driveway, the overgrown front yard resembled a miniature field of wheat, concealing junk piles hidden in the tall grass. Six months ago, when the doors of the garage began to bulge and crack from the unrelenting pressure, Jack started "temporarily" storing items in the yard—mostly *cleared objects* that his clients didn't want returned, and non-haunted objects that paranoid wackos from across the globe had sent him over the years.

Anna turned the radio on and the deejay's banter dissolved into static.

"We're getting zapped by the sun," Freddy said, "so the signal's scrambled."

"Zapped by the what now?"

"Don't you watch the news?" Freddy asked in his condescending tone. "The earth is getting hit by solar flares. It's when the sun releases a lot of energy at once. Like a massive solar barf."

Freddy wore a T-shirt with a big photo of Neil deGrasse Tyson on the front at least once a week but was still cute enough to annoy the popular girls with his lack of interest. If he hadn't been Anna's friend, Freddy might have joined the ranks of the chosen ones, sashaying down the halls. But he'd always seemed content with her and Dor.

Two blocks down Eden Street, Doreen waited outside her house with her dark blonde hair in a ponytail, the hue of her cheeks accentuated by a red sweater with a tag sticking out in the back. Anna made a mental note to snip it for her later.

Dor got into the back seat and Anna turned to greet her.

"Mornin' sunshine. Do I look okay?"

The question was often on Anna's mind since the situation with Craig Shine was finally getting somewhere. Over the summer, she and Craig shared music and chatted online, and since junior year started a few weeks ago, they'd flirted in the hallways, exchanging a few heat-inducing glances.

"Hot," Dor said, "totally hot. What about me?"

"Super cute." Anna made a sympathetic face. "But your sweat-sucker lines are showing."

Doreen had an issue with excessive armpit sweat. The technical term was primary hyperhidrosis. It was a bummer, but she managed, mainly by wearing prescription antiperspirant and applying menstrual pads to the under sleeves of her shirts.

Doreen pulled at her sweater. "Better?"

Anna gave her the thumbs-up.

They drove on until the potholed roads of Old Bloomtown transitioned to smooth blacktop. "*Whooshh*," they all said in unison, marking the passage. It was a nod to the days, years back, when they'd explored the newly tarred roads from their bikes. Doreen's house used to be the last house on Eden Street, a dead-end, but then the area farmers sold their land to developers. The houses in New Bloomtown were huge bloated things that dwarfed the spindly, hair-plug trees that sprouted from their yards and lined their sidewalks.

New Bloomtown development began five years ago when a convoy of trucks and men arrived, ripping the large old pines from the woods next to Dor's house. Freddy, Dor and Anna rode their bikes through the two hundred acres of newly cleared land, soaring up and down the dozens of dirt hills, their stomachs floating up inside their bodies like they were on a roller coaster. After the McMansions were built, they cruised the new roads, black as ink and smooth as porcelain. *Whooshh.* But that first summer, the sun glared off the large New Bloomtown windows. The black tar roads shimmered in the heat and melted on their wheels. Realty signs were staked into newly seeded lawns, most featuring the tanned face and blinding smile of Saul Gleason. His eyes had seemed to follow them as they rode past, creeping them out.

While Doreen and Freddy discussed the high level of tedium involved in their calculus homework, Anna pulled down the sun visor and fidgeted with her hair. She was minutes away from a possible encounter with Craig Shine. Pink lip gloss couldn't hurt.

Anna made an effort to look *bright* to counteract the perception kids had of her. She once made the mistake of wearing a stylish black trench coat to school, and some jackass spray-painted an upside-down cross and "Satan's Slut" on her locker. She went home early that day and sobbed until her face blew up like a blowfish, and when her dad knocked on her bedroom door she refused to let him in. How could she tell Jack that his chosen profession made her different in a bad way? Freddy and Doreen had crossed out "Satan's Slut" with black magic markers, but the dark splotches remained for weeks until Principal Steuben finally had the janitor paint over it.

Freddy steered Major Tom off Eden Street and traveled down the back road that connected to local Route 33, a two-lane highway packed with stoplights, gas stations, fast food and strip malls in a bland montage of Anytown, America. In the distance a water tower loomed. Huge block letters spelled "BLOOMTOWN" across the giant bulbous tank.

Freddy snickered when he noticed Anna fussing over her hair. "What about me?" he screeched in a horrible impression of a teenage girl. "Am I hot, or *not?*"

"You are beyond hot," Anna said. "You are what hot looks like after a workout, a blowout and a new outfit."

Doreen giggled in the backseat.

"You are hot *after* hot's makeover," Anna continued, "when the audience goes nuts and friends and family cry tears of awe."

"Oh, am I?" Freddy screeched. "Am I *that* hot?"

Anna turned around in her seat. "Take it away, Dor!"

Doreen did her best to compose herself. "Freddy, you are *so* hot," she said. "You are what hot looks like…in a women's magazine—" She was giggling again. Dor could never get to a punch line without laughing. "*After* the Photoshop!"

Freddy turned off Route 33 onto the street leading to the parking lot of Bloomtown High, a large, squat building with one sprawling floor. Right as they were about to turn into the parking lot, Sydney White turned in from the opposite lane. She was driving Mackenzie Donald's BMW—the staple car of New Bloomtown spawn. Mackenzie sat in the passenger seat.

Sydney was the reigning queen of the New Bloomtown set, but she had Old Bloomtown roots. She'd been one of them

17

once, pedaling through the pines. But that was then. Sydney was now the feared ringleader of slut-shaming, whisper campaigns, sudden shunning and other mean-girl shenanigans. She had a feline, slinky grace and features of such otherworldly perfection—poreless skin and Disney-princess green eyes—that she looked almost inhuman. Her clothes wrapped around her like they were grateful, as did her long, highlighted hair that sparkled on the cloudiest of days. Next to her, Mackenzie looked like a gargoyle, but then most people did.

Freddy braked, waving Sydney through. From behind the wheel Sydney shot them her patented dull glare, simultaneously transmitting disdain and utter boredom. Sydney had a special contempt for Dor, Freddy and Anna, but they kept their eyes unfocused and their expressions neutral. Their strategy, as always, was to navigate the waters of Bloomtown High as they would an ocean of sharks, careful not to make too big of a splash. They stuck together to appear larger to predators and thus avoid battle. Any blood spilled could spark a feeding frenzy.

After parking, they walked up the concrete path that bisected the grassy lawn in front of the school. Approaching the large glass entrance doors, a cloud drifted in front of the sun, casting everything in shadow. Anna looked up. From behind the cloud, the sun looked rather meek, nothing but a circle in the sky. Whatever these solar flares were, they weren't visible.

First period bell rang and the trio parted. Anna hurried through the commons area, her footsteps silent on the trampled blue carpet. The dreary carpet extended into the cafeteria and beyond to the rows of yellow lockers along the back hallway.

At her locker Anna looked discreetly for Craig, but he wasn't around. Probably slept in again. Craig was the lead singer and guitarist for the Manarchists, a hardcore band with lyrics like "Screw you, screw it, screw me, I wanna screw you!" Not exactly Romeo and Juliet set to music, but Anna kind of liked that his band bit the big one. It made him more attainable, less like an untouchable Greek god. Yes, he was *that* hot.

• • •

The school day was uneventful until last-period biology. The teacher, Mr. Denton, turned on the flat-screen TV in front of the blackboard.

"Everybody know what this is?" he asked, pointing at the screen. An image of a churning ball of fire filled the monitor. "The sun," he said. "The star in the center of our solar system that will eventually incinerate us all. As your parents have undoubtedly mentioned to some of you, it brought you into the world…and it can take you out."

There was a pause as Denton waited for a reaction. From the back of the room Izzy Lopowitz issued a sarcastic "har, har, har," which was followed by a spattering of genuine laughter in the room. Bald and long-jowled, Denton always tried *so* hard to impress the popular kids, but Anna had empathy for him. Every afternoon he arrived with a piece of science news called The Big News of the Day. He cared, and it made the class more interesting.

Anna took out her phone and snuck a peek at Craig's Instagram while Denton took attendance. There he was, posed with his guitar and wearing jeans that sagged at his hips to reveal boxers adorned with the UK flag.

Tall and lean, Craig had dark eyes and thick black hair that was half-spiked in a careless, entirely sexy way. One day, if she had the balls and the opportunity, she would get to kiss those lips. But the question of the moment was *where?* In the back of an empty dark classroom? No. Down at the Shore. The best part of living in southern New Jersey. They could go for a night swim and allow the black waves to rise over them, temporarily erasing the stars. He'd draw her to him, brushing his salty wet lips against hers as her fingers found the nook of his collarbone…

Something light bounced off the back of Anna's head and fell to the floor, ending her fantasy: a small piece of notebook paper crumpled into a soggy ball. She turned around, knowing that the two people immature enough to throw a spitball sat in the back row: Izzy Lopowitz and Frank Mafay. They usually spent class gawking at some depravity or another on their phones, but their Neanderthal brains now focused on her.

Anna glared at them, mouthing the words *grow up*. Frank's hand was cupped in front of his face, muffling his wheezy, high-pitched giggling. Next to him Izzy pretended to take notes with one hand, using the other to casually point his cell phone at Anna. She heard a faint click and turned back around, squeezing the pen in her hand. *Damn it*. Izzy took her picture. He'd probably use it for something ridiculous and cruel, like pasting her head onto images of naked women. He'd done it before to other girls, posting the manipulated pictures online. One of the girls, a quiet sophomore, left school for good after swallowing a bottle of sedatives. A few vultures left comments on her Facebook page saying they were sorry she didn't finish the job.

Both Izzy and Frank were "porn-heads," a group of kids whose worldview was shaped by the extreme smut they spent their time watching, sharing and discussing online. Frank was Izzy's crude and stupid sidekick, a big goon with short arms, a stocky build and saggy dog eyes. He was always smelling his fingers, either doing it quick, like he thought no one could see, or absently, with a dazed look on his face.

Izzy was the more intimidating of the two because he fancied himself as a brooding tough guy—even though he lived a comfy suburban life and didn't have to work. Izzy's older brother was in jail for possession of marijuana with intent to distribute in a school zone. He got a harsh sentence, seven years, and everyone in Bloomtown knew about it. Ever since, his devastated parents let Izzy do whatever he wanted.

And right now—another soggy wad whizzed past her head—Izzy wanted to launch spitballs at Goblin Girl. She ignored him. *Don't feed the trolls.*

"Okay, kids, listen up! The Big News of the Day is not just big, it's *epic*," Denton said, as the animated sun on the TV cast a glow on his hairless head.

Groan. Anna began scrolling through her recent texts.

"As of this morning, we are being hit with the largest solar storms in many a decade. Solar flares shoot all kinds of stuff into the atmosphere. Electrons! Ions! X-ray radiation!" Denton paused. Nobody cared.

"Do we know what solar flares are, Ms. Fagan? We don't have our phone out, do we?"

Anna slipped her phone up her sleeve. "No on both counts," she said.

"Good! I wouldn't want to have to confiscate it and deny you your God-given right to take a hundred selfies before bedtime."

Har, har, har. Denton went on about the solar flares for a while and then handed out a quiz, reminding Anna that she should have spent the morning studying instead of obsessing over her scar.

CHAPTER THREE

THE ANNIVERSARY

That night, Anna dreamed she was floating on the ceiling and looking down at herself. The moment she screamed she woke up in her bed, her heart thumping. But something was wrong, something was *missing*. Her mother's picture wasn't on the bureau. There was a clattering sound, persistent and loud, coming from the floor underneath her mattress.

Trembling, Anna got down on the rug and looked under her bed. Her mother's picture was banging up and down on the floorboards. This was far too aggressive to be the work of a Trickster. Something else had gotten into her room. Anna reached her hand under the bed, petrified, but wanting the noise to stop. As soon as her fingers touched the edge of the wooden picture frame, a frame carved and sanded by her mother's hands, something cold and sharp—a *claw*—grabbed the nape of her neck. Before she could scream, Anna jolted awake, back in her bed.

It took a while to convince herself that she was awake this time. Eventually her heartbeat slowed. The photo remained on the bureau. Her breath deepened and she fell back to sleep.

When the alarm went off a few hours later, for a moment the world seemed light and full of potential. Slivers of sunlight snuck through the curtains and cast a cheerful hue on the lilac of her walls. But then a dread descended over her and she remembered. It was the anniversary of her mother's death.

Jack wasn't downstairs, and she didn't knock on his bedroom door to say good-bye. He probably had a rough night, too. He was always withdrawn on the anniversary, either shuffling around the house avoiding Anna or holed up in the basement, fussing with the haunted objects.

Stepping outside was like walking into an oven. It was at least eighty degrees and almost tropical with humidity. Up and down Eden Street, rows of sodden pine trees sagged under the sun's glare.

Freddy and Major Tom were nowhere in sight. Anna checked her watch: 7:39. Freddy was late. That wasn't like him. After waiting another ten minutes, Anna decided that she'd rather ask Doreen's mom for a ride than sit in strained silence in her dad's sedan while he avoided the subject of the anniversary. Anna was about to cross the street when the yellow elementary school bus came into view, chugging up Eden Street. She squinted to see if Old Lady Minx sat behind the wheel, aka Shady M.

Shady M was infamous to Bloomtown schoolchildren, partly due to the large mole on her left cheek that sported a crop of long, dark hairs that curled at the end like a villain's mustache. Hairs, Anna always thought, that she could easily just tweeze. Known and despised for her strict "load 'em and leave 'em" policy, Shady M would ignore the slightly tardy kids running toward the bus stop, pulling away as if she didn't see them. Anna had firsthand knowledge, maybe more than any kid in Bloomtown, that Shady M showed no mercy. In a way Shady M had contributed to the death of Anna's mother.

Filled with a sudden dumb horror, Anna's body went into autopilot and she felt her legs stepping off the curb. There was a glimpse of Shady M driving the bus, grim and focused, followed by a yellow and black blur and a sickening wind that blew Anna back to the final morning of her mother's life.

Anna was eight years old and hoping it was one of Mommy's good days when she walked down the second-floor hallway, clutching her favorite hair band. The hallway was hoard-free and sunlight filled the house. She poked her head into her parents' bedroom.

"Mom?"

Helen Fagan didn't answer. She was huddled under a blanket, facing the wall. Anna approached the bed, her hand hovering over her mother's swaddled figure, wanting to touch her but knowing to be afraid. She registered the rapid rise and fall of her mother's bedding and heard her faint but fevered whimpering. Feeling light-headed, Anna snatched her hand back—it was one of Mommy's *bad* days.

Anna backed out of the room, picking up one of her mother's barrettes from the vanity, the one shaped like a butterfly that she wasn't supposed to play with because it was expensive and had sharp bits. She was being bad, but Mommy was sick again and it wasn't *fair*. She secured the barrette around a section of hair behind her right ear and then walked down the stairs.

In the kitchen her father poured cereal into a bowl. "Bloomtown Plumbing—The Drain Whisperers!" was stitched on the back of his overalls.

Anna handed him her hairband. "Can you gimme a French braid?"

Jack admired the butterfly barrette in her hair: two pairs of ornate silver and peach malachite wings curving upwards to sterling silver tips. "Very pretty."

"It's Mommy's." Her mother had loved butterflies.

Anna squirmed as her father's large hands fumbled through her hair. He was doing it wrong, starting too low on her neck. Jack didn't know about braids, or barrettes that were for *looking not touching*.

"That's not how Mommy does it! It's a *French* braid, not a regular one." She wished she hadn't said it because now his face looked old.

Jack walked her to the back door and helped her get her backpack on.

"Okay, kiddo, gotta go to work. You're going to Doreen's after school. I'll pick you up after dinner."

"Can't Dor come over here? We wanna play with Peeps."

"Not today. Mommy's sick."

Anna sulked. "She's always sick."

Jack bent down for a hug before leaving. Penelope's small form scampered into the kitchen and greeted Anna with a flurry of paws, licks and hungry whines. Jack forgot to feed her! Anna poured puppy food into a dish and filled the water bowl from the faucet. Watching Peeps gobble up her food, Anna couldn't resist petting her for a minute. She giggled as the puppy's head whipsawed wildly between the bowl and Anna's hand. It was a minute too long. From outside came the heavy rumble of the school bus. Anna grabbed her backpack and bolted out the front door and into the street, making eye contact with Shady M in the bus's giant side mirror. She was fast, but Shady M was faster. The bus grew smaller and then disappeared around a bend. Out of breath, Anna looked back toward her house. There was no place else to go.

Her legs wobbled all the way up the stairs.

"I missed the bus," she said, stepping into her parents' bedroom. "Can you drive me?"

There was a long silence as the sour smell of sweat and sickness settled over her. But her mother wasn't in the bed. Helen was crouched atop the ceiling fan above the bed, baring her teeth at Anna, her ribs protruding through the fabric of her sweat and tear-stained nightgown. Locked in fear, Anna's legs refused to budge. Helen dropped down onto the bed with a light *thump*.

"So many questions for such a little maggot," Helen said, and Anna felt her knees clack together like magnets. Mommy wasn't herself again. Mommy was *sick*. Helen slithered off the bed. "I can give you knowledge, child. Do you want knowledge?"

Anna tried to swallow the terror in her throat, but her words came out reedy and shrill. "The bus left without me."

Minutes later, Anna sat strapped into the front seat of her mom's blue Volkswagen Jetta. Daddy would be mad that "sick Mommy" was driving her to school. Anna's stomach hurt and the seat belt made it worse. The thing inside her mother had grinned at her from the driver's seat, its yellow teeth, slick with saliva, shining in the harsh morning sun.

Anna stood on the street, breathing hard and blinking in the glare. Her shaky hand touched her forehead, wet with sweat. She tried to slough the horrible memory off like a bird shaking out its feathers, tried to think about good things so she wouldn't cry. There was Craig and the possibility of kissing him one day. There was a future, away from Bloomtown and Jack's Crap, where no one knew about her parents and no one called her Goblin Girl. Tears welled up but Anna swallowed hard, pushing them back down. Forget going to Dor's, she'd walk the two miles to school. She wanted to be alone.

• • •

When Anna made it inside the blissfully cool hallways of Bloomtown High, the bell marking the end of first period was ringing. Great, now she'd have to ask Jack to write some bullshit note excusing her absence. Feeling sweaty and gross, she rushed to her locker hoping that she wouldn't see Craig.

Freddy was waiting for her, wearing a NASA sweatshirt and a guilty grin.

"Where were you?" Anna asked. "I missed first period."

"Me too. My phone alarm didn't go off. The satellites are getting fried by the flares. The radiation bursts must be as potent as cosmic rays up there."

"Cosmic rays?"

"Pinpoints of high-energy radiation that can zap right through an astronaut's helmet and skull like they're not even there."

Freddy grabbed Doreen's hand as she snuck up behind him and playfully poked him in the ribs.

"So, ladies, space gaze tonight?" Freddy asked. "The aurora borealis may be visible because of the solar storms. Hasn't happened around here, in like, a hundred years."

"Sounds pervy," Doreen said.

Anna pulled open her locker and inspected her shiny face in the mirror she'd taped to the locker's back wall. The scar on her face had swollen to an angry red, and she quickly blotted it down with several layers of powder.

"No, you dirty-minded fiend," Freddy said. "It's charged particles from the sun reacting with gases in our atmosphere. You know, the northern lights? It's gonna be a clear night. No clouds means good visibility."

Inside Anna, irritation flared along with a dim headache. "Don't you think we're getting a little old to sit around staring slack-jawed at a bunch of stars?"

Freddy looked stung.

"They're not all stars," he said. "Some of them are distant galaxies, and who peed on your pop tarts?"

"I wonder if when aliens die, they become, like, alien ghosts," Doreen said.

"Yeah, and they need ghost hunters like Mr. Fagan," Freddy said.

Her father was the last thing Anna wanted to discuss. "Who cares?" It came out sharp and mean. Doreen wilted like a thirsty tulip.

"We do. You do," Freddy said, annoyed. He was protective of Doreen. Anna was, too, normally. "At least you used to."

"I used to be a lot of things."

"The anniversary," Doreen said quietly.

Anna flushed. Of course they knew. They were mourning, too. They had their own memories of Anna's mother, when Helen Fagan still danced around the house with Jack after a glass of wine. The summer that New Bloomtown started construction and they lost their bike trails, Helen had surprised all three of them with the to-die-for water guns of the moment. There were the rainy weekends that she made them peanut butter and jellies by the mound, quartered with the crusts cut off, and let them play video games all day.

Helen Fagan came from a snooty family in upstate New York who hadn't wanted her to marry Jack—"the plumber," as Anna's grandparents still called him—but she detested snobbery of any kind. Before the demon, Helen truly enjoyed her life, so she didn't have the need to make other people feel badly about theirs. She studied art and design in college and became a woodworker, making custom furniture for private collectors.

Anna's favorite memories were of the walks she took with her mom in the nature preserves of Ocean County. Helen liked to teach Anna about the tree species native to southern New Jersey. They tried to scare each other with gruesome tales of the infamous Jersey Devil, a deformed half-beast, half-man that was said to haunt the wild and desolate Pine Barrens. But while hiking through the thorny forest, pretending to be frightened by the slightest rustling of brush, they knew they were safe, that no evil bogeyman was really hunting them down. How wrong they were.

A swell of anger rose from Anna's core—but then she saw Craig Shine walking toward her.

Anna squeezed Freddy's wrist. "Pretend we're talking."

"We are talking," Freddy said.

Doreen gave Freddy a pitying look and escaped down the hall just as Craig reached his locker. He nodded at Freddy, giving Anna a brief, private smile.

Craig opened his locker, resting one hand on top of the metal door. He wore ear buds with one bud in and the other hanging down the front of his shirt. A detail that struck Anna as unbearably sexy. A string from one of the buttons on the wrist of his flannel shirt was coming loose, and she had an urge to reach out and tug on it.

Craig leaned toward her, the nearness of him making her face even warmer. For one nerve-jangling moment she thought he might kiss her, but instead he whispered in her ear, "Cut a new track last night."

He pulled back, reached into his locker for a book, then turned to look at her. His dark eyes made the noise and bustle of the hallway retreat to a blurred hush.

"And are you going to share this mysterious new track?" she asked.

Craig took his hand off the locker and placed it on her back, whispering in her ear, "Well, that depends, Fagan. Do you *want* me to share it with you?" He trailed his hand down her back, a rush of heat chasing the path of his fingers. "Ask me nicely," he said. The hair on her neck fluttered under his breath as her heart ignited in her chest.

Calm down, she told herself. *Above all, say nothing stupid.*

Freddy leaned against a nearby locker, pretending to be engrossed with his phone. He looked up at her with a pained expression. Freddy thought Craig was a simpleton with subpar musical talents. But Craig had a deep side. "I like to turn up the music so loud that it's impossible to think," he'd told her one night in August at a beach party where a bunch of them had gathered to mourn the end of summer. And that was sort of deep, wasn't it?

As if Freddy's death glare wasn't enough to ruin the moment, Izzy Lopowitz and Frank Mafay approached, no doubt trying to score popularity points by being seen in the vicinity of Craig Shine.

"Sup, Craig?" Izzy said, scanning Anna's body. "You hanging with the witch girl? Her daddy traps goblins and shit."

Frank emitted a rapid-fire spray of girlish laughter, getting a quick finger sniff off before fist-bumping Izzy.

"Let's go," Freddy said, placing his hand on Anna's arm. He was trying to get her out of the situation, but she gently shrugged him off. Izzy wasn't going to ruin the few moments she'd have all day with Craig.

"Girls always stick together," Izzy said, jabbing his index finger in the middle of the blue circle on Freddy's NASA sweatshirt. "Do you two go pee together, too?"

"Yeah," Frank said, getting in Freddy's face. "You need a tampon, gay boy?"

To toast that stroke of comic brilliance, Izzy and Frank fist bumped again and continued their swagger down the hall. Anna rolled her eyes at Freddy but he declined to give her a roll back, mouthing "later" and leaving for class. Izzy would have Freddy in his crosshairs now, and it was her fault. She'd make it up to Freddy later. What mattered now was Craig. But he had a strange look in his eye.

"That's some crazy shit about your dad. You into that stuff?" Craig asked, running a hand through his gelled hair.

"Not even remotely," Anna said. And it was true, mostly.

The bell rang.

"See ya, Fagan," Craig said flatly before walking off.

Great. He was totally turned off now, probably crossing her name off as any kind of possibility. Annoyed, Anna rummaged through her locker looking for a book. The second-period bell rang and she cringed as the clanging sound continued to vibrate between her ears.

Perfect. Not only was she late, but her ears were ringing. It was probably a brain tumor with her luck.

Heat shot down the back of her neck. Izzy was back, and way too close. His breath reeked of cigarettes and chocolate milk.

"You're kinda hot, Goblin Girl," he said. "You like getting scared? I got something that'll make you scream."

Disgusted, Anna slammed her locker shut, but Izzy blocked her way. His curdled breath surrounded her in a fog.

"Do you mind?" She gestured for him to move. "Your stench offends."

Izzy's smirk faded. "I'm saying I like you. I want to get with you."

It was shocking how much she wanted to *hurt* him. Her fingers curled into fists as she stifled the urge to punch him in the face.

"The scariest thing ever?" she said. "Your face."

Izzy, not sure what to do, grabbed his crotch. "You'd be lucky to get on this."

It was laughable, but Anna didn't laugh. Adrenaline was coursing through her, which was weird because she didn't normally let Izzy get to her. She broke past him and took a few steps before turning and flipping him the double bird.

She didn't have to see Izzy again until Denton's last-period biology class. Mr. Denton was droning on, oblivious to the large black pepper stuck between his front teeth. He had an angry rash of broken capillaries around his nose, made more garish under the fluorescent lights of the classroom. The harsh lights buzzed in her ears and bathed the classroom with an unforgiving glare, revealing every clogged pore and dandruff flake and all the dusty chalk smears on the blackboard behind Denton's desk.

The big news of the day was the Invasion of the Zombie Bees. The flat-screen TV, rolled out in front of the blackboard, was broadcasting night-vision footage of bloated bees, jerking erratically through the air. The bees, Denton explained, had been attacked by a parasitic fly that had injected its eggs into their bodies. The fly larva inside them somehow overpowered the worker bees' basic instincts, resulting in previously unseen behavior like night flying and the abandonment of their hives.

Anna rubbed her temples. Another headache.

"What do you think, Ms. Fagan?"

Denton looked down at her.

"About what?"

"I see you're not paying attention once again. Maybe that's why you failed your quiz yesterday?" Denton held up her quiz in front of the class. A large "57" was written in red at the top and underlined. Next to it Denton had written "Really??" in extra-large print.

Anna might have laughed it off if Izzy hadn't opened his mouth.

"Really, Fagan, a fifty-seven?" Izzy yelled from the back of the room.

A few kids snickered and Denton blushed with pleasure as he told the class to settle down. He was the type of teacher that treated his vulnerable students with subtle contempt, all in a bid for "cool points"—but this was extreme, even for Denton. Anna normally felt vaguely sorry for him, but now a visceral loathing exploded in a starburst behind her eyes and reignited the painful ringing in her ears.

"Is this part of your job description, Mr. Denton?" Anna asked.

The room froze in a collective silence. This wasn't the way Goblin Girl acted. Goblin Girl normally sat there and took it. Anything to keep the attention off her.

"Excuse me, Miss Fagan? I suggest you watch your mouth or—"

"It's a simple question," Anna continued. "Is sharing a student's grade with the rest of the class a part of your job or not?"

"I'll send you to Steuben's office," Denton said, the top of his bald head turning red.

"Great. I can ask him."

The class snickered, not at her now, but at Denton. Anna knew better than to get on the bad side of a teacher. She was surprised she had the guts to take him on. *Guts, or stupidity?* a voice inside her asked, but she ignored it.

"Everyone get back to work and keep it zipped," Denton said. It was over, for now.

When the bell rang, Anna found herself walking slowly past Denton's desk. She met his eyes straight on, and he was the first to look away.

Izzy approached her in the hallway. "Yo, G-girl, didn't know you were such a badass." Anna kept walking, but Izzy kept moving his lips.

"The ass ain't bad, actually. I'd like to crack that nut."

She didn't bother to flip him off. "Get some help," she said, already thinking about going home, where she could be alone in her room and mourn her mother's death in peace.

CHAPTER FOUR

SOURCE

There was a realm not of matter and form, but of spirit, from which the universe, and possibly countless others, had sprung. Jack called it "Source." Anna wanted to believe that Helen Fagan had crossed into Source, that she was free, that she was safe, but then why had her spirit remained elusive? When Anna felt hopeless—as she did today—she tortured herself with thoughts of her mother's spirit trapped in some sort of monstrous hell dimension, enslaved by the demon that murdered her. Jack had tried for years to contact Helen, hiring mediums and psychics and using his own connection to Source to try to communicate with her. He'd begged for any sign from her, but the phone lines were silent. One day he just gave up, and Jack's connection to Source grew weaker from then on.

Anna was with her dad the night he first encountered Source. She was ten years old and nodding off on a plaid loveseat in the living room of a haunted cabin in the Pocono Mountains. Jack dozed nearby in a recliner. Back then he'd taken Anna on many of his investigations. There wasn't money for a babysitter, and he didn't want her to wear out her welcome at either Freddy's or Dor's house.

That night Anna was on the edge of sleep, where perception floats unencumbered and the veil between the worlds can thin. As her eyes fluttered shut, a basketball-sized orb of light appeared in the center of the room, illuminating a poker hanging on a hook attached to the brick fireplace. A wispy mist, feminine in form, twisted around the poker like a tiny tornado.

As bizarre as seeing the spirit was, Anna's young eyes were drawn back to the orb of light. The light had a *belonging* quality that was somehow more credible than the room itself. It was like the living room had been reduced to a drab painting on a window shade, and the fabric of that shade was torn, allowing a ball of brilliant sunlight in. Anna stared at the light, transfixed. The light expanded and blissful warmth spread throughout her small body. Then, somehow, *Anna* expanded.

There were no longer any boundaries between Anna's consciousness and the wispy feminine spirit. Anna felt its desperate need to cling to the antique poker. She knew, as if the memories were her own, that the spirit was a girl named Mary who was forced to marry at thirteen. Mary had taken many beatings from her much older husband in their cramped hovel. She became pregnant, but her body was too small to deliver the child. The baby died and Mary barely survived, only to be attacked again by her husband before her wounds could heal. Anna was flooded with dark images and sensations—violations of the tortured girl's body and soul that Anna's young mind could not understand.

One night, after another attack, Mary-the-child-bride could take no more. Her husband passed out drunk on the floor, and she found the courage to beat him to death with a poker. When her husband's body was found, Mary was arrested and shackled in the town square. For three days villagers spit on her. Little kids poked her with sharp sticks. In a jail cell, waiting to be hanged, Mary died of her infected wounds, her soul rising from her body like seeds off a dandelion. When the light came for her, Mary was confused, ashamed, and terrified of further torture. She resisted it. Instead of crossing into Source, Mary's spirit had returned to the poker—the one thing that had given her safety, power, and justice, however temporary.

With Anna bearing witness, the light of Source had now returned to claim Mary once again.

"Go," Anna said.

The girl's spirit stopped spinning, curling tight around the poker. Details of the misty figure emerged: her dress was a quilt of crudely sewn rags, her long black hair snaked around her head in matted knots. But it was Mary's face that made Anna want to turn away. Mary's left eye was swollen shut, protruding from her broken eye socket like a bruised and rotting apple. Her nose was a crushed, boneless mass that hung under her right eye, an eye that peered at Anna with shock and suspicion.

"Anna. Shhhh," Jack said from the recliner, awake and sitting up.

The light of Source flared, fully illuminating the room. Mary turned toward it, and Anna saw the girl's spirit as the light saw her: beautiful despite her battered face, innocent and wholly loved. Mary's spirit drifted toward the light and then shot straight into it like an arrow. It was then that the vibrations began. Anna's teeth rattled and her body trembled as the overwhelming *want* to follow Mary's spirit into that light encompassed her. Anna had never wanted anything so passionately, but the light disappeared.

This first encounter with Source left Jack with the gift of discernment, the ability to sense spirits, and from that day forward he could "sniff out" contaminated objects without any special instruments. It also left him with another lucrative gift, the ability to make holy water. But over time that ability had slowly weakened and finally evaporated. Jack now bought holy water on the open market, an expense that was eroding his already slim profit margins.

When Anna got home—still unsettled from her encounter with Denton—Jack was at the kitchen table, scrolling through emails on his phone. He rubbed his red eyes.

"How was school?"

"Swell," Anna said, almost tripping over a pile of books. There were more books, yellowed paperbacks, occupying her chair. Jack had been to the thrift store and the kitchen was apparently no longer a hoard-free zone. Anna was disappointed but not surprised. She spotted a pile of identical copies of a two-year-old issue of *Paranormal Times*. On the cover, a picture of her father smiled up at her above the caption "Plumber to Prodigy," his salt-and-pepper hair and permanent five-o'clock shadow eerily lit for effect. The corners of the pages were curled up like dead rose petals.

"That magical Internet thing you told me about sure came in handy," he said. "I'm hearing from a lot of impressive job applicants."

Anna's shoulders ached. She wanted to say that she didn't give a flying frig about Jack's new assistant. There was nowhere now to drop her backpack, and suddenly the weight of it seemed too heavy to bear. It was like a chain around her shoulders, trapping her in place to await the inevitable homicidal avalanche of Jack's Crap.

"One in particular really stands out," Jack said, handing her a sheet of paper. Anna scanned the information at the top: Geneva Sanders, University of California, Berkeley, PhD in Electrical Engineering, 2012.

"If this Geneva Sanders is so smart," Anna said, offering it back to Jack, "why does she want to work with you for *free*."

"Oh, she's not only smart," Jack said, "she's an inventor, and if what she says is true, her latest invention could be a game changer, not just for the field of paranormal investigation, but for us. We could open the new office with a heck of a lot of buzz."

Buzz. Anna knew what that meant. Stories about Jack's business in the newspaper, Jack parading around on the local news. In short, more public humiliation. Everyone at school would be snickering about it. *Craig* would hear about it. Dor and

Freddy would face consequences too, just for being her friends. Not that they ever complained—hell, they were used to it by now—but Anna knew it had to get to them.

"You're going through with this office thing?" Anna said. "You deal with it. I have my own problems."

She started to walk off, but Jack put a hand on her shoulder. "What problems?"

His hand on her backpack strap sent a bolt of pain up her neck and into her head. He wanted her to carry his burden, too, and it was too much.

"It's nothing I want to talk to you about, okay?"

"Well, who do you want to talk to?"

Bitter tears welled in her eyes before she could stop them.

"I know it's a tough day," Jack said softly, "but you should be grateful your mother crossed over and isn't earthbound."

Anger flared like a struck match. "You don't know that. You only know that *you* haven't been able to contact her."

The hand remained, a lead glove.

"We have to accept that we don't have all the answers. That's part of life."

"Maybe you've given up on her, but I haven't."

Anna went outside to feed Penelope, who lumbered over to her dish with her tail low. One of the puppies stumbled over the dog's hind legs and Penelope snapped at it, growling. A wave of guilt hit Anna. *She was too old to have them, and it's your fault.* Anna hardened. No. It was Jack's fault. She thought about going over to Freddy's. They could pick up Dor and drive somewhere, to the mall, to McDonalds, anywhere. But upstairs her laptop waited. Maybe Craig was online.

When she came back inside, Jack was sitting at the table grimacing. In front of him on the table was an object covered with layers of soiled hand towels.

"Gross," Anna said. "What is that?" The stench coming from the table was a nauseating blend of sulfur and wet dog.

"Same old song. Some curious dimwit bought a haunted object on eBay, screwed up his life and now it's my problem."

Jack peeled away the crusty towels, revealing a corroded iron box. A figure was etched into its hinged lid, some sort of muscle-bound mammal with large spikes protruding from its back. Anna sat down to get a closer look, placing a clean hand towel over her nose. Jack bought hand towels by the bushel at Costco.

Jack's eyes narrowed. "Do you see that?"

"See what?" Anna leaned in. And then she saw it. The box was no longer metal. It was...*meat*, sinewy and alive, puckered with beads of white fat and drops of liquid.

"Is that...sweat?"

Jack frowned. "It's messing with us."

Anna blinked. It was an iron box again. The attachment was clearly powerful, a spirit with a century or more of practice manipulating the natural world. It was almost a shame that it would soon be wrenched away from its pseudo home, but Jack had a job to do.

A large glass bowl and a jug of holy water sat on the kitchen table. Jack emptied half of the holy water into the bowl, careful not to spill any. He picked up the iron box and immediately cried out, letting the box drop. It clattered on the table for far longer and louder than it should have.

"Nasty thing," Jack said. He placed an oven mitt on each hand before picking the box up again and lowering it into the bowl of holy water.

The water instantly corrupted. A hissing gray-brown foam rose inside the bowl, almost to overflow, and then slowly fizzled. They sat staring, waiting for the water to lose its cloudiness as it normally did during a successful clearing, but instead it settled around the box in a murky soup. The vein in Jack's forehead made an appearance. Anna knew what that meant. He'd need more holy water to finish the job, which meant any profits from this gig were history.

Jack scowled, lifted the box out of the water and placed it back on the table. He soaked a new batch of towels in a fresh bowl of holy water and then rewrapped the box. Smothering the box with the soaked towels should take the fight out of it for a while. The next dunking would either send the spirit attachment into Source or weaken it enough so that Jack could store the box safely in the basement until the spirit crossed on its own.

But within moments the towels around the box grew brown and putrid.

"What are you going to do with it?" Anna asked. "Move it to the basement?"

Jack shook his head. "It might agitate the dormant objects." The basement was home to dormant objects whose spirit attachments had been weakened and bound with holy water. Most bound spirits eventually chose to cross into Source, and the newly-vacant objects were then officially cleared.

"Send it back to its owner," Anna said.

He wouldn't and she knew it. His compulsion to hoard would claim another victory, and the box would never leave his house.

"I'll deal with the box later," Jack said. "For now I need to concentrate on setting up the new office. And, kid"—he looked at her pointedly—"I could use less attitude and more help."

Jack's vein throbbed as Anna stood from the table, repositioning her backpack on her sore shoulders. "Stay away from this box," he said. "The attachment is an ugly one."

The box rattled on the table. The lines on Jack's face, the bags under his eyes, were deeper than ever. Anna left him there, surrounded by the evidence of his compulsive hoarding, in kinship with the fearful spirits that clung to the earthly realm, entrenched in the most meaningless of things.

At long last, she was alone in her room. The first thing she did after unloading her backpack was settle on the bed and pull up Craig's Instagram on her phone. Craig's page occasionally highlighted new music by the Manarchists but consisted mostly of heavily filtered selfies of him and his bandmates making angry faces. Today Craig posed with his guitar, wearing a black knit cap pulled low on his forehead. Vaguely aware that her obsession with Craig was no longer fun, Anna typed a comment—"nice hat"—and then cringed. How lame. Her phone buzzed, causing her heart to jump, but it was only a text from Freddy.

space gaze yay or nay?

not 2nite, Anna replied.

On Anna's wall a picture of Doreen, Freddy, and herself stared down. They were camping in Freddy's backyard on his eleventh birthday. It was a cute picture of the three of them, and Freddy's mom had given them each a framed copy. Anna was ten years old in the photo, when she still loved the feel of warm summer rain and never worried about her hair frizzing. She was a tomboy in those days, probably taking after her mom.

Helen used to wear clothes splattered with wood finish around the house. Her hands were always stained, and she hardly ever wore makeup. Anna struggled to remember her mother's hands, the calluses on her palm, her stained and tapered fingers.

Although the memories of her mother were fading, at least she still had Freddy and Doreen. They were her *tribe,* small but reliable. The camping picture tugged at her from the wall, as if whispering something just out of range. Anna blew the feeling off and snooped through the comments on Craig's page.

Her phone vibrated. *Please be Craig.*

It was a text from Doreen.

moms driving me crzy

least u have a mom? call u later, Anna replied.

The ringing in Anna's ears had shifted into another pounding headache, but she continued to snoop around Craig's page. Sydney had posted a comment thanking him for turning her on to some band Anna had never heard of. So, he was sharing music with Sydney now? She threw her phone on the mattress.

What was she thinking? Someone like Craig would never really be interested in Goblin Girl, especially not with girls like Sydney around. Anna picked up a fashion magazine and flipped through it to the back pages, where ad after ad for breast implants, butt implants, hair removal, liposuction, nose jobs, and even "vaginal rejuvenation" flashed by.

With the magazine curled into her fist, Anna stood before her full-length mirror and assessed herself. All she could see was a pimple on her forehead and the small bump on her nose. Her brown hair was drab, mousy. The hair of a rodent. She should get highlights like Sydney. She'd need money for that, a real job that *paid*.

She leaned closer to the mirror, inspecting her pores. *You're so disgusting.* The thought was punctuated by a sharp prick of pain behind her eyes.

Anna winced, glaring at her reflection. *You stupid ugly bitch.*

She froze, gripped with an intense urge to punch the mirror. For a moment her image in the mirror distorted into a grotesque mound of flesh and hair, a puckered blob of blackheads and bony protrusions. Instinctively, she threw the magazine at the mirror. It hit the glass with a loud thud, bringing the mania and pain in her head to an abrupt stop. In its wake was bone-deep exhaustion.

Anna turned off the light and crawled under her covers, falling asleep almost instantly. Hours later, when she opened her eyes again, it was dark. It was night, yes, but the *air* itself was dark. The air was *black* and she was choking on it! Before she could register what was happening, Jack burst into her room and slammed her window shut. Anna thought that she was dreaming for a few bewildered seconds. Then it hit her. *The backyard is on fire. Penelope.*

Anna flew out of bed and down the stairs. Jack trailed her, screaming at her to stay inside. But Anna ran into the kitchen, stumbling over Jack's hoard, and flung open the back door, stopping for a moment to take in the alien scene before her. Flaming tendrils of leaves and paper danced through the air, curling in and out of the doghouse. The *P* on the doghouse roof was warping; the melting glue and rhinestones crackled and popped. Along the side of the house a pile of newspapers and leaves smoldered, glowing orange through the black smoke as the wind spit embers across the yard.

Anna lunged for the burning doghouse, the hot air singeing her eyebrows, but Jack grabbed her and yanked her back.

"She's by the gate," he said.

"Where?" Anna yelled, disorientated by the thick smoke and swirling debris. Then she saw her.

Penelope was lying still, her two puppies squirming next to her. There was something *off* about Penelope's stillness. *Burned,* Anna thought. She prepared for the smell of scorched fur and sound of agonized whines as her legs carried her forward, but when she reached Penelope there was only silence. The puppies were safe, huddled together next to their mother, their tails low.

"Don't touch her," Jack said.

But Anna reached out and felt the horrible coolness of Penelope. *Dead.*

A wailing filled her ears. A fire truck, followed by an ambulance, pulled into the Fagan driveway. Anna tore her eyes from Penelope's body and looked up. Freddy and Doreen were standing a few feet away. Each of them lifted up a puppy without saying a word, looking like wide-eyed children, younger versions of themselves, like they had when Helen Fagan still breathed air and felt the wind on her face. Life wasn't perfect then, but it was pretty good. But now, nothing could ever be good again.

Neighbors were gathering in small groups, arms folded like they were watching a Little League game, a few of them shooting video with their phones. Anna wanted to scream at them, but her attention turned to a fireman who was picking something up from the ground near the charred newspaper pile. Her numb legs carried her over to the fireman to see what was in his hand. It was a clove cigarette butt, half smoked.

CHAPTER FIVE

READY TO REENIE

The last-period bell rang and students swarmed out of classrooms and into the hallway. Two days had passed since Penelope's death. Anna was miserable, but she'd made it through the first day back at school after the fire. There were stares and whispers, but being Goblin Girl she was used to it. Tomorrow was Friday, at least, and that helped to push her through the day, despite her broken heart.

Yesterday she and Jack dismantled what was left of the doghouse. They didn't talk much while they did it and cried on and off. Neither of them showered, and they still had soot under their noses and around their mouths when the skinny red-haired man from the *Bloomtown Gazette* showed up and started taking pictures. Jack didn't say anything when Anna threw globs of melted rhinestones at the man until he left. In return Anna kept quiet when Jack lugged the burned wood from the doghouse down into the basement.

Anna, Doreen, and Freddy found each other in the crowded hallway and made their way through the commons, discussing Penelope's puppies. Anna wanted them out of the house as soon as possible. It wasn't safe there.

"We'll find them a great family," Doreen said as the threesome left the school and headed to Freddy's Jeep.

"At the very least, only moderately dysfunctional," Freddy added.

Izzy, Frank, and a couple of other porn-heads stood on the curb in front of the parking lot, passing around a phone and scrutinizing the screen.

"Whoa, that shit is nasty," Frank said.

"The bitch loves it, though. Look at her face," Izzy said, then spotted them approaching. "Hey, gay boy," Izzy shouted to Freddy, waving his phone, "check this shit out. I found a girl that just might let you bang her."

Freddy ignored him.

"What's the matter, got your period?" Frank said, then sniffed his fingers as he guffawed.

Anna saw Freddy's green eyes narrow.

"Don't feed the trolls," she said.

Doreen nodded. "So not worth it."

"Don't you like pussy?" Izzy called after him. "Shit. You really are queer."

Freddy kept walking, but Izzy kept at it.

"Look at them go!" Izzy shouted. "The three G's. Geek, goofball, and Goblin Girl."

Anna tried to lighten the mood. "So, which one of you is the geek and which one is the goofball?"

Doreen giggled, but Freddy wasn't laughing. He glanced over his shoulder at Izzy. "That's four G's, you ignorant homophobe."

"Oooh. Look at gay boy talking tough!" Izzy said, and then *whack*. He darted toward them and sucker punched Freddy in the back of the head. Freddy managed to get his arms out in front of him before he hit the ground.

Anna whirled around. "You coward!" she shouted at Izzy.

A small crowd formed and quickly encircled them. Anna helped Freddy up. His face burned a deep crimson. Adam Letcher, a large football-playing senior, stepped forward, took out his cell phone and started filming.

"Can we just go?" Doreen asked, after Freddy got to his feet.

Izzy lunged at Freddy and made him flinch. The crowd laughed. Satisfied, victorious, Izzy lit a cigarette.

Time seemed to slow as Anna stared at the clove cigarette sticking out of Izzy's smug face. Izzy tossed it on the ground, still burning. She closed the distance between them.

"You were at my house the other night," Anna said.

"Shit," Izzy said. "Maybe if you begged me."

She picked up the cigarette butt. "Who else is stupid enough to smoke this thing?" Anna flicked it at his chest.

Izzy slapped burning embers off his shirt, his features twisting in surprise.

"You killed my dog," Anna said, and threw a punch. She was aiming for his nose but missed, so she threw another, connecting with his stomach. Izzy grabbed both of her wrists and held them in one hand, aware of the eyes on him.

Freddy lunged at Izzy, but Frank tackled him and pinned his arms behind his back. Anna dug her nails into Izzy's hand and bit down hard on his wrist. Izzy roared in pain and anger and put her in a headlock.

"Drawing blood, Fagan?" Izzy said. "Wanna suck something, vampire bitch?"

Doreen, her face pale beneath the rosy splotches on each cheek, made a strange primal noise, a combination of the words *stop* and *no*. She launched herself onto Izzy's back, pulling his hair and slapping his ears. The crowd loved it, cheering and laughing. With one heaving shrug, Izzy threw both girls onto the pavement. Doreen managed to land on her feet, but Anna fell hard on her back. The breath left her lungs in a quick blast, and she couldn't pull any air in.

From the pavement she saw Jimmy Pitz in his Honda Civic, squealing to a long and loud stop in the parking lot. Jimmy stuck his wide, acne-clogged face out the window, ogling the fight. His hand followed, holding out a cell phone. *Damn it.* Anna didn't want this to be her YouTube debut.

Her vision narrowed as her brain screamed for oxygen. Jimmy Pitz and the parking lot became a receding square at the end of a long black tunnel. And then it wasn't Jimmy Pitz she was seeing anymore. It was the demon inside her mother on the last morning of Helen Fagan's life.

On their drive to school that morning, eight-year-old Anna had cowered in the passenger seat while the thing inside her mother sped through the streets of Bloomtown without even glancing at the road. It turned corners and screeched to a stop at stop signs and red lights, all with its grinning face turned to Anna. Finally, What-Was-Helen screeched to a stop in front of Bloomtown Elementary.

"Give Mommy a kiss good-bye," it said.

Anna groped for the door handle and launched herself out of the car and onto the pavement. She wanted to run into the elementary school, to Freddy and Doreen, even the teachers, even the *mean* teachers, but then she heard her mother's voice, her *real* mother's voice.

"Anna."

She peeked into the car window. Her mother was herself again.

"It wants me to hurt you, honey," her mother said. "You and Daddy. But it can't make me. I won't...and it knows it. I love you, Sweet Pea. You know that, right?"

Anna nodded, but then her mother's sad smile morphed into a maniacal, teeth-licking grin, and What-Was-Helen slammed its foot on the gas. Her mother's car lurched forward and peeled across the parking lot for what seemed like forever, but was probably only a few seconds. There was a loud crunch as the Jetta smashed into the dumpster by the soccer field and the hood crumpled like an accordion. And then the blaring of a horn, stuck and broken. A cloud of green glitter, knocked loose from a discarded "Happy Earth Day" banner, rained back down into the dumpster. A high-pitched sound blotted out the horn and Anna realized, dimly, that she was screaming.

Jill Flanagan's mother, her mouth thin as a blade, had grabbed Anna and pulled her toward the front doors of the elementary school. Anna tried to look back at her mother's car, but Mrs. Flanagan covered Anna's eyes with one of her hands. "It will be alright, Anna. Just don't look." It was said with such authority that Anna had slapped her own hands over Mrs. Flanagan's, pushing hard and squeezing her eyelids together as tightly as she could. Mrs. Flanagan's coat smelled like the soap in the library bathroom. That smell was the last thing Anna registered before going numb.

Anna didn't feel her mother's poorly fastened butterfly barrette spring loose from its clasp. She didn't feel the sharp tip of one wing pierce the skin behind her ear and then scrape across her cheek as she'd staggered blindly into the school. She was placed on a cot in the nurse's office and sat there, cold, stunned and bleeding until her father came to get her. The look on his face when he showed up would haunt her nightmares for years. Hours later, in the hospital waiting room, a doctor came and told Jack that his wife was dead.

"Something *bad* got her, didn't it?" Anna asked when the doctor left them alone.

"It wasn't Mommy's fault."

He wasn't *answering* her. Anger rose from the depths of numbness inside her. The numbness began to peel away, allowing in the first jolts of ragged pain. The seven stitches in her face tightened and throbbed.

Anna's voice cracked. "Does it still have her?"

"She's in heaven now, Sweet Pea, with God."

Anna no longer believed in a god, but she suspected there were fates far worse than death.

"What if she didn't make it? What if the bad thing's still hurting her?"

"She made it."

"But how do you *know*?"

Jack got down on his knees and took his daughter's small hands in his. "I'll find out. I'll make sure, okay? That's a promise."

A promise he failed to keep.

Anna's lungs finally sucked in air. She was lying on the warm, rocky pavement, her head aching. Jimmy Pitz was still gaping at her from his Honda, and Doreen's tear-stained face hovered over her. Anna sat up too fast and her head spun. Frank let go of Freddy and pushed him toward them.

"You okay?" Freddy asked, rushing to Anna's side. She nodded.

"That shit was like a horror movie," Frank bellowed to the crowd. "Attack of the freaks!"

Izzy forced a laugh. His wrist was imprinted with Anna's purple bite mark, and his ears were red from Doreen's thrashing. For a moment Anna's heart thudded with glee.

"Can we please go?" Doreen begged.

Anna took Freddy's hand and pulled herself upright. But Frank was still at it.

"Damn, Izzy, you killed the hoochie's dog?" Frank said. "No, hold up. You killed the bitch's bitch?" Frank went for a high-five but Izzy skulked off.

The disappointed crowd made disappointed mutterings as Freddy, Anna, and Doreen ambled off with as much dignity as possible, crossing the street into the parking lot.

"That dirtbag killed Peeps," Anna said as they limped toward Major Tom.

"He must've been peeping in your windows," Freddy said.

"No surprise. He's a total perv," Doreen said.

"Speaking of surprises," Anna said, looking at Doreen with a smile. It was hard to fathom that her shy, conflict-avoiding friend had unleashed a fury of blows to Izzy's head.

Despite their fresh humiliation, Anna's long-absent smile seemed to energize her two friends. Freddy clapped Dor on the shoulder. "I didn't know you had moves like that."

Doreen threw jabs into the air and danced from side to side.

Freddy cupped his hands like a bullhorn. "And in this corner, standing five foot three inches tall...ladies and gentleman...let's get ready to Reeeeeenie!"

They were almost to Major Tom when they passed Craig Shine leaning against his SUV, his legs crossed casually at the ankles. A sliver of his tanned stomach was showing in between his jeans and the bottom of his vintage Sex Pistols T-shirt. Sydney White leaned against him, whispering in his ear. Craig grinned at whatever she said, his hand on her waist, his eyes cold.

"Yo, Fagan," Craig said when he saw Anna. "What was up with that throw down?"

Craig's mocking tone hit her like a gut punch. Freddy and Doreen got into Major Tom. Freddy opened the passenger side door for Anna, willing her with his eyes to *get in*. He must have guessed what was coming.

"You really need to chill, Goblin Girl," Craig said.

It was the first time he ever called her that.

CHAPTER SIX

PUPPY RUN

D or had to go home to help her mom with something, so Anna took Freddy back to Jack's house to wait for her. Freddy's eyes went wide when they stepped through the front door and into the path-tunnel of Jack's hoard. He hadn't been over for a while to witness the progression of Jack's Crap, or maybe *regression* was more like it. Entering the kitchen, they found Jack at the table reading a thick hardcover book with a well-battered spine.

Jack sneezed, his face haggard beyond his years, and then trained his bloodshot eyes on Anna.

"I won't survive another night with them inside," he said. "Allergies are killing me."

Anna was keeping the puppies in her room.

"We're on it," she said, filling two glasses of water and handing one to Freddy. "Dor and Freddy are going to help me find homes for the pups."

Jack looked over at Freddy as if just noticing that there was a teenaged boy wearing a Neil deGrasse Tyson T-shirt in his kitchen.

"Hi, Freddy. How's your mother doing?"

"She's great, Mr. Fagan. What's that book you're reading?"

"*The Origins of Faith*," Anna said. "It came to Jack through a client, some rich Manhattan bachelor who collects rare books. We call it *Oof*."

"A client, huh?" Freddy's eyes lit up. "Any little creepsters still hanging on to it?"

"Sorry. All clear," Jack said and went back to reading.

"It had an attachment that Jack cleared years ago," Anna said. "The spirit specialized in filling rooms with the smell of flatulence, especially when a woman was present. The client didn't want the book back so, of course, Jack was happy to keep it. *Oof* turned out to be useful, especially for researching objects."

"So it's no longer passing gas? That's a bummer," Freddy said, grinning at Jack—but Jack didn't look up.

They left Anna's father bent over *Oof* and went upstairs to greet the puppies. Hyper from being stuck in Anna's room, the puppies rushed them, barking and nipping at their sneakers. Freddy played with them for a bit and then went to Anna's window, looking out at the shingled slant of roof directly underneath it.

"Remember when we used to sit out there at night with your dad's binoculars playing the what-if game?" he said.

Anna remembered. They'd stay out there for hours, watching the stars and asking what-ifs. *What if the whole universe is a cell in the body of an inconceivably large being? What if we are those beings and every time we skin a knee, entire cosmos explode?*

Anna stood beside Freddy—a puppy in her arms, licking her nose—and looked out the window, down past the shingled roof to the burned, blackened ground where the doghouse used to be. Izzy's smug face flashed before her, and a fast rage built in her throat.

"I'd come over with my remote-controlled rockets, but you didn't like them, remember?" Freddy said. "You said it would be easier to take an escalator to space, like at the mall."

"You remember everything," Anna said. She put the puppy down, sat on her bed and pulled up Craig's Instagram on her phone. "It was a stupid idea."

"It wasn't stupid. They're studying it," Freddy said. "It could happen."

"Huh?" What was he babbling about?

"The escalators to space. But it would be more like an elevator. What they'd do is anchor the cable at the equator and extend it up into space, then inertia would counteract the forces of gravity. It would have to be pretty long, though."

"Uh-huh," Anna said. Mackenzie Donald had posted a comment on one of Craig's selfies.

ur band rox!

Ugh.

"I could be a part of it," Freddy said. "The studying of it. I'm thinking about applying for the Young Physicists Scholarship at a private school in Florida. I could do my senior year there maybe."

Anna didn't look up from her phone. Freddy sat on her bed next to her.

"Leave, like, forever," he said and snapped his fingers in her face. "Did you hear me?"

"I hear you," Anna said.

"I said I might move to Florida."

"Lucky you." Yeah right. He wasn't going anywhere.

Freddy leaned over to see what she was looking at. "Pining away for Shine again?" He stood and put his hands in his pocket. "Where's Dor? Maybe she'd like to talk about something other than Shine's shitty band."

Anna's head snapped up, ready for a fight. But the color had drained from Freddy's face. He looked so *lost*. She thought about giving him a hug but stayed where she was. Sometimes when she hugged him it was like he didn't want to let go, and she wasn't sure she did either. It felt nice in Freddy's arms. It felt warm. But he was one of her best friends.

Besides, Anna suspected that Doreen had a little crush on Freddy, not that Dor would ever admit it. Either way, it was better to keep things the way they'd always been between the three of them. Freddy and Dor were like extra limbs at this point, keeping Anna steady.

"Dor said she'd be here," Anna said.

"Well, I have other things to do," he said.

And just like that, Anna was seething. "Don't worry about it. Penelope gets murdered and it's inconveniencing you, so go home."

Doreen rushed in the door, flustered and more red-faced than usual. She opened her mouth and then, taking in the thick fog of tension in the room, closed it again.

Freddy put the puppies into a basket. "Let's just do this," he said.

Anna was about to put her phone away when Izzy posted a comment to Craig's page.

up 2 party?

Penelope was dead and that scumbag wanted to party.

Freddy started toward the door. "C'mon, Dor. She wants to stay here and worship Shine."

No. What she wanted was *revenge*. Anna slipped her phone into her pocket. "*Okay*, I'm coming."

• • •

Faint traces of the aurora borealis snaked across the dusk sky, but no one in Major Tom was looking up. They decided to drive around Bloomtown, scanning houses for signs of kids, the demographic they'd pegged as the most likely puppy-wanters. When Freddy spotted a basketball hoop outside an Old Bloomtown brick ranch house, they parked, and with the puppies in tow, knocked on the front door. Danny Pickens opened it, shiny with sweat and wearing a tank top and tiny shorts.

"Miss Fagan, Miss Lee, and Mr. Simms," Pickens said.

No kids in this house, just creepy Danny Pickens. Pickens was a gym teacher and football coach Anna's freshman year. Supposedly, he got fired because the football team had a crappy season, but she knew all too well that Pickens was a sicko and never doubted that there was more to it. She felt Freddy tense and wondered which one of them would say that they had the wrong house. Then Doreen said, "Hey, Coach Pickens."

"Not a high school coach anymore, Miss Lee, strictly Little League now. Consider me a civilian."

"We have puppies," Doreen said. "Um, for free."

"Well, come on in. Let's take a look-see."

Pickens stepped back, and before Anna or Freddy could stop her, Doreen walked into the house, giving them no choice but to follow. Framed pictures of a Boy Scout troops hung on the dark wood paneling covering the walls. Pickens led them into a large, stark kitchen. The tiled floor was pockmarked with dents, and dumbbells of varying sizes were stacked in the corners.

Pickens pulled out three chairs from the kitchen table. "Plant those buns of yours," he said, and then slurped water directly from the kitchen tap. Doreen and Freddy sat. Anna remained standing. She wanted out of there.

Pickens opened his fridge, taking out four beer bottles and placing one down in front of each of them.

"Our secret," Pickens said, pulling another chair out and sitting down in his micro shorts. He cracked open his beer and chugged it in loud, wild-eyed gulps, and then picked up a dumbbell and launched into a set of arm curls. They watched in mortified silence as he counted twelve reps aloud, grunting in between each one.

"So tell me," Pickens finally said, "what am I going to do with a little puppy?" His knees were wide, way too wide.

"Yep, I guess it's kids that really go nuts for them," Freddy said, then blushed furiously and stood up. "Sorry to have wasted—"

Pickens cut him off, perking up. "They do, huh?"

Freddy picked up the puppy basket from the floor. The puppies jumped over each other, playfully snapping at his fingers.

"C'mon Dor," he said. "We gotta go."

"You two girlfriend and boyfriend?" Pickens asked Doreen.

Freddy's eyes narrowed. Doreen giggled and shook her head, cheeks blazing.

"What about you two?" Pickens swung his finger between Freddy and Anna.

"Dor, *get up*," Anna said. Why the hell was she still sitting there? Doreen took a gulp of beer before rising out of her seat. Pickens put his free hand on Doreen's arm, coaxing her back down. Anna's heart raced. She didn't breathe again until his took his hand off of Doreen.

"C'mon, you can tell me," Pickens said to Doreen. "Kids tell me all kinds of stuff. I don't snitch." He dropped the dumbbell, which clanked loudly on the tile floor, then winced and rubbed his temples. "That one really rattled the old noggin!"

Something inside Anna squirmed. Pickens had a headache, too. He looked up and grinned, but there was something violent in it.

"Come *on*, Dor," Freddy said.

Doreen had the insane nerve to take two more gulps of beer while Anna and Freddy shot death glares at her.

"One for the road," Doreen said, and burped.

"You guys do stuff, though, you know," Pickens said, his eyes wandering over all three of them. He made the quote sign with his fingers. "Friends with bennies?"

They laughed politely in the reflexive, hollow way they did when authority figures tried to be cute. Pickens laughed, too, a chuckling that went on and on in the otherwise silent kitchen until he stopped to suck in air.

"We have to get going," Freddy said. "Our families are expecting us for dinner."

Pickens's eyes narrowed. "You know, I might want one of those pups after all. Why don't you stick around? We can chillax, watch a movie"—he stood and whispered in Anna's ear—"smoke a doobie?"

"No, thanks," Anna said, her stomach rolling from the sour smell of Pickens's body odor. Her eyes met Freddy's and an agreement passed between them. They were done being polite. Freddy grabbed Doreen's arm, yanked her up, and pulled her toward the front door. Anna was right behind them with the puppies, but Pickens rushed by her, seemingly *racing* them to the door. Freddy quickly yanked it open, shoved Doreen out and then held the door open for Anna.

"Come on back anytime," Pickens called after them, his voice strained. The three of them half-ran down the driveway.

Safely inside Major Tom, they drove away in stunned silence.

Eventually, Doreen said, "Gross, did you see his—"

"Let's not discuss it," Anna said, turning around to face Doreen in the backseat. "What were you thinking, drinking his beer?"

Doreen shrugged and looked out the window. Freddy and Anna gave each other the side eye. Something was definitely up with Dor, and when they were done with this puppy business Anna would drag whatever it was out of her. The puppies were restless in Anna's lap, and she reached in the basket to comfort them. Wet noses nuzzled her hand and tiny warm tongues lapped at her knuckles. But Anna felt only the cold grip of grief. They probably missed their mother.

They drove on in silence until Freddy slowed down in front of an Old Bloomtown colonial with a small pink bike on the front porch.

"Boom," Freddy said, parking Major Tom.

The mailbox was stenciled in primary colors: "The Catilanos." Freddy knocked while Anna stood next to him on the front porch, holding the puppy basket. Doreen lingered behind them, burping. Mrs. Catilano answered the door, thin and stark-faced with big bleached Jersey hair. There was a curly-haired girl clinging to her hip and sucking on a pacifier, which was odd because the girl looked about eight years old.

"Yeah?" Mrs. Catilano said.

"We have free puppies if you're interested," Freddy said.

"What do you know," Mrs. Catilano said. "The cat just died."

Anna lowered the basket so the girl could see the puppies. The pacifier swung around wildly in the girl's mouth like she was really gnawing on it.

A male voice boomed down from the second floor. "Who is it!"

Mrs. Catilano shouted up the stairs. "Shut your gaping piehole!" She turned back to Freddy. "The last thing I need around here is another freeloader."

"Squeeze puppy!" the little girl shrieked, and a puppy squealed in pain.

Anna jerked the basket up and away from the girl, who launched into a tantrum.

"No! Want puppy! Squeeze puppy!" the girl screamed, her hands clenching and unclenching. Anna lifted the basket out of the kid's reach and the brat punched her in the ribs, *hard*. Maintaining her frozen smile, Anna backed away and bumped into Dor. Together they shuffled backward onto the front step.

"Why don't you think about it?" Freddy said, following suit.

The male voice bellowed down the stairs, "If the kid wants a puppy, give her a goddamn puppy!"

"You gonna clean up the dog crap?" Mrs. Catilano yelled back. "You gonna scrape up what's left of the thing when she's done with it? Mr. Big Hero, right? Always making me the bad guy!"

After Mrs. Catilano slammed the door, Anna, Dor and Freddy walked quickly past a peeling birch tree in the Catilanos' lawn. At the base of the tree, partially obscured by grass, a Popsicle-stick cross marked a tiny fresh grave. Anna shuddered and glanced back toward the house. The youngest Catilano watched them go from the living room window, wringing her hands and chewing hungrily on the pacifier. After reaching Major Tom, they huddled on the street in the night shadow of a giant pine. Freddy opened his mouth to say something, and a muffled scream came from a nearby house, making all of them jump and sending a splinter of pain through Anna's skull.

"Something is *wrong* with this town," Freddy said.

"You want to talk about wrong?" Doreen swayed slightly on her feet. "You should see what's going down at my house!"

Anna winced. "Dor, can you use your inside voice?"

"But...we're outside."

"Good point."

Anna rubbed her temples. The damn headache again. What Freddy said was true—something *was* wrong in Bloomtown. She thought about cosmic rays slicing through her head like it wasn't even there.

"Do you think this has something to do with the solar storms?"

Freddy frowned. "The radiation can mess with satellites. But with people? I mean, if it did, it would be headline news."

Could it be a coincidence, the solar storms and the creep factor in Bloomtown rising simultaneously? Anna wasn't so sure.

"Not if they hadn't discovered it yet," Anna said, "or…if they were trying to cover it up."

Freddy smirked. "Anna Fagan, a budding conspiracy theorist. Who'd of thunk it?"

"You guys," Dor said quietly. "Not that you care, but I have to go home."

A deep growl came from behind Anna.

"Watch it!" Freddy shouted, knocking into Dor as he yanked Anna away from the jaws of a bullmastiff, pulling her against his chest. The dog had charged out of the dark yard next to the Catilanos' house, its sharp teeth missing her arm by inches. Thankfully, the muscled bullmastiff was held back by a heavy chain attached to something in the darkness. If that chain had been just a *few* inches longer. Anna's mouth went dry. She cold almost feel the dog's teeth rip through her skin, cracking bone. The dog struggled against its metal collar, drool dripping off its muzzle as it retched out strangled growls.

Shaking, Anna opened the back door of Major Tom.

"Dor, get in before that thing breaks loose." But Doreen was gone.

• • •

Anna ran through the backyards of Old Bloomtown, enduring the punishing ache in her skull as she chased after Doreen. It was the beer, Pickens's stupid beer. Why else would Dor run off like that? But then she remembered the hurt on Dor's face when Freddy had elbowed her aside, instinctively reaching for Anna. Whatever the reason, Dor was buzzed and acting like a loon, and there was no way Anna could let her go home like that. Up ahead were the sounds of twigs snapping and the soft crunch of pine needles being pushed into sand and gravel, but Dor was far enough ahead to remain out of sight. Anna didn't call out to her, hoping the run would sober Dor up. Besides, she knew where Dor was headed—they'd worn paths through these yards years ago, pool-hopping on hot summer nights—and she almost enjoyed the old, familiar rush of wind whipping through her hair.

But soon her lungs burned and acid rose from her chest, bringing a sour taste to Anna's mouth. Doreen, more than most, knew what Pickens was capable of. Why didn't she refuse his beer? Doreen was like one of the puppies, eager and cloying, never getting enough love and attention from her and Freddy—it was exhausting sometimes—but from Pickens, too? From *Pickens*?

Anna's side cramped and she stopped and leaned against an oak tree, breathing heavily and gripped with a sudden fury at Doreen. Anna was the one who'd lost Penelope. Doreen was supposed to be helping her, not running off like a toddler. Anna spit on the ground and struck the tree in frustration. When her hand hit the bark, an image of Izzy's smug face popped into her head. She was mad at the wrong person. This was all Izzy's fault. He was the one that killed Peeps. Anna would make him pay, and she was pretty sure she knew just how to do it.

For a moment she thought about cutting left and crossing the back road to the parking lot of the Yo! Yogurt shop. Anna could get a chocolate cup, load up on sides and let Doreen fall on her own beer-covered sword. But instead she turned right and ran through another dark yard, toward the last Old Bloomtown house on Eden Street, in the shadow now of grand McMansions, but still a dead-end.

Dor was standing at her mailbox sorting through a stack of junk mail, the underarms of her T-shirt soaked with sweat.

"That dog was messed up, huh?" Anna said gently, approaching her. "I don't blame you for taking off, but you should chill for a few minutes before going inside. You smell like a brewery, and the last thing you need is to get on Cindy's shit list."

It was a joke. In fifth grade, Doreen's mom, Cindy, had announced that Dor was on her "shit list" for leaving her wet Uggs on a leather recliner. This struck Anna and Dor as hilarious, and they hadn't stopped laughing about it since. But tonight Dor looked at Anna with no trace of a smile. In her hand was a white envelope adorned with a stamp and a glaring blankness where the return address should be. Anna knew what lay inside. It was a check signed by Anthony Caputo, Doreen's so-called father.

"She's making me bring it to her now. It's so humiliating," Doreen whispered. "She had that back surgery a few weeks ago, remember? She's supposed to be in physical therapy, but just lies on the couch all day and night watching TV."

Anna nodded. She vaguely recalled Dor telling her something about Cindy needing surgery, but it didn't really register at the time.

"She *never* gets off the couch now. I don't even know if she *can*."

Never? Anna let that sink in, unsure what to say. It wasn't like she could tell Dor to turn to her father for help. She and Dor had always bonded over both having only one parent, but Doreen had never known her father. Well, that wasn't quite true. Doreen did have *one* brief, but vivid, childhood memory of him—one that she'd repeated to Anna many times over the years. Doreen was three years old and in the living room. Her mother, Cindy, was wearing gloppy red lipstick and a strong perfume that made Dor nauseous. Cindy had pushed her toward a strange man with cold hands and hairy arms, and Dor cried and squirmed until he let her go. That was it, Dor's only recollection of dear old dad.

When Doreen was seven and old enough to ask questions, her mom told her that her father was a missionary in Cambodia and that his heroic passion to help the disadvantaged kept him away from both of them. But when Dor got old enough to pick up on the raised eyebrows and pointed silences from relatives whenever she mentioned her father's noble calling, she knew it was a lie. On her thirteenth birthday, Doreen's mom finally told her the truth. When Doreen was conceived her father was a married man with his own family. Cindy sat her down and opened a white envelope with no return address. Inside was a check for four figures made out to Cindy. It was signed by one Anthony Caputo of 233 Garden Drive in North Portersville, NJ. Doreen was the mistake he paid for every month.

That same night Doreen went to Anna's and told her everything. But how could they believe Cindy? She'd lied about so much for so long. The two girls decided to track down Doreen's dad and see for themselves. They took two buses and then walked for an hour around North Portersville until they found 233 Garden Drive. There was a basketball hoop in the driveway and an SUV with a "Proud Father of an Honor Student" bumper sticker. They snuck around to the backyard of the white, blue-trimmed colonial, finding camouflage among the moon shadows. Through a sparsely curtained window, they saw Anthony Caputo watching television with two gangly teenage boys. Doreen had elbowed Anna: "Look at his hairy arms." Before Anna could respond, Doreen picked up a rock and hurled it at the window. They ran away, the shattering of glass so loud in the quiet night.

Doreen made Anna pinky swear to never tell anybody about that night, and Anna had kept the promise.

"Do you have any gum?" Anna asked.

Dor rummaged through her bag and pulled out a crinkled bag of Skittles, offering them to Anna.

"Not for me," Anna said. "For your breath."

Doreen shoved a handful of Skittles in her mouth and chewed dutifully. She let out one last burp, which had them both bent over with their hands over their mouths, stifling laughter. It felt good.

"Okay," Anna said, collecting herself and assessing Doreen. "You good to go in?"

Dor nodded. "Will you come with me?"

"Sure."

"Tell me something first."

"Anything."

The sadness crept back in to Dor's eyes. "What's going on with you and Freddy?"

Dor did have a crush on Freddy. Of course. That's why she ran off like that. Anna could still feel the lean-muscled warmth of Freddy's chest radiating in her own, but she wasn't about to tell Dor that. She thought about icebergs and cold ocean swims.

"Nothing! Why?"

"I just…" Dor dropped her head. "I don't want anything to change between us. It's been kinda weird lately."

"It won't!" Anna was talking too loud.

"Shhh. Okay fine. C'mon."

Anna followed Dor up the pathway and through the front door. Inside, garbled static and flickering shadows emanated from the television in the otherwise dark living room. Anna made out the form of Dor's mom sleeping on the couch. One of Cindy's arms had fallen off the side, and the tips of her fingers were grazing the floor. They tried to creep toward the stairs, but a betraying floorboard creaked underfoot.

"Did the check come?" Cindy asked from the dark living room.

Doreen stepped into the living room and Anna followed. There was a horrid stench. Cindy struggled to raise her head from the pillow on the brown leather couch, her bloated face scrunching from the effort. Her hair hung off her head in greasy strips.

"Yes," Doreen said, reaching for a pill bottle on the mantel above the fireplace. She placed two pills next to the cup of water on the coffee table.

"Leave them here," Cindy said, eyeing the pill bottle in Doreen's hand.

Doreen ignored her, returning the bottle to the mantel.

Cindy scowled. "The TV's busted."

"It's the satellites," Dor said. "They're wacky because of the solar flares."

"The 'solar flares,' huh. Think you're pretty smart, don'tcha, Miss Fancy Pants?" Cindy looked over at Anna. "You're such a good little helper to your dad. But my daughter"—she glared at Doreen, practically snarling—"is pretty much useless."

Anna held her breath and her tongue—she'd never heard Cindy talk to Dor like that. Embarrassed, Dor glanced at Anna, a clump of her dark blonde hair stuck to her face with sweat.

"Did you call Dr. Williams like you said you would?" Doreen asked, steeling herself.

Cindy ignored her, crossing her arms over her chest like a defiant child.

"You have to eat something," Doreen continued.

"Did you not hear me? *Fix. The. TV!*"

Doreen opened her mouth as if to say something, but instead turned and thundered up the stairs. Anna followed, finding Dor on her bed, her face burrowed in her pillow.

"What can I do?" Anna said.

Dor picked her head up, her face a patchwork of blotches. "That's how she talks to me before the pain pills kick in. In half an hour, she'll get all dumb and smiley like nothing happened." She reburied her face in the pillow. "I'll call you later," she said, her voice muffled. "You better leave now before it gets worse."

When Anna stepped back out onto Eden Street, she breathed in the warm, moist September air and looked up at the luminous streaks of pink and green trailing across the sky. The aurora borealis was visible at night now because of the solar storms. A part of her recognized its beauty, but she was scared, too, for herself and for her friends. Penelope's murder,

Cindy's uncharacteristic viciousness, the way Pickens boldly offered them alcohol and drugs—it felt like a palpable evil hung in the humid air.

Anna thought about the Catilano girl, desperate to harm the puppy. She thought about her own anger, boiling inside, making her want to hurt someone. If something evil was brewing in Bloomtown, Anna had to figure out how to stop it. She'd lost her mother, but would be damned if she'd sit by and lose anyone else. She'd rather cross into Source.

But her sense of purpose and clarity was quickly over-whelmed by a thumping in her skull. The pain behind her eyes mocked her. *Who are you to figure anything out, Goblin Girl?*

PART TWO

ELECTRICAL GHOSTS

CHAPTER SEVEN

THE NEW ELF

F riday afternoon, Anna and Jack were shoulder to shoulder by the front door, peering over the Mountain of Mail through the sliver of accessible window to the street outside. Jack's new assistant had called from Route 33 and was due to arrive at any moment.

When the bright yellow hybrid hatchback came into sight, its right front wheel was already on the sidewalk. The extremely blonde woman behind the wheel hit the brakes, but her front bumper still banged into the Fagan mailbox. She put the hatchback in reverse and backed off of the sidewalk, bouncing onto the street before slowly pulling into the driveway with one hand covering her mouth.

"That must be Ms. Sanders," Jack said flatly, opening the front door. Anna trailed behind him to the driveway, trying not to smirk.

After parking behind Jack's sedan, Geneva Sanders, aka the New Elf, flung the driver's-side door open, frantically apologizing as the busted GPS inside her hatchback repeated, "You have reached your destination. You have reached your destination." She turned the engine off and emerged from the car.

Clearly not someone concerned with the latest trends, Geneva wore a rainbow-colored tie-dye tank top accessorized by a thin chain necklace adorned with a quartz crystal. There was a wet stain on her long, billowy yellow skirt. She had a thing for yellow, it seemed. Not exactly what Anna imagined from a woman with a PhD in electrical engineering.

"What was I thinking?" Geneva said. "Well, I wasn't think-ing." She took a much needed inhale. "I was on the phone—dumb, I know—and spilled my coffee." She looked down at the stain on her skirt. "Turned the wheel by mistake and then overcorrected and—I am *so* sorry. How embarrassing."

Geneva's expression became unreadable as she assessed their overgrown front yard.

"Are you hurt?" Jack said.

"Just my pride." The sound of harps and a soft rain billowed from Geneva's hatchback. "That's my phone," she said, rummaging through her purse. "Oh it's in my car. Do you mind?"

"Please," Jack said. "Go ahead."

Geneva opened her passenger-side door and searched for her phone. She emerged with her cell in one hand and a long black case in the other.

"Geneva Sanders," she said, walking over to Anna. "So great to meet you. You must be Jack's daughter."

Before Anna could reply, Geneva's phone started ringing again. Birds were now chirping in the harp-filled rainforest.

"I'll just send this to voice mail," Geneva said, tapping her phone—but instead of ending the call, her cell was now in speaker mode. A man's baritone voice boomed out.

"What's up, Genie? We got cut off?"

"It's my lawyer and if I have to call him back, he'll charge me," Geneva whispered to Anna and Jack.

"Take your time," Jack said.

Anna gave Jack a look. He was quite accommodating to someone who'd just smashed the mailbox.

Geneva resumed tapping on her phone to no avail. "It's frozen," she said, frowning.

"Gene-genie, is that you?"

"Bill?" she said, "Real quick, because I'm busy at the moment. I got the final papers. Thank you for that. But there was also another invoice from you, and I thought we were all settled up."

"Yeah, well, what's-her-name, your ex-husband's lawyer, had some kind of issue locating my office. So she calls and needs all this information, during my lunch, giving me indigestion—annoying woman—so, I had to charge you."

Geneva rubbed the crystal on her necklace between her thumb and index finger.

"What I hear you saying, Bill, is that she called to…verify your address?"

"Yeah, something like that. I had the receptionist handle it. This ain't a sweatshop, know what I'm saying? A man's gotta eat!"

Geneva rubbed away. "I'm not judging you, Bill, but I feel uncomfortable with you charging—"

"Correspondence! You makin' me go through this again, my little Genie in a bottle? An email, a phone call, a letter, it's *cor-re-spon-dence*! Every correspondence is billable. Not my fault your ex hired a bonehead to represent him. You married him. Responsibility! Gene-genie-bambini! Own it!"

Geneva inhaled and let the air out slowly.

"So, we're done now, Bill? No more invoices?"

"You're done with that cheatin' S.O.B., thanks to me. Move on and god bless. This call will be another two hundred and fifty, then you're done with me, too. I'm gonna miss you, Gene-genie. Better pay me, though, or I'll sue you. Ha! I crack myself up."

He hung up.

Geneva released her crystal and looked at Jack and Anna.

"Your mailbox," Geneva said.

"Oh, don't worry about that," Jack said, dismissing the mangled mailbox with a wave and eyeing the long black case that Geneva had retrieved from her hatchback. "Whatcha got there?"

"Oh! My invention." Geneva lifted up the case and something rattled about inside it. "Might need to tighten a few screws after that fender bender."

A gust of wind swept through the tall grass in the Fagan yard, revealing an upside-down blue sled, the paint chipped and weathered, that served as a makeshift trunk for bundles of Frisbees wrapped with twine. Back when Jack mowed the lawn and Helen sanded table tops in the garage, sending clouds of dust into the driveway, Anna, Dor and Freddy had invented a game for the hottest of summer days. To score a point, they had to jump through the sprinkler in the front yard while catching a Frisbee. They called the game Up Chuck, a name they were required to scream when a point was scored. The neighbors weren't amused. Little did those neighbors know how bad living next to the Fagans would get.

Geneva squinted at the hoard pile for a moment and then moved on. "Anyway, my invention," she said, "is revolutionary. What I mean is that it will...revolutionize the industry."

Now she was gazing past Anna and Jack to the bulging, cracked garage door. In one high corner, a stain crawled over the paint. Something was leaking *through* the door. Impressive. Even for Jack.

Thrown, Geneva continued. "That is...I could use your influence to help market it and...it could be marketed."

Geneva rubbed her crystal and closed her eyes, taking several breaths while Jack and Anna fidgeted.

"Mr. Fagan, what I meant to say is that my invention makes it possible to view 3-D, real-time images of electro-magnetic fields. Paranormal investigators, such as yourself, have been held back for decades by the use of EMF readers that only give needle readings. With my invention you can isolate, visualize and document EMF anomalies in a way that's never been done before. Now"—Geneva fumbled in her purse, taking out a checkbook—"I owe you for the mailbox."

"I'd love to take a look at that invention of yours once you settle in," Jack said. "As for the mailbox, let's worry about that after we set up shop at the new office." He looked at her hatchback. "Have room in there for a box or two? I'd ask you inside for some coffee but the place is a bit of a mess."

A bit of a mess. Jack had a never-ending supply of euphemisms for his hoard.

Anna helped load up Geneva's hatchback and Jack's sedan with boxes—without having to be asked. She was trying to stay under her father's radar because she had a plan, one he'd definitely not approve.

Despite the distraction of Geneva's presence, the ache of Penelope's death remained so acute that Anna barely registered the thudding in her head. Relief would only come with some semblance of justice. Izzy needed to *pay* and Anna was going make sure he did, all by herself. First revenge, then she could focus on whatever bad juju was unfolding in Bloomtown. She dropped a box of case files into Jack's trunk with stony resolve, wondering if this was how it felt to be an adult.

Once all of the boxes were crammed into the cars, they drove seven blocks up Eden Street, made a right on Washington and pulled into the sand and gravel driveway of a gray-shingled ranch house shadowed by towering pines. There was a "Rented by Saul Gleason, Bloomtown's Top Realtor!" sign planted in the front yard. It featured a head-shot of Saul grinning with the condescending charm of a game-show host. Anna avoided his plastic eyes.

Jack unlocked the front door and the three of them stepped inside a spacious living room. Sunlight hit freshly painted cream-colored walls. Furniture delivered the day before was unpacked and ready for assembly. The living room would serve as Jack's new office, while Geneva would be provided with free room and board in a bedroom down the hallway.

"So that's what a floor looks like," Anna said, admiring the newly finished wood floor.

An hour later, Anna and Jack were sliding drawers into a file cabinet when Geneva came in the front door holding a large round mirror.

"It'll make the room look bigger," Geneva said.

"Where did you find that?" Jack asked.

"My trunk. It miraculously survived."

"You're not responsible for any of the furnishing. It's included in your room and board."

"Oh!" she said, self-conscious. "I thought I'd contribute. Am I overstepping?"

"Not at all." Jack was adamant. "I appreciate it. Thank you."

They smiled at each other like goofballs.

The sugary exchange made Anna shudder. Who was this fancy new assistant with a PhD, anyway? When Jack left to pick up more boxes from the Eden Street house, Anna asked Geneva about her background in the supernatural.

"I studied incidents of paranormal activity in a lab setting: a psychic describing hidden objects, a medium communicating with the dead relatives of grad students," Geneva said. "But I have little real-world experience. Why don't you fill me in on the family business?"

Geneva sure turned that around quickly. Impressed, Anna searched for how to begin.

"Let's start with your standard ghost, a human spirit," Anna said, filing a poltergeist case in the new cabinet. "Who's confused and doesn't want to leave their home, dorm room, favorite restaurant, whatever. Those cases are simple. You get their attention, tell them they're dead and that it's time to move on.

Most of them get it and leave. If not we'll do a cleansing to push them out, or bring in a medium to talk them over.

"Jack also works on nonhuman spirit cases, but nothing genuinely evil. Tricksters, for example, can attach to and move objects. They like to hide keys, wallets, glasses, socks, remote controls. Slide furniture around a room a little each day, stuff like that. They play head games but don't do any real harm."

"If they're not human spirits, what are they?"

Anna shrugged. "We can't say for sure. Jack thinks they might not be spirits at all, but some kind of life-form we don't understand. Maybe from another dimension. Holy water works on them, too, though. You only need a small spritz to send them packing. Where they go—into Source or back to wherever they call home—is unknown."

"Tricksters," Geneva said. "Fascinating. I hope I get to see one."

"You won't. They're invisible. And you might change your tune if you had one blowing in your ear all night or snagging one of your favorite earrings, but yeah, I guess the brats are somewhat intriguing. Next on the rundown of pesky nonhuman spirits are the infamous, but again, not *that* dangerous, shadow people."

Geneva's eyes went wide. "I heard about them. The tall ones, right?"

"Yep, tall, scrawny, humanoid in shape. Also of unknown origin. They give off an icky vibe but rarely attack people. When they do, they just kind of rush *through* them, scaring people but not injuring them. They prefer to hover in corners of dark rooms, observing people, which can be terrifying, obviously, for anyone who sees them. But those who encounter a shadow person are normally terrified to begin with, because shadow people appear in homes already experiencing paranormal activity. Lucky for us, they are skittish and avoid confrontation, and, like Tricksters, a quick spray of holy water usually gets rid of them.

"It's the human spirits who attach to objects and hang on tight; they'd rather spend eternity in a hatbox or an accordion than cross over. The powerful ones can also attach to people, even possess them temporarily, but it's rare. Clearing haunted objects of their spirit attachments is my dad's specialty, and the real moneymaker."

Geneva furrowed her brow. "Why wouldn't they want to cross over?"

"Some have no idea they're dead, but it also depends on the spirit's belief system. Some were mean as hell when they were alive, and they're afraid to face judgment. Others were decent enough but taught to fear the afterlife, so they panic and latch on. If a spirit won't release their grip on an object, we weaken them by binding them with holy water. It's their choice to either cross into Source or remain attached, but they can't do much harm after the binding."

They took a break and Anna began scrutinizing herself in the new mirror, pulling a section of hair forward to hide her scar. She tried not to think about how much she missed Penelope and hated Izzy, or the hateful way Cindy had lashed out at Doreen. But the sound of Dor's pillow-muffled sobs remained fresh in her memory.

Anna's gut told her that the solar flares were somehow behind the malevolent upsurge in Bloomtown, but now she wasn't so sure. The sun storms were affecting a large part of the hemisphere, and the world wasn't falling apart any more than usual. If it wasn't the solar flares, then what else could bring out so much ugliness in people? Anna sucked in air. *Tricksters.* Of course. Driving people crazy was their jam. Maybe Bloomtown had been invaded by an unusually hostile breed of Tricksters not content with simply annoying their targets. Maybe they wanted to hurt them too. A fresh pain flared in her head, redirecting her focus. First she needed to avenge Penelope's death, then she'd ask Jack to help tackle Bloomtown's possible downward spiral. Anna was so engrossed that she didn't notice Geneva standing beside her until she spoke.

"Mirrors can be a doorway into your soul," Geneva said, "if you really look at yourself."

"Huh? I am looking at myself."

"True," Geneva said, "I mean, look *into* yourself." She addressed Anna's reflection in the mirror. "Supposedly, if you can quiet the chatter in your mind and then look deeply into your own eyes, your soul can leave your body and travel through the astral plane, the first level of Source, as you call it."

"What do you call Source?"

"I think of it as an infinite sea of quantum possibilities."

"Where does your soul go?" Anna asked.

"Anywhere. Any *time*," Geneva said. "It's been reported that there are no limits, that your thoughts guide your journey. Whatever, *when*ever, you think about. *Pop.* You're there. It's not easy, though, I hear. Going out of body isn't for the weak. You have to be brave."

During Anna's encounter with Source, that night years ago with Mary-the-child-bride, the light had been beautiful. But it frightened Anna, too, how the light had *pulled* on her, and how badly she'd wanted to disappear into it, even if it meant leaving her father behind.

As if on cue, Jack appeared, paintbrush in hand. "Want to see your new room?"

Geneva squeezed Anna's shoulder. "You come, too."

Anna followed them down the hall into one of the ranch house's two small bedrooms. The other bedroom was for "storage," and Jack had sworn not to stuff it with his *things*.

Geneva's bedroom was bright, airy, and clean, just like the rest of the house. Jack had painted it a pale shade of warm yellow. He hovered by the doorway, not sure where to put his hands.

"It feels so good in here," Geneva said.

Anna had to agree.

"I ordered you a mattress." Jack cleared his throat. "Not just a mattress, but...a headboard, too, bedding, the whole shebang. It should all arrive tomorrow."

Oh my god. Was he *blushing*? He was. All afternoon he'd stole glances at his new apprentice, and Anna wasn't sure how to feel about it. Had he looked at her mother like that when they first met, before they fell in love and began dreaming of a life together? The thought thickened her throat.

Geneva ran her finger along the top of the bookcase next to her bed.

"I have the strongest sense of déjà vu," she said. "Some people think that's a sign, that you're right where you're supposed to be."

Jack nodded like he knew exactly what Geneva meant, but his puzzled eyes told another story. Anna, however, did understand. There was something about Geneva that felt familiar.

"Tonight," Jack said, "I'll clear off space on the couch for you to sleep on back at the house."

"Nice sales job, Dad."

"Um, thanks, but a hotel is good," Geneva said.

Once they finished for the day, the three of them took a last look around.

"Looks great," Jack said.

And it did, like a new beginning.

CHAPTER EIGHT

DIRT BATH

When Jack pulled up to the battered Fagan mailbox, the wheat-like grass in the front yard swayed in the wind, and the house loomed dark and unwelcoming in the dim evening light. Anna's relatively good mood snuffed out like an air-starved candle.

"So, whatcha think?" he said.

Reaching into the now lidless and crunched mailbox, Anna removed the mail that the letter carrier had dutifully shoved into the twisted metal. She knew better than to try to sort it. Most of it would be tossed unopened on the Mountain of Mail.

"About?" Anna said, even though she knew he was asking about Geneva.

"Ms. Sanders, um, Geneva."

"Kind of granola for a scientist." Anna said. "But she's cool."

"Yep," Jack said. "She seems pretty cool, pretty groovy."

What a goof. Jack was unusually cheery, and she probably should be grateful that he was at least normal enough to have a crush on someone. But it still made her uneasy, aside from being kind of *gross*.

Jack hadn't dated anyone since her mother's death. There was one woman, Sheila, a divorced neighbor who used to come by in sundresses and strappy sandals to check on them in the months after Helen's funeral, bringing over food and toys and then, discreetly, bottles of wine. Jack made excuses to cut her visits short until they stopped altogether.

Sheila was now firmly in the anti-Fagan camp (and who on Eden street wasn't?). Anna couldn't blame her. Jack's yard was a blight that undoubtedly brought down the value of every house on the street.

Her head suddenly thudded with resentment. Her father was too selfish to think of anyone but himself. *And what about you? Where were you when Dor needed your help?* But Anna ignored the fading voice of her conscience.

Once inside, the oppressive bulk of Jack's hoard felt heavier after spending the day in the airy new office. As usual, Jack seemed oblivious to it.

"I'm going to grab some dormant objects from the basement for tomorrow's training with Geneva," he said, winding through the path toward the kitchen. "It's gonna be a busy weekend!"

"Yip-a-dee-doo-dah!" Anna replied sarcastically, following him to search for something edible.

The basement was off-limits and therefore not of much interest. The spirits down there were either struggling against their bindings or in the process of transitioning into Source. The latter especially needed a peaceful environment and, according to Jack, Anna's presence in the basement would be disruptive. Spirits, he said, were drawn to the raw, chaotic energy surging from teenage bodies and minds.

Jack reemerged from the basement carrying a filthy burlap bag full of tagged objects. Anna's nose wrinkled as a musky, chemical smell wafted toward her. She was about to complain about the stench when Jack removed the iron box from the bag and placed it inside an open steel briefcase on the counter. The box was wrapped in dirty hand towels, moldy with crusted brown slime.

Anna ceased rummaging through the fridge, suddenly at full attention. The spirit inside the box was still strong and no doubt ready to do some damage, if it had the chance.

"Where do you think it's from?" she asked.

"Looks early European," Jack said, scooping up an armful of old newspapers from under the kitchen table.

He was acting weirder than usual, hovering by the basement door with the newspapers, tapping his feet as if waiting for her to leave.

Anna reached for the basement door.

"Hey!" he snapped. "The basement is off-limits."

"I was getting the door for you. Geez! I can't even touch the doorknob?"

"What's with your sudden interest?"

"What's with the trash reshuffling?"

"They're newspapers," Jack snapped. *Trash* was one of the words on the do-not-say list.

Anna threw her hands up. "Fine." She feigned a casual interest. "You keeping that box up here now?"

"You're a little too curious about the damn box," Jack said. He shuffled over to the kitchen counter without dropping a single newspaper and shut the briefcase with his elbow. "It's going in my bedroom. I don't want it agitating the dormant objects."

She eyed the useless trash in his arms and felt another surge of resentment.

"Wouldn't it feel better to toss that crap?" she asked.

Jack remained rooted by the basement door, wheezing slightly.

"Give it a rest," he said, "and go to your room."

On her way out of the kitchen, Anna picked up *Oof* from the kitchen table, discreetly tucking the book under her arm.

Jack stood by the basement door until he heard the mattress in Anna's bedroom creak. It floored him sometimes, how much she looked like her mother, especially when she was frustrated: her chin jutting out in defiance, her almond-shaped eyes growing subtly rounder. He balanced the papers in his arms while using his pinky fingers to twist the doorknob on the basement door. Grimacing, he swung the door open with his foot. His sinus infections were acting up again, keeping him awake at night with their unrelenting pressure and squeezing.

The light switch unreachable, the darkness unnerved him as he shuffled down each wooden step. It became harder to inhale, as if something heavy crouched on his chest ready to spring at his face, teeth bared. His foot kicked into some errant trash on the steps and he stumbled, throwing his shoulder against the wall to catch himself. A sharp pain dominated and his mind almost cleared. He should go outside, take a walk around the block, maybe take Anna to a movie. But no—the pressure in his sinuses returned—the neighbors would be seething at him from their perfect yards and tidy, monochromatic cars. Besides, Anna wouldn't want to be seen with him.

As he struggled with the physical and mental unease that accompanied the shrinking of his airways, Jack puzzled over how it came to be that he was now too much of a coward to face his neighbors. He wasn't altogether sure, but he knew exactly how it had begun.

It started with nightmares. For days Helen Fagan had barely slept, waking, when she did, overwhelmed by indefinable dread. Then came the scratching noises on the floorboards under her side of the bed. Jack couldn't hear them, but there was Helen every morning with bags under her eyes, insisting that the scratching had kept her up all night. After several weeks, the scratching migrated to the inside of her pillow. "Here," she'd say, "listen," but Jack heard nothing.

Helen was drugged the night it took full possession of her. She'd taken two sleeping pills, hoping to sleep until morning. Jack awoke later that night to the sound of gurgling. He turned to his wife and the demon was staring at him, staring into him. At first it could only hiss and spit. It had to learn to manipulate Helen's vocal cords. "The sow is mine," it finally said, and Jack felt his bowels loosen and quiver. "Helen, stop," he said stupidly, knowing it wasn't Helen. The demon's eyes grew wide, sensing his terror. Its cackling reached a crescendo along with Jack's racing heart until, slowly, Helen managed to gain back control of her body.

"Don't leave me," she'd begged, and Jack held her, although it sickened him, and said he never would, although he wanted to. After that night, Helen offered to sleep in the guest room. She couldn't hide her relief when Jack said no; they were in this together. Till death do us part. Had she known, he now wondered, that death was coming?

Suicide. Schizophrenia. Those were the words doctors wrote in their charts and filed away after Helen's death. Jack hadn't wasted time arguing with them. They were fools. He focused instead on contacting Helen's spirit, sure that if he lost sight of that goal, he'd sink into the quicksand of despair tugging at his heels.

He became obsessed with studying religions and the occult but was unable to connect to Helen's spirit. Although he couldn't reach Helen, he went on to help others find peace, both the living and the dead. But now his connection to Source was gone.

He'd lost his wife, his daughter was ashamed of him and his business was failing. Jack descended into the dark basement thinking that he should have been the one to die.

After midnight, Anna crouched in the dark hallway outside Jack's bedroom, waiting for her eyes to adjust and listening to her father's labored breathing. She crawled into the room, the carpet muffling her movements. The steel briefcase was on his nightstand on top of a pile of books. He was sleeping right next to it! She wouldn't have to go searching through the hoard piles in his room.

Holding her breath, Anna lifted the metal case from the small table inches from Jack's head. She darted out of the room, pausing in the hallway to listen for any signs he was awake. Her heart felt both fluttery and leaden. She was stealing from her own father. Could she get any lower? She thought of Izzy's smug face and the horrible coolness of Penelope's body. *She could.*

Back in her room, Anna spent an hour thumbing through *Oof* and searching the Web before leaning back in her chair, satisfied. *Oof* was open to a chapter titled "Celtic Animism and Polytheism," which featured sketches of animal images, one of which was a very close match to the beast etched into the lid of the iron box. On her laptop a website on ancient Ireland contained another near match, and a confirmation. It was a boar. The animal carved into the lid of the iron box was a pig. How fitting. How perfect. It was a sign.

Anna switched off her lamp, looking out her bedroom window and down to the burned patch in the backyard. Tears wet her eyes, but she was sick of crying. She was *sick* of grieving. Instead, she would get justice. She went downstairs and removed Jack's car keys from their hook on the kitchen wall and left the dark house through the back door.

Twenty minutes later, what she saw through Izzy's bedroom window had her biting her fist to keep from laughing. Anna was on her toes in Izzy's backyard, watching him through the glass. He slept in his bed, curled up in the fetal position with his thumb in his mouth. If she had her phone, she could show the world what big, bad Izzy was really like. What she was about to do to him would have to suffice.

Izzy's bedroom was dimly lit by the moonlight filtering through the window and the glow of a screen saver scrolling across his computer monitor. It was the image of a naked woman wearing a dog collar. Typical. But there was something very *off* about the angle of the woman's head. Anna pressed down further on her aching toes and leaned closer to the window, squinting to get a better look. The air caught in her throat.

A picture of Anna's face had been digitally attached to the naked woman scrolling across Izzy's monitor.

The potato salad Anna had for lunch made a bitter re-appearance in the back of her throat. She turned her back to the window, sliding down the aluminum siding to the grass, and picked up the iron box from where she'd left it on the ground. Anna ran her hand over the closed lid, feeling the dulled vibration of a spirit muted by holy water.

"I'm going to set you free," she whispered to it.

Anna dug into the grass with both hands, scooping up cold, moist soil. Using her thumbs, she massaged the dirt into the shallow crevices of the pig etching, smearing it along the hinges, covering the box with the musty dark earth. She filled her hands with more dirt and continued to caress it onto the box. Once saturated with soil, she brought the box close to her face, looking for signs that the *attachment* was responding to the ritual. A blast of hot, wet air, like a sharp exhale, swirled across her cheek.

"I wash away your binding," she whispered, her mouth almost touching the box. Another blast of hot air, wet and pungent, fell across her lips like a grateful kiss. She wiped her lips off with her sleeve (she wasn't that desperate), got to her feet and tucked the box into the nook of a pine tree a few yards from Izzy's window. From the landscaping around the base of the tree, she collected several pinecones and threw them—*one, two, three*—at Izzy's window. As the *thwacks* echoed in the empty yard, Anna sprinted down the block to Jack's car.

She didn't take a deep breath until she was out of Izzy's neighborhood. Now all she had to do was get back home undetected. There was also the matter of dealing with her father once he realized the box was missing, but she'd handle that later. A block from her house Anna turned the engine off, coasting into the Fagan driveway with the car in neutral, lights off. But through Jack's hoard in the windows, she saw a sliver of light. The kitchen light was on. *Crack balls!*

Jack didn't look up when she walked in. He sat on the stairs facing the front door, his head in his hands.

"Where is it?" he asked through gritted teeth.

Minutes later Anna was back in Jack's car, sitting slumped and cross-armed in the passenger seat, a black baseball cap pulled down over her eyes. Jack turned around in the driver's seat, searching through the mess in the backseat. He pulled out a blue velvet bag with a cross stitched on it and stuffed it into his jacket pocket. After pulling out of the driveway, Jack broke the loaded silence between them.

"Do you have any idea what you've done?"

Anna met his withering gaze with one of her own. "I know exactly what I did. Peeps was murdered and *I* did something about it."

Jack bristled but said nothing. These digs at him about her mother weren't altogether fair. It wasn't his fault Helen Fagan was dead, Anna knew that. But it *was* his fault that he gave up on trying to contact her spirit, that he'd trashed the house and made them both objects of fear and ridicule.

Jack kept his eyes on the road. "This is our goddamn *livelihood* you're messing with, not to mention exposing this poor Izzy kid to god knows what. I didn't raise you to hurt people."

They spoke to each other in grunted monosyllables as she directed him to Izzy's house. Jack parked a few houses down and they darted between neighboring houses to Izzy's backyard. The box was no longer in the tree outside Izzy's window, and his bedroom light was on.

"He's in there," Anna whispered, gesturing to Izzy's bedroom window. "I'll wait in the car."

"I may need you to assist," Jack said.

"Are you kidding? I can't risk him spotting me."

"Possession victims have little to no recall of what happens when they're possessed, you know that."

"I'll ponder that in the car."

Jack placed a firm hand on her forearm. "Maybe it's time you took some responsibility for your actions."

It felt like all of the blood in her body was being pumped in hot pulses from her aching brain. She wrenched her arm out of his grasp, ignoring the shock in his eyes. "Fine."

They crept up to the window. Anna crouched down by the siding while Jack peered inside.

"I don't see him," Jack said. "What is that..." he trailed off, suddenly rigid.

Anna's stomach dropped. *Oh no. The screen saver on Izzy's monitor!* Anna stood just as Jack bent down toward her. They bonked foreheads.

"Ow," she said, rubbing her head. The last thing she needed was more pain in her friggin' head.

Jack's sunken eyes were full of horror. "What is that... picture?"

Anna's cheeks burned. She hadn't done anything wrong. Why was he looking at her like that? "It's not *me*, Dad. He just put my head on it."

"Is that little...that *boy*, is he bothering you?"

"Yeah, he's *bothers* me. He killed Peeps!"

Jack's struggle to find something to say ended when Izzy levitated into view behind the window. Izzy was horizontal, wearing only unfortunate black briefs adorned with a white skull pattern. The skin on his grinning face was puckered and ridged the way fingers and toes get after a long bath, aging him half a century.

Anna and Jack ducked beneath the window, breathing hard, their backs against the siding.

"It's a full possession," Jack said, "and the spirit is strong. What did you *do*?"

"Not much. Gave the box a little dirt bath."

"You must have been pretty enthusiastic about it," he said, with a hint of pride. After seeing that screen saver, Jack no longer seemed overly concerned about Izzy's well-being. "Okay," he said, standing up, "you have permission to go to the car."

As Jack pushed open the window, Anna speed-walked around the side of Izzy's house. She was almost out of the driveway when she heard a loud grunt and a string of muffled curses. *Crap.* Jack was in trouble. She crept back around the side of the house and saw her father's legs sticking out of the window.

By the time Anna reached him, he'd collapsed belly-first onto the windowsill, gasping. Before she could grab one of Jack's feet, he tumbled into Izzy's room, landing with a loud thump.

Anna stood on the tips of her sore toes, her fingers gripping the windowsill. "You okay?"

Jack nodded from the floor of Izzy's bedroom. He put his finger to his lips, shushing her. Izzy slowly turned in midair like he was being roasted on an invisible skewer, still wearing a vacant grin as if unaware of their presence. Izzy's reddish hair, normally cropped to his head, looked lethal; the short spikes came to sharp points and had knife-like edges, mimicking the spikes in the crude pig etching on the lid of the iron box. Whatever was in the iron box was now inside Izzy. And where was the box? Anna scanned the room. Besides a dirty couch, there was no furniture other than his messy bed and desk. Izzy's clothes were in a pile on the floor of the closet—not a single item hung on a hanger. Posters of naked women lined the walls, their faces and bodies twisted in either contrived ecstasy or pain. The room was gross, just like Izzy.

Jack struggled to his feet. "Go back to the car," he hissed, and then launched into a coughing fit, stifling the noise with his hands.

Anna sighed. She wasn't going anywhere. Jack was clearly in no shape to deal with this alone. She pulled herself through the window and into Izzy's bedroom.

CHAPTER NINE

THE PIG MAN COMETH

I zzy sure was pissy about something, or maybe it was the spirit from the iron box who was pissy. Floating in the air, his facial expressions shifted between fear and a defiant glare. He was snorting, too, and squealing. The irony wasn't lost on Anna. Izzy, the piggish bore, appeared to be possessed by an actual boar-pig. Sometimes life was fair.

Jack pulled the blue velvet bag with the cross on it from his jacket pocket. From the bag he removed a crucifix and a small "sprinkler" vessel containing holy water that was attached to a thin chain.

"By the power of Christ, I command you to be gone!" Jack said, swinging the vessel at Izzy. Drops of holy water soared through the air and landed on Izzy's bare chest with tiny pops.

Izzy raised his head from his horizontal position and turned to Jack with a puzzled expression. "What's up, bro?" he said. The small burns were merely a nuisance. His attention moved to the wall behind Jack, to a poster of a woman with her breasts exposed.

"Titties! Titties! Titties!" Izzy said, and soared through the air with his arms and legs splayed, pressing himself against the poster, nuzzling it, drool falling from his lower lip.

Jack flicked holy water. "By the power of Christ…"

Damn it. Jack's approach was all wrong. Crouched behind Izzy's bed, Anna spotted the iron box between the folds of

Izzy's smelly blanket. They needed to get this pig spirit, or whatever it was, out of Izzy and back into that box.

"Dad!"

Jack whirled around, his eyes widening at the sight of Anna's head peering from behind the mattress. "I said get the hell out of here!"

"On the bed. The box. *Look at it.*"

Annoyed, Jack grabbed the box off Izzy's blanket.

"The Jesus stuff won't do it," Anna whispered. "It's from ancient Celtic times—pre-Christianity, *B freakin' C.*"

Jack brushed some dirt off the etching. "Pagans?"

"Sort of."

"And you know this how?"

"Research first. Isn't that what you taught me?" Anna wasn't above a little butt-kissing in her predicament. At least Izzy's lustful attentions were still focused on the poster.

"What now?" she said, standing next to Jack on the crusty carpet, hoping that he was right and Izzy wouldn't remember any of this.

"We need to ramp up the power of Source in the last traces of this holy water or we're out of luck," he said. "To do that we have to tap into the spirit's belief system. What do you know about it?"

"The Celts worshipped nature," she said. "Animal spirits. Water spirits, too. Important bodies of water were considered, like, spiritual crossroads."

Izzy stopped slobbering on the mangled poster. "Goblin Girl?"

Anna froze. As Izzy turned to her, the razor-sharp spikes on his head sliced through the poster and into the wall, sending plaster, paint and paper shavings to the floor. Izzy dropped to the carpet and walked toward her, sniffing the air and snorting. Large swaths of saliva oozed from his lower lip.

Jack raised his hand, flicking more holy water. "Get back!"

Drops of water sizzled across Izzy's chest and he shot upward, the spikes on his head lodging into the ceiling. Izzy grunted as plaster rained down around him, and then, realizing he was stuck, *roared*.

Anna cringed as Izzy's rage compounded the pain behind her eyes. She'd gotten in *way* over her head on this one. This spirit attachment was stronger than expected, and they were almost out of holy water. While Izzy thrashed about, pedaling his feet while impaled in the ceiling, Anna spotted a deep and inflamed gash on one of his ankles. She suppressed a grim smile. Penelope went out fighting.

Jack began pumping her for more information about the box, and Izzy managed to swivel his eyes toward Anna. They flared for a moment with hate and recognition and then shifted, unfocused and wild, sinking further into his wrinkled face.

Surrounded by endless darkness the only sensation was that of a light wind. No, not a wind, Izzy realized. He was moving, sailing through the darkness into more darkness. He saw two faint, twinkling stars in the distance and grew desperate to reach them. The wind hastened as he picked up speed, flying through the blackness toward the pair of lights.

Growing closer, he saw that the stars weren't twinkling. They were static. But something bobbed up and down in front of them, jerking from one to the other. Closer still, Izzy saw it was a skinny, barrel-chested man, his face lined with deep wrinkles. The man had a blond scraggly beard and wore an oversized vest made of bronze on top of a blue robe. And the lights weren't stars. They were holes. A way out!

Izzy rocketed toward the holes, crying out with need. But the bearded man dug one of his hands into Izzy's hair, yanking him back from the light holes. No longer surrounded by blackness, Izzy was dragged down an endless hallway lined with doors on either side. *The bearded man pulled on each doorknob with his free hand. When he found one that opened he shoved Izzy through the door and slammed it shut. Izzy's eyes adjusted to the murky light, his scalp burning. He heard a lock engage.*

Izzy sat on the floor of a vast warehouse, filled as far back and as high as he could see with columns of open air racks. Naked mannequins were stacked on the towering shelves. He stood, stumbling on his infected ankle toward one of the columns, arms outstretched and expecting metal to brace his fall. But the base of the column bent like cardboard under his hand. The column quickly snapped back, but the damage had been done. From a great height a mannequin whistled through the air, crashing to the floor and kicking up a dust cloud. I'm in hell, he thought, for killing that bitch of a dog.

Izzy hadn't meant to kill the dog. He'd gone to the Fagan backyard almost every night for a month, but that night he'd finally jumped the fence. He wasn't sure what he wanted to do to Anna, bang her, choke her, maybe both. The plan was to figure it out when he got her alone. There'd been a weird pulsing in his head, urgent and cold. But now that he was there, closer to doing it, it was more of a satisfied hum. Lately, he imagined every girl he saw screaming in pain, but liking it. Even the most extreme videos now bored him. Izzy needed more pain, more screaming. He wanted Anna to scream. He wanted to make her scream.

He'd heard the growl when his sneakers touched the ground and crouched in front of the doghouse. Sneering at the girly paint job, Izzy flicked his lighter, illuminating the beagle and her litter. There was another growl, wolf-like, as the dog shot out and bit into his ankle. He'd kicked at her with his free leg, lost his balance, and fell. When the dog came back at him, snarling, Izzy kicked her again, this time connecting hard with her side. Something inside the dog cracked, and she retreated into the doghouse.

After limping back to the fence at the edge of the Fagan yard, Izzy lit a cigarette to settle his nerves. He thought about getting another kick in, maybe stomping the dog's head. The visceral want of it sent hot blood rushing to his face. Instead, he'd taken a last mournful glance at Anna's dark bedroom, flicking his clove cigarette on the ground before pulling himself back over the fence and bracing against a sudden wind.

A low rumble in the warehouse became a roar as mannequins tumbled down by the dozens, crashing to the floor and kicking up huge plumes of dust. They all had faces now, Anna's face. The mannequin closest to him twisted its neck toward him, its Anna-face coming to life. "Do you mind?" it said. "Your stench offends."

Izzy turned away, distracted by a movement in the air. A great cloud of dust was slowly funneling into the darkest corner of the warehouse, about a football field away. There was something else in the warehouse, lurking in that dark corner. It was blacker than the dark abyss and, every instinct told him, exponentially more evil than the bearded man. Through his growing panic, Izzy registered a pulling sensation beneath his shoulder blades. As his hands went to his chest, his fingers were quickly lost in the soot-colored fog rising off of him. One of the dust plumes funneling toward the dark corner was coming from him. The thing in the corner was sucking it out of him. It was eating him alive.

Izzy screamed, scrambled to his feet and sprinted toward the door. He threw his shoulder against it until it opened and then sprinted back down the corridor. The doors and floor evaporated around him, and he sailed again through the dark abyss, searching for and then finding the pair of lights, knowing now what they were. The bearded man no longer scared him and Izzy flew at him, shoving him aside. Izzy floated close to the light-holes—which were actually eye holes, his eye holes—and looked into his bedroom. The bearded man roared in surprise and came at Izzy, fists raised. They battled for control of Izzy's eyes.

Anna forced herself to look away from Izzy's crazed and wrinkled face. "The Celts believed that water spirits were links between Source and the earthly dimension. That seems relevant, right?"

Jack nodded. "I can use that."

Izzy grunted and pushed hard against the ceiling, freeing his spiked head. He dropped to the floor, snarling at them as Jack swung the vessel. The small sprinkling of holy water missed him entirely. When flustered, Jack had crappy aim. Izzy crawled toward them drooling on the carpet, snorting and sniffing, his nose pointed in the direction of Anna's crotch.

Jack wrapped a hand around Anna's bicep. "You're getting out of here, *now*!"

Part of her wanted nothing more than to do a running dive out of Izzy's bedroom window, but this was her mess to clean up. Anna yanked the vessel from Jack's hand and held it up toward Izzy.

Her voice booming, she yelled, "You have totally pissed off Sequana, goddess of the River Seine!"

Izzy cocked his head at her and snorted, his puckered face pinched with fresh alarm.

"You dare to defy her natural order of death and rebirth!" Anna brought her arm back. "This water holds the venom of her wrath!"

Anna flung the vessel at Izzy. The last few drops of water soared through the air, landing on his face. A series of large, sizzling blisters spread down his neck. Izzy shrieked and retreated, cowering in the corner of his room, emitting the keening, high-pitched squeals of a piglet.

"The spirit," Anna said to Jack. "It really is a pig, isn't it?"

Jack shook his head. "Animals always cross over. This thing was once a man, and men have egos. If we can get him to show off, it might wear him out."

Jack poured a circle of salt on the floor around him and Anna.

"This circle represents the center of our souls," he shouted at Izzy, "that which is eternal and cannot be harmed."

Izzy sniffed around the perimeter of the circle, but did not cross the salt barrier. Jack and Anna relaxed a smidge. It was a win. If the spirit inhabiting Izzy's body believed the circle was an un-crossable boundary, it would act as one.

"What did boars mean to the ancient Celts?" Jack asked.

"They were brave beasts," she said, "hard to hunt and kill. Soldiers had boar hair weaved into their armor." Anna pointed to the boar's spikes on the lid of the box in Jack's hand. "They thought the boar hair made them fierce warriors, upped their odds to survive."

Jack studied the box.

"I think I know what this is," he said, stepping to the edge of the circle. "We have to provoke it."

Jack stood at the edge of the circle, taunting Izzy. "So, the mighty boar seeks shelter inside a puny boy?"

Hot air puffed from Izzy's nose.

"Perhaps you're just the runt of an old swine's litter and not a warrior at all." Jack laughed derisively, then nodded at Anna. Her turn.

Anna used her best Sydney mean-girl voice. "Are you afraid of real girls, too, like the waste case you inhabit?"

Izzy stomped his back legs and snorted, sniffing the barrier resentfully.

"Could it be you're not a mighty boar at all, but a *man*, a lowly tailor?" Jack said. "A soldier's servant? Did your armor fail them? Did you pay with your life?"

Izzy's spine stiffened, his eyes circles of shock and rage. He roared and charged, crashing into the invisible barrier surrounding Anna and Jack, squealing in pain as a few of his spikes snapped off on impact. Injured, Izzy ran back to the mutilated poster and nuzzled it for comfort.

"We command you, abhorrent spirit," Jack screamed at him, "return to your hiding place! Back to your bristle box!"

Anna had to admit, Jack's supernatural sleuthing skills were on point. She braced herself for Izzy's charge, digging her heels into the scuzzy carpet, but he only whimpered, his spikes wilted and torn.

Jack raised the vessel. "This is your final warning!"

Beaten, Izzy slumped and slid down the wall. His mouth went slack and then opened wide, his chest heaving as he vomited. But it was no ordinary puke stream. It moved with intelligence. Long and thick with coarse bristles, the vomit shot across the room, slapped against the open lid and oozed down into the box. The lid slammed shut unceremoniously and Izzy collapsed, his head lolling to one side. His hair and features returned to normal, but several bald and bloody patches remained on his scalp.

Someone pounded on Izzy's bedroom door.

"Izzy? What's going on in there?"

Izzy's eyes fluttered open at the sound of his mother's voice and he trained them on Anna. She stood there stunned by the hate and fear he radiated until his eyes rolled up into his head and he lost consciousness. Anna and Jack made a hasty exit out of the window, bringing the box with them, and hurried back to Jack's sedan.

• • •

Later that night, back home at the kitchen table, Anna held the iron box while Jack poured the last splashes of a jug of holy water into a glass bowl. The box zapped her fingers lightly, out of gas but still trying to punish her for her betrayal.

"Doesn't look like enough water," she said.

Jack took the box from her and dropped it into the bowl. The water instantly corrupted.

"When the entity's weak, like Pig-Man the Tailor here, you don't need much. It's also the last of what we have in stock."

Scum-filled foam rose in the bucket, close to overflowing.

"It's not working," Anna said.

"Patience."

The foam died down. The water calmed to a murky cesspool and then *cleared* to a pristine brilliance. It was done. The Pig-Man had moved on to a sty in the hereafter.

Anna slapped Jack on the back. "Nice!"

It was the wrong move. Jack started wheezing. He tried to catch his breath, failed, and then, racked by a sudden convulsion, retched up a large, black loogie on the table.

Anna was repulsed. "What *is* that?"

Jack coughed and wiped off the edges of his mouth. "Must be from the fire."

Anna went to the sink, filled a glass of water and handed it to Jack.

"Allergies, the smoke inhalation, years of exposure to troubled spirits. It's all taken a toll. I'm getting older," Jack said, "not recovering as fast."

"So quit," Anna said, sitting back down. "Drains still get clogged, right? Go back to being a plumber and we'll just be normal again."

It was a nice dream, but she could tell by the look on his face that he wasn't hearing her.

"What you did tonight..." Jack said. "You have all the right instincts. Maybe tonight was supposed to show you that. Maybe—"

"Right," she said, "everything happens for a reason. Like what happened to Mom?"

Jack's eyes darkened, but then he placed a hand over one of hers.

"The Fagan name means something in the paranormal community," he said. "We have a real chance right now to expand.

Now that Geneva's working with us, think about all the people we can help, people who have nobody else to turn to. There are plenty of plumbers in Bloomtown, but only one person who does what I do. And we need the money." He squeezed her hand. "Can I count on you or not?"

Did she really have a choice? "Sure," she said, taking back her hand, "I'll keep training the new elf, but only if this office thing is kept on the low. No interviews or ads in the *Bloomtown Gazette.*"

"The *elf* is working for free. More importantly, if what she says is true about her invention, she could be our ticket out of this mess. Imagine how easy it would be to track spirit attachments if we can see them in 3-D! Not to mention the cash people will pay to get a look at what's keeping them up at night."

"Okay, but you have to get yourself checked out, and soon."

"Soon as I get insurance."

Anna started down the path to the stairs and then stopped, calling back to her father. "Is it true that animals always cross?"

"It is," Jack said.

Anna nodded, grateful that she didn't have to worry about Penelope. She climbed the steps, eager for her uncluttered bedroom and soft mattress.

"And you're still in trouble!" her father called after her. But she knew she wasn't.

Anna needed to sleep, but first she should email Doreen and ask how things were going with her mom. Freddy, too. He'd definitely want to hear about the goings on at Casa Izzy. But she was unsettled by the cloying withdrawal of not having gazed upon Craig's loveliness in several hours. She would go online instead and see what he was up to. Her decision made, the pounding in her head settled, pulsing softly like a distant but ominous tribal drum.

CHAPTER TEN

NERDGASM

Anna left for the new office on Washington Street at ten o'clock on Saturday morning. After six days of the world's longest headache and barely any sleep, she longed for a dark room and icy washcloth. But with Jack unwell, it was up to her to continue working with Geneva. Instead of resting or seeing a doctor, Jack planned on spending the day checking the "release status" of dormant objects in the basement. When a bound spirit let go of their object and crossed into Source, the object had to be retagged and either returned to the client or stored with other cleared objects to avoid any "cross pollination."

It was an important task, but Anna was surprised that Jack didn't jump at the chance to see Geneva. His *things* in the basement trumped everything, she guessed.

Trudging down Eden Street, Anna checked her phone for any Izzy-related news or threats, praying that Jack was right and Izzy wouldn't remember the exorcism. She'd hoped that memories of Izzy drooling and terrorized would bring her closure, but instead they made her nauseous and uneasy, as if she'd somehow diminished herself irretrievably.

The moment Anna walked into the ranch house's bright living room, the pain of her headache subsided, but just a little. Geneva knelt on the wood floor, surrounded by boxes of files and office furniture in the latter stages of assembly, screwing the base of a battery compartment back into the belly of her mysterious EMF invention. It resembled a smooth, bulbous super-soaker type of water pistol, but smaller, sleeker and encased by dark-tinted fiberglass.

Geneva looked up and smiled, her eyes crinkling at the corners. She wore a long flowing sundress in the same shade of yellow as the walls on her new bedroom. Her sandals had a vibrant floral design. Anna figured this was the kind of look that was easier to pull off in California.

"So, where's Jack?" Geneva asked.

"He had stuff to do at home," Anna said, registering Geneva's disappointment. "How's your hotel?"

"Lovely," Geneva said, "but I'm looking forward to the day I can move in. This place already feels like home."

Anna sat at the large white drafting table that was to become the main workstation and got to work untangling a printer cord. She was squinting at the back of a computer, trying to find the printer port, when the doorbell rang. Pete, as his name tag stated, stood on their doorstep.

"Delivery from holy water dot com," he growled when Anna opened the door, wheeling in a cart stacked with three jugs. His goatee looked ridiculous hanging off his baby face.

"I need your signature."

Pete handed Anna a pen and then snatched it back the second she signed her name, scratching her hand with his thumbnail. Anna glared at him. He wasn't even going to apologize? The cold glint in his eyes made her think twice about saying anything, but she shut the door after him with extra vigor.

Anna returned to the drafting table with one of the jugs and began pouring small amounts of holy water into the array of vessels and spray bottles that Jack liked to keep handy.

Geneva abandoned her invention, wheeled an office chair next to Anna, and sat down.

"Do you mind if I watch?"

"Nope," Anna said, funneling holy water into a spray bottle.

"So," Geneva said, "if a spirit attaches to an object or person you do…an exorcism?"

"If it attaches to a person, you do an exorcism. To an object? It's a clearing."

"But isn't holy water strictly a priest kind of thing?"

Geneva had watched too many movies. "Rituals to purify water for the purpose of warding off evil were done by the early Egyptians, Greeks, Romans, Jews…everybody did it," Anna said, "because it works."

Geneva lifted the jug of holy water off the drafting table and examined it. "There was a study suggesting that water molecules react to their emotional environment," she said. "Maybe that's why anyone tapped into Source can make holy water."

Anna nodded. "My dad used to make it when I was a kid, but he lost his mojo and now has to order it, and it ain't cheap."

"What about nonhuman, negative entities?" Geneva asked. "Does holy water work on them?"

"Demons?"

"Have you ever come across one?"

There was a stretch of silence before Anna answered. "Years ago."

Sensing the subject was better off dropped, Geneva busied herself with a box of files. After a few minutes, the doorbell rang again. It was Freddy, wearing jeans that seemed to bag more than usual. He was late, *again*. Anna bit the inside of her cheek to keep from admonishing him, reminding herself that he was there to help. It was getting harder to control her temper.

"Where's Dor?" Anna said.

Freddy shrugged. "Didn't pick up her phone. She's been kinda weird lately."

Anna wouldn't mention Dor's situation with Cindy until she and Freddy were alone. She felt a twinge of guilt for not checking on Dor last night, but then the pain behind her eyes sharpened. Jack's illness, setting up the office, Doreen's mom, the creep factor in Bloomtown—how did it all end up on her shoulders? Freddy stared at her as she struggled to calm her sudden anger.

Anna pointed to the beginnings of a smaller workstation in the corner. "You can start with getting that scanner working."

"Hi, and you're welcome," Freddy said. He stood inside the door, arms crossed. He was cute when he was feisty and had agreed to give up a weekend to help her out. So why was she fighting off another wave of irritation?

"*Thank you* for coming over," Anna said.

Freddy brushed by her, smelling like a mix of fresh laundry and the slightly musty Freddy smell Anna was very familiar with. He must have ridden his bike over.

"Freddy," Anna said, "this is Geneva. She's working with my father—um—with us."

Freddy's eyes went a little wide. Was it Geneva's clingy yellow sundress or that Anna was stepping up as the heir apparent? Probably both.

"Nice to meet you," he said.

Geneva bowed her head and clasped her hands together. "*Namaste.*"

Freddy blushed.

"It means she recognizes the soul part of you or something like that," Anna said. "Right?"

"Pretty much," Geneva said, winking at Freddy.

The woman really knew how to throw a guy off balance. Anna imagined trying that *namaste* stuff with Craig. Nah, he wouldn't go for it.

Freddy wheeled an office chair over to the workstation in the corner. "What's this?" he said, picking up a small plastic box with a series of lights on it.

Anna squinted. "An EMF reader." She grinned at Geneva. "The old-fashioned kind." She took it out of his hand to get a closer look. "Looks like it's busted. Stuck on the highest reading."

"Really?" Geneva said. "May I see that?"

"What's an EMF?" Freddy asked.

Geneva scrutinized the device. "An electromagnetic field. It's a physical field that emits a low-frequency radiation. You'll find one around anything electrical."

"Oh yeah, sure," Freddy said, "so wiring, cell phones, appliances, all that stuff?"

"Yes," Geneva said, "and more."

"Spirits, too," Anna said. "You can use it to track the location of an entity, or the object they are attached to."

"Ghosts are *electrical*?" Freddy was dubious.

"Not exactly," Geneva said. "It's possible that they gather electrical energy from the living, harvest it from our auras. And when they get enough of it they can use it to get people's attention, do spooky stuff."

Freddy gave Anna the side eye. "Our auras?"

Geneva graced him with a patient smile. She took the batteries out of the EMF reader and popped them back in.

"All living things are electrical, Freddy. There are low-frequency bio-electromagnetic fields inside cells. Even nonliving things like rocks have magnetic fields." Her fingers found the crystal on her necklace. "One theory is that the magnetic fields of certain elements can intermingle with our auras and potentially strengthen them."

"You study the supernatural?" Freddy asked.

"Well, yes, I'm here to learn, but I'm also an inventor." Geneva pointed to her invention, lying on top of the glass coffee table, still in pieces.

"Cool. What is it?" Freddy asked, coming alive in a way Anna hadn't seen in a while.

"Something that will make this"—Geneva held up the older EMF reader—"obsolete." She turned to Anna. "According to this thing, we're standing on power lines instead of wood."

Anna nodded. "Broken, right?"

"That, or something in this house is throwing off massive electromagnetic fields."

"Nothing is even plugged in, except for one computer and that radio." Anna walked over to the radio. "And it's not even on."

Anna flicked a switch on the radio and the smarmy voice of Bloomtown's very own shock jock filled the room.

"The geniuses at NASA are now saying we're getting one or two more big blasts from the sun, and I mean mongo big, and then this once-in-a-lifetime solar storm will finally be kaput. Let's hope the chumps at NASA know better than the local chimps we got predicting the weather. That Channel 2 guy with the big ears, now am I nuts, or does he look—"

Static overwhelmed the signal and a series of deafening cracks boomed out of the speakers, making them all wince. Geneva shut the radio off.

"Could the storms be causing those high readings?" Freddy asked Geneva.

Geneva shook her head. "Not levels this high. Not on the ground."

Anna took out her phone. "Let me see if I can get online."

"Internet's down," Freddy said, fussing with the radio as Geneva knelt next to her invention. "That's why I was late. I spent the whole morning trying to check my email to see if I got into that school in Florida. Then my mom made me clean my room. She wants to rent it out if I get in."

Wait. *What?* "What school in Florida?" Anna asked.

"I told you about it," he said.

That's right. He had mentioned a school on the day of the failed puppy excursion, but she hadn't taken it seriously.

"Some stranger will stay in your room?" she said, shaken. "*Gross.*"

"Chill, I haven't even gotten accepted yet. If I do get in, the rent money will keep me off PB&J."

Freddy, leaving Bloomtown? Leaving her and Dor? Anna pushed down a growing panic, imagining Freddy in a new, palm-treed town with new and cooler friends, a *girlfriend*.

"Can I take a look?" Freddy asked Geneva, gesturing to the pieces of fiberglass on the coffee table.

Geneva nodded.

"How will this make EMF readers obsolete?" Freddy asked.

"It's an electromagnetic field imager," Geneva said, "an EMI—or Emi, as I like to call her. EMF readers"—Geneva pointed at the older device, still registering through the roof—"can only pick up energy, but they can't show you exactly where it is and what it looks like."

Anna tipped the jug on the drafting table, pouring holy water through a funnel into an empty bottle of Windex. Was Freddy flirting with Geneva? No, he couldn't be. She was old enough to be his mother. He was probably just excited to meet a real scientist. Besides, why would Anna care if he was flirting? She wouldn't. Holy water splattered on the wood floor. Crap. She needed to pay attention.

Geneva got to her feet. "After I finish unpacking, I'll do the last couple tweaks on Emi and give you two a demonstration."

Freddy stared longingly at Emi. "Any way I can help?"

"You good with a screwdriver?"

Freddy nodded.

"I can vouch for his total geekness," Anna said.

"*Gently* reattach the base of the signal trigger." Geneva pointed to Emi's underbelly. "Right here."

"I'm on it!" Freddy said with unnecessary loudness. He cracked his knuckles and dropped to the floor like a spaz.

Geneva raised an amused eyebrow at Anna, said her good-byes and disappeared down the hall to her bedroom. Anna watched her go, perplexed. The woman just gave Freddy free rein over her invention. Anna wasn't sure if she was a good judge of character or just flaky. Probably a bit of both.

"Wow," Anna said to Freddy. "I think you just had a nerdgasm."

CHAPTER ELEVEN

HEY GIRL

B ack at home, Anna made her way down the second-floor hallway and heard the faint creak of the basement door closing downstairs. She knew better than to disturb Jack when he worked down there. The door was always locked and Jack kept the key in his back pocket. Like the grass on their front lawn, Jack bent easily with the wind on certain subjects, but when it came to his all-important *things* in the basement, he was a brick wall.

Anna closed her bedroom door behind her, finding relief, as always, in the orderly structure and soft palette of her bedroom. She sat cross-legged in front of her full-length mirror, tweezers in hand. She had her mother's brows, full with a nicely shaped arch. She didn't mess with them much, but it had been a while and she was due for a pruning.

In the mirror she could see the framed photograph of her mother's face behind her on the bureau. The faded freckles on Helen Fagan's nose and cheeks were visible on her clean and smiling face.

Jack took the candid shot on their honeymoon in Puerto Rico. It wasn't posed like other pictures of her parents, both of them wearing pasted-on smiles. Those were all lost long ago in the ocean of Jack's hoard. There were no pictures of Helen on display anywhere else in the house. Anna suspected that seeing his wife's picture was painful for her father, that he saw the demon and its gleeful, malevolent grin instead of the woman he married. So why then did she leave a large picture of her mother centered on her bureau, knowing it was the first thing he'd see if he came into her room? Was it to punish him or to keep him and his mess out? She wasn't sure.

Anna braced against a stab of grief, raking her fingers through the small rug in front of the mirror. The grief deepened the pain thudding behind her eyes. Pain that built into a tortuous crescendo until, finally, something clicked inside her skull and a chaotic need flooded through her. Anna had to see Craig's Instagram, *now*.

The pain settled when Anna found her phone. She began reading the comments that girls, especially Sydney, had posted on his page. She looked at the mirror, seeing the inadequacy of her frizzy hair, the small bump on her nose, the dull pallor of her skin. Disgust rose in her chest. There she was in all of her non-glory, not *her* exactly, but the collection of parts and blemishes that were so obviously *not good enough*. How could she help Dor, or anyone in Bloomtown, if she could barely stand her own reflection?

Geneva's faint voice echoed inside her. *Mirrors can be a doorway into your soul, if you really look at yourself.* Was it possible? Geneva said that one must be brave to mirror gaze. Anna had her share of imperfections, but bravery she had in spades. Didn't she?

Anna dropped her phone and locked eyes with her reflection, fighting the urge to dismiss the whole thing and go back to analyzing her enormous pores. But after a minute or two of quiet breathing, a distant calm began to soften the edges of her unease. She continued to hold her own gaze. Who *was* she anyway?

There were gold flecks in the hazel of her eyes that she'd never noticed before. Anna stared, fascinated by this undiscovered part of herself. Then, a stirring in her solar plexus, a strange *awakening* that felt both light and powerful, a force that lifted her head, making space in her chest and throat. A rush of cool air filled her lungs, muting the pain in her head.

This *lightness*, it reminded her of something: a memory, a glimpse of a fireplace illuminated by beams of light. Her breath tasted mildly sweet, as it had when she was a kid in gymnastics class. She would tumble and bend so much that after a while, muscles hot and loose, she felt almost detached from her body yet in total control of it. But that wasn't quite it.

Anna felt more like she had in the hours after swim practice in junior high. Swimming lap after lap through the water, she'd catch flashes of her coach standing poolside when she turned her head to suck in air. Always the swimmer in front of you and counting breaths; stroke, stroke, stroke, *breath*e. At the wall, a flip turn and push off, followed by moments of coasting, arms straight, head down. Stroke, stroke, stroke, *breathe*. Over and over, slicing through the water until it became mind*less*. After practice she'd felt clear and calm, her body warm and tired, her breath sweet.

Her phone emitted a loud *ping*, the alert for an incoming text message. Anna ignored it, keeping her focus on the mirror. More *pings* erupted from her phone, louder than usual and demanding her attention. The dull pounding in her head lurched back to life and fought for dominance against the new lightness inside her.

What the hell was wrong with her phone? The pain behind her eyes surged and she closed her eyes, gritting her teeth against the wave of rage that accompanied it. *No.* She didn't want to be taken over by this dark mood. She looked to the mirror again, determined to reconnect with the glimpse of serenity she'd discovered. But something caught her eye, a movement.

Every muscle in Anna's body stiffened. The picture of her mother in the mirror no longer reflected Helen Fagan. It was the demon from eight years past, its tongue flickering out of its grinning mouth. Anna's jaw clenched, and the picture once again framed the face of her smiling mother. The loud *pings* continued from her phone. Anna picked it up with shaking hands. It was a text from Craig Shine.

hey girl

And just like that a crazed joy bloomed inside her, despite the foreboding atmosphere that now surrounded her phone. Even in her frazzled state Anna recognized that foreboding as a warning from her intuition, a warning she'd had before.

At ten years old, Anna had wandered away on a class trip to a nearby park. She ran ahead of the group, planning to jump out of the trees to scare Freddy and Dor. But she quickly lost her bearings and came across a path in the woods. The trees around the mouth of the path took on the same dark quality now encompassing her phone. *Stay away.* But danger and excitement are often interchangeable in young minds, and Anna started down the deserted path. Almost immediately a man came out of the trees, clean-cut and dressed in a blue tracksuit. She moved aside for him to pass but he followed her stride, remaining directly behind her, quiet and menacing.

The panicked teacher yelled her name, out of sight but close by, and the man darted into the trees. He wore sneakers without shoelaces, his shoes flopping open as he ran. Long white cords dangled from his clenched fists. Anna still thought about Park Man and what he would have done to her. Would she have fought back or remained frozen in terror, succumbing to some nightmarish, violent fate?

And here she was again, pressing on into possibly dangerous territory. Or maybe she was just losing it? It was just a phone, not a pedo in a park! The transformation of her mother's picture was probably a hallucination brought on by stress. Anyway, it wasn't important. Nothing was more important than Craig.

hey girl.

All of existence shrank down to those two little words, and her jittery heart flapped about in her chest like a newly caged bird. Another jolt as her phone rang. It was Doreen. Anna forwarded her call to voice mail and replied to Craig's text.

what r u up 2? ☺

Craig texted right back.

blasting tunes so mom stays out. Ur webcam on?

He wanted to see her. A webcam box appeared on Anna's laptop across the room. She scrambled over her bed, reaching the laptop on her desk in record time. It was Craig's face! Live-action Craig! His tousled black hair was slightly matted and his face had an oily sheen, but Anna barely registered it. A longing for him welled inside her, pulsing along with her quickening heartbeat. Moisture drained from her mouth.

Another text from Craig on her phone.

u alone?

yes, she replied.

turn ur cam on wanna c u

k hold on

Anna rushed to her mirror, applied lip gloss, flipped her hair, brushed it, flipped it again and then took the black tape off the camera on her laptop. Craig smiled in response and typed on his cell.

u look hot

Can u turn ur mic on? she asked. Why were they still texting? She wanted to hear his voice.

Craig shook his head.

wanna listen 2 tunes and c ur sexy body. K??

☺, Anna replied.

serious, he texted.

The butterflies in her stomach morphed into a murder of crows. Was she supposed to act like the women in Izzy's posters? Was that what Craig wanted? Arched back, pouty lips, that kind of thing? Or should she just pose and flex like a bodybuilder? She stepped back and then playfully sashayed toward the camera, hands on hips, lips parted. Craig was smiling and singing to himself. He was into it. He was into *her*. It was a rush like no other.

u r hot lemme c ur bra

Was he kidding?

no way, she texted.

its no big deal? I know about hastings, he replied.

A gut punch. Craig knew about Michael Hastings and her last year. Anna cringed at the memory. The beer on Hastings's breath, her wanting to know what the Fuss Was All About, their complete lack of chemistry. And if that wasn't letdown enough, Mike went and ran his mouth about it, after swearing on his little sister's *life* that he wouldn't. It went buzzing through the whole school. Sydney and her cronies were all over it, telling anyone that cared to listen (pretty much everyone), making him out to be this big player and Anna a slut. Such a glaring double standard, but that was how the Mikes and Sydneys of the world liked it.

So what? Craig assumed that because of Hastings she was fair game? An urge to tell Craig to go screw himself was on the verge of manifesting.

Jk hastings is a doosh, just wanna c u, Craig texted. *think about u all the time.*

Heat blew through her. She felt light and giddy like the time she drank wine at Freddy's house during a Seder dinner. Attention from Craig was an elixir that made everything else fade away, and this was her chance to connect with him, to give him what he wanted. For a quick second, Anna lifted her shirt at the webcam, grateful as hell that she had a cute black bra on. Craig was singing again, bobbing his head and wearing a smirk that didn't quite reach his eyes. He typed.

take the bra off

115

There was a muffled crash from downstairs. No, the *basement*. Whatever Jack was up to, he wasn't going to screw this up for her. She texted Craig.

not gonna happen ☺

But then a second muffled crash rattled the walls. Something was wrong. She sent Craig a final text.

Brb

Anna rushed out of her room, down the stairs and into the kitchen. She yanked on the basement door handle, but it didn't budge.

"Dad! What's going on?"

She rattled the doorknob hard, hearing only muffled coughing until Jack finally screamed, "I'm okay!" And then a strangled, high-pitched "Tripped!!"

"Come upstairs!" she yelled through the door.

This was ridiculous. She pulled on the doorknob, feeling resistance from a middle and upper latch. But there wasn't an upper latch on the outside of the door. The basement door was locked from the *inside?* What the hell? Bending down she peered underneath the door. Nothing. Total blackness. Jack couldn't work down there without a trace of light.

Anna foraged through the hoard under the kitchen table, finding an old wire hanger. After straightening the hanger's pliable tip, she poked it under the basement door and then withdrew it. Pieces of dark blue foam were stuck to the metal tip. Jack had placed some kind of a barrier, a *seal*, on the inside of the basement door. To keep her out or to keep something else in? Below, Jack's coughing fit ended in a nauseating retch.

"Can you move?" she yelled into the door.

"I'm fine!"

"Then come upstairs!" She was screaming through the keyhole now.

When Jack didn't reply, Anna decided that she'd had enough. She followed the path into the unlivable living room and starting kicking around the hoard piles, looking for something with some weight. *Ow.* Her foot found something heavy, all right. Who knew they had a bowling ball? Was there anything that Jack wouldn't hoard?

Anna lugged the ball back into the kitchen, stomping on any of Jack's hoard that had fallen into the narrow path. Back in front of the basement door, she held the bowling ball with both hands and swung her arms between her legs, gaining momentum. One, two, *three.* She let go, heaving the heavy bowling ball at the doorknob. Bull's-eye!

The door buckled inward and the doorknob popped off, falling to the kitchen floor along with the bowling ball, which bounced heavily, cracking the tile. But the top lock of the basement door was still stubbornly latched from the inside. Anna picked up the bowling ball, her arms burning, and hurled it again, higher this time. The bowling ball hit the top of the door, cracking the molding and breaking the inside top latch. The basement door busted inward, exposing the dingy light below. The bowling ball went crashing down the basement steps, and Anna was right behind it.

CHAPTER TWELVE

ANOTHER LEVEL OF SICK

The fumes hit Anna on the way down the basement stairs. She pulled her T-shirt over her mouth to filter the dreadful stench. Flies littered the steps, most of them dead, some listlessly hopping, using their last throes of life to try to escape. When she reached the bottom step, she saw what had attracted them.

A rotting mess of garbage littered the concrete floor at the base of the steps. Vegetable scraps, banana peels and moldy pizza formed a putrid brown collage. She stepped around it and turned left into the large, unfinished basement. Anna wheezed as her lungs rejected the foul air. The smell of harsh chemicals and rotting garbage was nauseating. But what lay before her was much worse. Open trash bags sat atop the massive hoard piles throughout the basement, dangerously close to several dingy lightbulbs hanging from the ceiling on wires.

Below the blanket of rotting garbage were piles of broken furniture, artwork and stacks of rusted pipes that had crushed the boxes of books and appliances beneath them. In one corner, the rusted green handlebar of her childhood bicycle stuck out of a chaotic pile of toys and gardening equipment. A rat ran over Anna's foot and she stumbled and then gagged, more from the stench than the rat. There was a stirring in the edge of her vision—something moved inside one of the garbage bags atop the hoard pile to Anna's left. She reached up and pulled the soft plastic further open. A rotten piece of raw chicken fell out of the bag and flopped down to the concrete floor, infested with dozens of squirming maggots.

Anna spun around, looking for Jack, but it was hard to see *specifics* in the chaos. The overstimulation of the basement was too much for Anna's battered mind to process. She was used to Jack's hoard. But this was a whole other level of *sick*. Another rat ran by her feet and Anna jumped, startled, and sucked in rancid air. She gagged, struggling to breathe, pulling at her throat. The so-called air was thick with mold spores, fumes and cobwebs. Something else moved, and Anna whipped toward it, ready to fight.

It was Jack. She hadn't seen him crouched in the shadow of a looming hoard pile. He got to his feet, stepping into the murky light. His eye sockets threw shadows over his face, turning his features skeletal. The sliver of pity she felt for him turned into anger.

"What did you do, Dad? What *happened* here?"

"I was rooting around in there and slipped," Jack said, gesturing to one of the large canvas bins of exposed bound objects. Each object had a tag that identified the owner and date of binding, and from what she could see, every tag was now stained and unreadable. "Cracked my head on the side of the table." He gestured to a broken folding table that was now supported at an odd angle solely by the hoard underneath it.

She'd forgotten about the crash she heard. "Not that," she said, throwing her hands up. "This!"

Fumes from concentrated drain cleaners and other harsh industrial-strength solvents hung in the air in a toxic fog. The thickest part of the rancid chemical cloud clung to the ceiling above several rows of steel shelving that had long since collapsed atop one another. The containers of chemicals, remnants of Jack's plumbing days, had all either burst or cracked.

"You're always down here," she said through her shirt. "How do you survive?"

Jack didn't answer, just stared back at her dumbly. Disgusted, she turned away from him. Something twinkled in a dank corner. Anna stomped her way over hoard and garbage to the filthy and cracked wooden trunk where the tiny gleam of light originated. Squatting next to it, she touched the lapel of a stained and tattered corduroy blazer. A rusty butterfly pin on the blazer's lapel somehow sparkled in the murky light. The wooden trunk was full of clothes, jewelry and shoes.

"Anna," Jack said, from behind her. She felt his pleading eyes boring into her back.

But Anna couldn't look at him.

"These are Mom's?"

"I wasn't sure...how to let them go."

So he had destroyed them, like he did to everything else. She looked inside another nearby box. Pictures of her mother and Jack, of Anna as a child, her grandparents' wedding portrait—all exposed to the filthy air and ruined. Stuck to the back of the wedding portrait was the worn image of Freddy blowing out seven birthday candles, accidentally spitting all over the cake. That day the other kids had yelled *eww*, but Anna and Dor ate it anyway, not making a big deal of scraping off the top.

"I'm going to fix it," Jack sputtered. "I promise."

She turned to face him. "Your promises are worthless."

Anna kicked and climbed her way over to one of the three bins of bound objects, each the size of a small dumpster. She reached in and picked up a mold-covered box of "Christmas Sausage" that had been smothering one of the bound objects— an old-fashioned typewriter. There was other garbage in the bins, strewn over the objects Jack had once so meticulously documented.

The poor spirits! Even if they wanted to cross into Source, they were trapped. The thick and putrid atmosphere was keeping the spirits from moving into Source. It was against everything she thought Jack stood for. Instead of providing them with a safe environment where they could make peace with their earthly existence, he'd created a hellish trap.

Jack stepped toward her.

"I was going to take them outside this week, air them out," he said. "Let me just…my head." He ran a hand through his tangled mop of hair, and it came away smeared with blood.

"You're bleeding," she said.

"It's okay, just a scratch."

Yeah. Just a scratch, like the house just needed *a little cleanup*.

"None of this is okay!" she yelled, her voice cracking. "Look!" she screamed, pointing at the garbage rotting over hoard piles, kicking at the ground carpeted with dead bugs and rat droppings. "It's this place…*this* is what's making you sick."

It wasn't allergies that caused Jack's illness. Penelope should have been kept inside. Peeps should have been *safe*. Anna's vision blurred. She was going to faint if she didn't get some fresh air.

There was a small window near the top of each of the side walls in the basement. Anna clambered up a hoard pile and tried to force one of the windows open, but it was hopelessly rusted and stuck. She kicked around the hoard pile, her hair dark with grime, looking for something heavy, and then— *ouch*—her tender toes found a wooden coat stand.

Anna's arms already ached from swinging the bowling ball, and her knees threatened to buckle as she pried the coat stand free. Jack sat on the diseased floor, watching her with a dazed expression, his tall frame leaning against his hoard. She rammed the window with the coat stand, breaking the glass. Heading for the second window, she scrambled up another pile of debris, wincing as her foot cracked a piece of burned plywood from Penelope's doghouse. In a single thrust, Anna smashed the second window with the tip of the coat stand.

The chemical fog wafted toward the broken windows, pulled by the fresh air. A few ectoplasmic wisps of souls rose from the large bins of tagged objects, and one by one, they soared out of the small windows. A spirit flew by Anna's head. The trail of relief it radiated penetrated her anger and disgust, giving her brief respite.

"I started to smell lilacs."

Anna whirled around. Jack's sunken face looked back at her blankly.

"What?" she said.

"I started to smell lilacs," he said. "It...it smells like lilacs down here."

Lilacs. Her mother used to dab lilac oil on her wrists every morning. Was he kidding? It smelled like a toxic waste dump.

"I don't smell lilacs," Anna said.

Jack was running his hands through his hair, smearing the dirt and blood on his forehead.

"And then I started thinking about the garbage in the kitchen. That maybe something was in there that had been thrown away by mistake, like a button or nail, something I could wash off and put away, where it wouldn't be forgotten, where it could be used someday. But then it dawned on me that even food scraps could be saved. That right there"—he pointed at a mesh bag full of rotting onions—"I can turn into compost, and those"—he pointed at a stack of crushed shoe boxes—"can be used to *package* the compost to sell on eBay."

Her father had finally lost his mind. And she'd thought that *he* could help find out what was screwing up Bloomtown? Doreen's mom, the puppy-squeezing brat, even Pickens and Izzy—they were all paragons of mental health compared to Jack Fagan.

"Okay," she said, wiping her hands on her jeans. "Let's go."

"Where?" Jack said, as a drop of blood trickled down his forehead.

"To the hospital," Anna said. "I'll drive."

Jack was shaking his head. "It's not that bad, doesn't even hurt, and we're in the hole enough as it is."

He was worried about money, but had no problem wrecking the house? Fine. Let him get a nasty scar, but she couldn't let him stay in the basement.

"Well, you're going upstairs," she said, coughing. Her lungs were closing up. "At least until this cesspool airs out."

She walked to the base of the stairs, stepping directly in the garbage she'd so carefully avoided before finding the mother lode in the basement. The mess at the bottom of the stairs seemed almost quaint now. Jack had the gall to hesitate.

"Come on, Dad," Anna said, doing her best to speak calmly, "up to your room. Get cleaned up and I'll check on you later."

Jack looked almost comfortable in the toxic fog. He opened his mouth, about to protest.

"Let's *go!*" She stalked over to him and held out her hand. Reluctantly, he took it and got to his feet.

• • •

An hour later, Anna wore two cloth face masks, one right over the other for extra filtration, as she pulled a large, industrial-size metal fan down the basement stairs. Chunks of the wooden steps flew off as the heavy fan banged down, but she didn't much care. The *Better Homes and Gardens* shoot would have to wait. She'd already brought down two buckets of soapy water, a gallon of bleach, a mop and a box of extra-large garbage bags. In her back pocket was a pair of mongo barbecue tongs for picking up anything too gross for rubber gloves alone.

Anna positioned the fan in the meter-wide circumference of concrete floor that she'd cleared of garbage so far. She'd found the fan in the living room underneath a pile of moth-eaten bedspreads that Jack had "collected" from Goodwill.

Taking a deep breath, she snapped on a pair of plastic gloves and trudged to the top of a hoard pile, reaching for one of the dim lightbulbs hanging from the ceiling. The thick winter boots she wore crunched into a box of petrified Cocoa Krispies as she screwed in a new high-wattage bulb.

Anna surveyed the stark ugliness of the now brightly lit basement. Something was bothering her.

Well, a lot of things were bothering her: a sick, injured and apparently completely off-his-rocker father, her raging headache, and that Craig was probably pissed she'd disappeared in the middle of their webcam chat. But there was something else nagging at her, something she couldn't quite access. Anna turned slowly in a circle, taking the basement in. And there it was.

There were garbage bags that she didn't recognize. The Fagans used black garbage bags, but scattered around the basement were white bags, clear bags, and even blue recycling bags. Jack was taking *other people's* garbage down there, too.

But why? It was a stupid question. To rifle through them, searching for God-knows-what? Something he could never find because it wasn't there, wasn't anywhere? Things to fix and hold on to for a goddamn rainy day? Jack's reasoning never made any sense. But this was way over the top, even for him. Her dad was crazy, bonkers, gonzo and probably belonged in a mental institution. Fear overwhelmed her and she knew she had to move, had to do something, or she might remain there, paralyzed forever on top of Hoard Mountain.

Anna skidded down the hoard pile and returned to the small but reasonably clean area of floor space. Stubborn grit remained in the cracks of concrete under her feet. She reached into her bucket of cleaning supplies and took out a roll of paper towels and antibacterial spray. Squatting down, she scrubbed the grit on the floor, turning the paper towels black with soot. Anna pulled more paper towels off the roll, but no matter how much she scrubbed and sprayed, the paper towels still picked up dirt.

She knew she should stop. But this one small piece of floor was *going* to be clean, completely clean. Anna blew through the roll of paper towels and opened a second one. When she was done the small circumference of concrete gleamed. Anna sat in the clean spot and let herself cry for a few minutes before getting back to work.

• • •

It was almost dawn when Anna dragged the last of seven full extra-large garbage bags to the curb in front of the house. She'd made a dent, not a large one, in fact a relatively minuscule one, but at least a dent, in the basement. Anna hadn't allowed herself to be sentimental; everything at all porous was ruined and would be trashed. The few things she'd saved, like her mother's butterfly pin, would need a thorough disinfecting. Jack had stayed in his room, icing his head, and for that she was grateful.

The garbage bags on the curb would be picked up later, but the three plastic storage bins she dragged up the basement stairs had salvageable contents. They contained rare books on paranormal phenomena, old case files and even a few tagged objects. Anna decided to drive the plastic bins to the new office, but first she needed to scrub the outside of each one. She went through another full roll of paper towels, and by the time she finished her knuckles bled from the sharp-edged plastic lids. Using every muscle, Anna lifted two of the bins into the trunk of Jack's sedan. The last bin went in the backseat.

It was a short drive and she rolled down her window, hoping the late-September air would energize her. The houses of Eden Street were dark and it was dead quiet outside, perfectly still but for the glowing ribbons of green and red that flickered in the sky. Anna turned onto Washington Street, hearing not a single insect, bird, or barking dog, not even the wind, only the sound of her own breath.

There was a light, though. Anna saw it as she pulled up to the new office. Saul the realtor's blue SUV was in the driveway and a light was on in Geneva's bedroom. She drove a few houses down from the ranch house and parked. What was Saul Gleason doing in Geneva's bedroom, especially when she wasn't even there? Geneva and her hatchback were both ensconced at a Holiday Inn on Route 33. Maybe Saul was checking on the property. Maybe he kept weird hours. Who knew? She did *not* want to have to explain what she was doing there in the middle of the night without her father.

The light in Geneva's bedroom shut off, and moments later the front door opened. Anna was relieved to see Saul get into his blue SUV and drive away. She pulled Jack's sedan into the driveway and spent the next half an hour maneuvering the plastic bins out of the trunk and into the ranch house, not giving Saul's odd presence too much thought. Anna had her own job to do, and it was a doozy.

After hauling the last bin into the main office area, Anna allowed herself a few minutes of rest. She sat on one of the new office chairs, surveying the emerging work space that would hopefully reinvigorate the family business. But the house, originally so light and hopeful, radiated a dim gloom. For the first time it occurred to her that the office could fail and ruin Jack for good. Once a flicker of hope the office now felt like another burden, heavy enough to crush them both. Anna drove home with a heavy heart.

CHAPTER THIRTEEN

EMI IS OPERATIONAL

A nna parked Jack's two-toned sedan next to Geneva's dented hatchback and trudged back up the pathway of the new office, wincing as the noon sun hit her eyes through the canopy of pines. She was surprised Freddy wasn't there already, drooling over Geneva's invention. Then again, a late Freddy was the new normal.

She'd managed to sleep for a few hours after scrubbing the basement grime off her skin in a hot shower. Anna wanted nothing more than to be back in her bed curled up in her comforter, but she was meeting Geneva and Freddy to continue setting up the work space. If the office ended up as the final blow to Jack's sinking financial ship, then so be it. For now it was still their only chance. Getting Jack away from his hoard on a regular basis might help salvage the remaining splinters of his sanity, assuming there were any.

Entering the ranch house Anna didn't see Geneva, but the large living room still felt crowded. The light streaming through the curtain-less bay windows no longer made the room feel fresh, but it did reveal encrusted dirt on the plastic bins that she'd missed the night before. Anna swore. She didn't want remnants of the basement cesspool corrupting the new office, but with the bulky plastic bins scattered about, the room bore a faint resemblance to Jack's Kingdom of Crap. And where was Geneva? Anna dropped her backpack on the drafting table and peeked down the hallway. Geneva's bedroom door was closed. Anna called Geneva's name, but there was no response.

She was about to knock on Geneva's door when a sweet, smoky smell hit her. A sickening chill wrapped around Anna's spine. Not another fire. She flung the door open, bracing herself for an onslaught of smoke, for the sight of Geneva's body slumped on the floor, unnaturally still. But Geneva was sitting on the floor next to two boxes of books, wearing jeans and a T-shirt with "Go with the Flow" printed across the front. She held something in her hands, a piece of paper. No, a photograph. A wisp of smoke rose from a small stick that Geneva was pressing *into* the photograph.

"Geneva!"

The woman's head snapped up. Her eyes flashed with a cold anger and then softened in recognition.

"What the frig are you doing?" Anna asked.

Geneva stubbed the stick out in a small metal dish on the floor.

"Of course, the smoke must be upsetting for you. I'm so sorry."

A spicy smell wafted toward Anna along with the last puffs of smoke. It was incense. Geneva really took the whole hippie thing seriously. Then again maybe not, since she appeared to be using it as a weapon of sorts.

Anna stepped into the room. "What's going on?"

Geneva swiped her hands through the ash that had fallen on her jeans, leaving dark smears on the denim above her knees.

"Not much," Geneva said. "An old photo fell out of one of my books. It brought back some not-so-happy memories, I guess. I thought I'd cheer the room up a bit with sage, but—" She laughed bitterly. "Well, you saw what happened."

Anna wasn't loving the vibe in Geneva's bedroom either, despite the yellow paint job that had made it homey and bright only yesterday. It must be the smoke in the air. Would Anna ever smell smoke again without feeling that suffocating dread?

Geneva tossed the photograph at the small metal pail by the bookcase, but it bounced off the rim and lay face up on the floor. It was a picture of Geneva and a man. Even with half of his face obliterated by the incense, he was clearly handsome, lean and square-jawed with amber-colored hair pulled into a low ponytail. His arm was slung over Geneva's shoulder as she curled into him, looking radiant, tan and in love.

Anna couldn't help but think of Craig. She hadn't heard from him after abruptly leaving their webcam chat. A pain crept up the back of Anna's neck and joined the ever-present thudding behind her eyes. What if he was with Sydney somewhere? Anna had an urge to go online and conduct a frenzied investigation into both of their social media accounts. With effort she pulled her thoughts away from Craig. *Keep it together, Fagan.*

As far as the photograph Geneva torched, Anna figured that moving on and not asking questions was the kindest option. She sat on the floor next to Geneva and leaned against the bed. Subject-changing time.

Feigning interest, Anna peeked inside one of the cardboard boxes. "Are these textbooks?"

"In a way," Geneva said. "They're your typical hard science standards. I brought them from my office at Stanford."

Anna lifted a few books out of the second box and checked out the titles: *The Power of Now, Life after Life, The Seat of the Soul.*

"These, too?"

Geneva gave her a wry smile. "Oh no, definitely not. Subjects like those are largely ridiculed in academia. They're from home."

"I thought college was about exploring different ideas."

Geneva snorted. "Not when it comes to matters of the soul. Well, if you're a theology student, yes, but not in the sciences. It's ten times worse with the supernatural. Depending on the institution, even bringing up the subject is enough to win the ridicule of your peers, lose precious funding and maybe your career." Geneva sighed, twirling a lock of blonde hair around her finger. "Things are changing though, slowly, at least in some universities."

"But the whole *universe* is a mystery, right? I mean, we don't really know what's out there." Anna thought about Freddy's lanky frame bent over his telescope and felt a sharp pang.

Geneva nodded. "Astrophysics is the exception, a field of study that allows itself a lot of leeway. Long-held theories can be disproved and new theories embraced, much easier than in other sciences."

"What kind of theories?"

Geneva tapped on the floor until it came to her. "Here's a good one. You've heard of the Big Bang, right—the birth of the universe?"

"Yep."

"Well, until fairly recently it was widely accepted that the universe was still expanding from the explosive power of the Big Bang fourteen billion years ago, an expansion that would eventually slow down due to the force of gravity. But, as it turns out, the universe isn't slowing down at all. It's *speeding up*."

Geneva stretched out a leg and used her bare heel to drag the photograph toward her. She crumpled and squeezed it into a smaller and smaller wad, tossing it at the garbage pail again. This time it sailed right in.

Anna was about to go in for a high five, but a pained expression returned to Geneva's face.

"Do you want to talk about it?" Anna asked. "About him?"

Geneva shook her head. "Your dad wouldn't appreciate me sharing my adult problems with you. It's inappropriate."

"Oh, please. It's not like I've exactly been *shielded* from the horrors of the world." She didn't tell Geneva that Jack had been sneaking around the neighborhood pilfering people's garbage and was in no position to judge.

"All I will say is that he cheated on me with a grad student he was mentoring." Geneva swallowed. "In our home."

"*Gross.* Did you catch them together?" Anna's cheeks burned. She shouldn't have asked that. It was none of her business. But Geneva drew into herself again, and she either didn't hear or ignored Anna's question.

"It's strange because I thought I'd moved past all of it," Geneva whispered, more to herself than Anna. "I *had* moved past it." She pushed the base of her palms into her eyes, either in frustration or to thwart brimming tears.

Anna wanted to open the window and gulp a lungful of fresh air. But Geneva's room wasn't a toxic dumpsite like Jack's basement. Her eyes darted around the room. Was some *thing* in there with them? She wanted to flee but couldn't abandon Geneva in her current state. It was subject-changing time again.

"Let's leave that jerk in the trash where he belongs. Tell me more about this universe-speeding-up thing. I'm not sure I get it."

"No one does," Geneva said. "All those great minds?" She kicked at the box of textbooks. "They were wrong. Turns out some invisible force that we don't understand, previously known as empty space, is pushing the universe out at an increasing rate of speed. They call it Dark Energy. And it's tearing everything apart."

Geneva's hand went to her right temple, massaging the skin. Her lower lip trembled.

Panic stirred inside Anna. Was Geneva losing it too?

"Have you experienced anything strange lately?" Anna asked.

"Strange how?"

"I'm not sure. Maybe just feeling really *off,* or like something is harassing you?"

"What," Geneva said, "like one of those harmless Tricksters?"

"Yeah, but not so harmless."

Geneva shook her head, looking down.

"No," she said softly. "Nothing like that. I think I just need to sit in meditation for a while."

The doorbell rang and Anna got to her feet.

"That must be Freddy. Come say hi when you're ready."

Anna let Freddy in through the front door. He crinkled his nose.

"Is something burning?"

• • •

An hour later, Freddy clicked something into place on Emi. The sound made Anna look up from the files she was sorting just as he pressed Emi's trigger. The black device shuddered, and a wide beam of blue light shot out of the chamber and onto the drafting table where Anna sat.

The beam turned the table a pale shade of aqua and revealed a series of flickering, white, hair-like loops that curled around the wiring connected to the printer, laptop and lamp. Surrounding these bow-tie loops of energy was an army of tiny electrical teardrops. These glowing teardrops moved around the magnetic loops as the loops pulsated and shook.

"EMFs," Freddy whispered, awestruck.

Anna stood from the drafting table, hypnotized by the beauty of the charged particles bound to their magnetic tracks. Freddy, too, gaped at the display, his finger tight on the trigger of Geneva's invention. He pointed Emi up to the light fixtures on the ceiling, exposing the twitching magnetic loops around each bulb, as well as the electric orbs undulating around them. But on the last bulb he scanned, the electromagnetic energy wasn't looping in a closed figure-eight pattern. As if the bow tie came undone, several loose and wiry magnetic hairs jutted down from the bulbs, thrashing about and throwing electric particles into the air like sparklers on the Fourth of July.

"Faulty wiring on that one," Freddy said, clucking his tongue. "We have to tell Geneva!"

Freddy headed for the hallway with Anna right behind him. They burst, rather rudely, into Geneva's bedroom. Geneva was sitting on her bed with her legs crossed. Her eyes opened and she regarded them with a mixture of surprise and amusement.

"Emi works!" Freddy yelled. He pulled the trigger again and Emi's blue beam roamed around Geneva's lamp and the overhead light, revealing flickering white loops and radiant particles.

"Good for you," Geneva said evenly. She knew exactly what her creation could do. "But take it easy, John Wayne. You're draining the battery."

"Who's John Wayne?" Freddy asked.

Geneva laughed. "Never mind." She turned to Anna. "We should show your dad."

"He's sick," Anna said. "Maybe tomorrow."

Anna peered at Geneva. The woman seemed brighter and it wasn't just her mood. She was glowing. No, it was the air *around* Geneva. It was *lighter* than the rest of the air in the room.

"Do you see that?" Anna asked Freddy.

But Freddy moved Emi's beam away from Geneva and toward the closet next to the bed.

"Do you see *this*?" he said.

Emi's beam exposed a gray mist of electrical static hanging in the air. The room was cloaked in it, but it was thicker toward the back wall. Freddy centered Emi's beam above Geneva's headboard. There was a *hole* in the wall above the bed, and a cluster of gray-tinged electromagnetic lightning bolts were shooting out of it in a giant hair ball. Anna made a noise deep in her throat. The bolts were thicker than the white bow-tie loops above the drafting table, and decidedly more ominous. There were hundreds, maybe thousands of the tangled, wiry bolts, and mists of gray static-like particles flew off the ends of each one into the air.

Geneva scrambled off the bed and stood next to Anna and Freddy, all of them transfixed by what was, moments ago, just a patch of yellow wall. It was as if a giant, electric, thousand-legged spider was climbing out of the hole above Geneva's bed, legs first, while shooting its choking gray web everywhere.

Geneva snatched Emi out of Freddy's hand and turned it off. The bedroom and wall looked perfectly ordinary again.

"What was that?" Anna asked.

"Some sort of EMF distortion." Geneva sounded calm, but her hands were shaking.

"But there isn't an electrical source," Freddy said.

"We don't know that for sure," Geneva said sharply. "But I've never seen anything like that...*thing*."

"Could there be wiring behind the wall?" Anna asked.

Geneva frowned. "Even if there were, it wouldn't explain that heavy electric *rain*. And I can't imagine what kind of wiring would generate that large of an EMF."

Geneva eyeballed Anna and Freddy with new alarm, as if realizing that she had two minors on her hands while something very unusual was going down. She quickly herded them out of her bedroom. Back in the main office area, Geneva activated Emi and swung the device in a wide arc around the room. The same gray static mist hung in the air, but less densely than in her room.

"It's *everywhere*," Freddy said.

Geneva had no trace of her former smile. "Honey, you should go home."

"But maybe I can help," he said.

"I'm sure you can once we have a better idea of what's going on," she said, "but for now, I need to let Mr. Fagan know about this situation."

Freddy slumped in disappointment.

"You *better* call me tonight and tell me what's going on," he said to Anna as she walked him to the front door.

Anna bristled. "Chill out. I will."

"Yeah, well you've been kinda unreliable lately."

The animosity that had been simmering inside of her for much of the last week rose to an instant boil.

"I have enough going on without your drama. See ya," she said.

Anna slammed the door, her adrenaline on overdrive. But she'd been too harsh. She opened the door again, ready to apologize, but Freddy was climbing into Major Tom. He started the engine and music blasted through the windows.

Anna met Geneva back in her bedroom, and the two of them stood at end of the bed, facing the headboard.

"I'd feel more comfortable if Jack was here," Geneva said.

"That makes one of us." The last thing Anna wanted was to involve her father.

Geneva fired up Emi and once again illuminated the monstrous, electromagnetic fur ball.

"I want a better look at this thing," Geneva said, handing Emi to Anna. She walked around the bed to view the spew-hole from the side. A particularly long wiry hair lashed out of the hole, whipping a thick trail of static mist inches from her cheek. Geneva retreated back next to Anna, her face pale.

Anna held Emi as steady as possible despite the trembling in her arms. Her headache had shifted from behind her eyes to the top of her head, and a tunneling pain drilled into her skull as if determined to make mincemeat of the gray matter inside. Through gritted teeth she asked Geneva to get the Windex bottle on the drafting table. Geneva reappeared moments later with the bottle in hand.

"It's holy water," Anna said. "Let's spray this thing down."

"How many ounces should I use?"

"We're not in a lab. Just start squeezing!"

Geneva pumped the bottle at the wall and the electro-magnetic hair ball immediately began to evaporate. She kept pumping until the last traces of the "spider hole" disappeared.

"Yep, it's evil, whatever it is," Anna said. She released Emi's trigger. "The good news is that it's not that strong."

"Jack needs to know about this," Geneva said. "Sick or not."

Chapter Fourteen

The Energy-Sucking Vampire

Geneva drove Anna to the Fagan house, making the seven blocks in about as many seconds. Anna saw Saul's blue SUV parked in the driveway next to Jack's sedan. What was he doing there? The guy was friggin' everywhere.

Anna and Geneva entered the Fagan house and maneuvered through the pathway into the kitchen. Saul sat at the kitchen table, talking on his phone and jotting notes onto a notepad. His powder-blue polo shirt featured the green crocodile logo that might as well have spelled out *d-o-u-c-h-e*. He bared his teeth at Anna in a blinding smile and ended his call.

"Anna, perfect. I was just trying to track down your number. I have an appointment with your dad and rang the bell a few times, but he didn't answer. His car's in the driveway, and the door was open, so—"

"So, you just let yourself in?"

Saul leaned back in the chair and regarded her coolly.

"If Jack has a problem with that, I'll address it with him." He gestured to the basement door. "What exactly happened here?"

The shattered door had been crudely patched up with plywood and adorned with a shiny new doorknob. Anna jiggled the doorknob. Unsurprisingly, it was locked. She pounded on the door, the cheap plywood grating against her fist.

"Dad!"

Anna pressed her ear against the door and heard a faint scuttling in the basement. The rats, no doubt, but she'd bet anything that they weren't alone. Jack was supposed to be resting in bed, but it looked like he'd found something else to do. She turned to Saul.

"I can hear him," she lied. Bleary-eyed and exhausted, Anna doubted that she could break the basement door again. "You'll have to kick the door in."

Saul smirked. "That's a bit dramatic, don't you think?"

"He's sick, okay? And hurt. He might need help."

"I'm Jack's colleague," Geneva said, extending her arm to shake Saul's hand. "Dr. Geneva Sanders, and I can assure you that this is somewhat of an emergency. So, *please.*"

Saul grumbled but got to his feet. He kicked the door with his shiny leather shoes, *once, twice,* and the third time it broke open. Anna descended the stairs with Geneva and Saul at her heels, barely registering the soft crunch of dead flies under her feet. She turned left at the bottom of the steps and there was Jack, sitting on top of a hoard pile under one of the new hanging lightbulbs, his hands deep inside a black garbage bag. His eyes, shifting and nervous, narrowed at the sight of them. Scattered atop the debris in the basement were the tattered remains of the *same* garbage bags that Anna hauled to the curb the night before.

"What have you *done?*" It was Saul, turning in a circle and taking in the colossal mess before him. He stumbled as his foot kicked into a busted bottle of drain cleaner.

Jack didn't seem to hear him. He peered sheepishly at Anna. "You know," Jack said, "I realized that Uncle Pete's stamp collection might have been in one of those bags."

Shock rumbled in Anna's gut like milk way past its expiration date.

"You brought all of it…*back* down here?" She struggled to comprehend it as the words left her mouth.

The wrinkles around Jack's eyes were deep gashes. He searched for words, looking like a stranger, looking like the freak everyone at school thought he was.

"It's like an itch in my brain," he finally said. "It won't let me be."

Everything inside Anna sagged. She'd been a fool to think that she could rein in any of her father's chaos. The downward spiral that started with her mother's death had finally reached its sorry conclusion. He couldn't get any lower, any loonier. She thought about Jack in the institution she'd have to visit on the weekends, eating apple sauce with a plastic spoon. She'd need to live with either Freddy or Dor until graduation. She could still count on them. Couldn't she? Why did they suddenly feel so far away?

Saul took a tentative step toward Jack, the ground beneath his feet creaking. He took another step and a charred plank of wood snapped in two.

"Ah, geez, Jack," he said. "Now that I've seen this, how the heck am I supposed to get you that loan? You're nowhere *near* ready for an inspection. I gotta tell you, buddy. You really let me down. I'll have to check on that new office and make sure you're not trashing that property, too."

"But…you checked on it last night," Anna said.

Saul turned to her. "You're mistaken."

"No, I'm not. I saw you there at, like, three o'clock in the morning."

Jack and Geneva exchanged a puzzled glance.

"Is that true, Saul?" Jack asked, relieved that the focus had shifted away from him.

Saul made a big show of looking insulted. "This is ridiculous."

Anna wasn't backing down. "You were there, and you know it."

Saul crossed his arms. "Jack, I'd appreciate it if you would control your daughter. Let's not make this situation any worse."

"Dad. I *saw* him."

"Anna, cool it," Jack said. "Just answer the question, Saul. Were you there?"

Geneva spoke up.

"Can we all calm down, please? Everyone just take a moment and get centered. Whatever's going on"—she looked around warily at the hoard-laden basement—"I'm sure it can be worked out. But right now there's something urgent we need to talk to Jack about, so, Mr....?"

"Saul."

"Saul. If you wouldn't mind..." She nodded at Anna.

Anna took Emi out from her backpack. "Emi is operational," she said, pointing the machine at one of the exposed lightbulbs and pressing the trigger. The blue beam revealed the electrical orbs moving like a flock of starlings around the twitching magnetic field that encircled the bulb.

Jack gaped at the display and then at Geneva.

"You'll get the Nobel Prize for this," he said, making his way off the hoard pile, his blackened sneakers alternately crunching into debris and slipping over scraps of wet garbage.

"Either that or an infomercial," Anna said. The machine was getting heavy, and she moved Emi's beam down, off the lightbulb, giving her arm a rest.

Suddenly Jack's hand dug into her sleeve. As he yanked her toward him Anna instinctively pulled back, looking down, as she did, into the dark hole beneath her, licked with pale flames. *A hole she was falling into.* She tightened, bracing for the ensuing fall. But then a wiry magnetic hair whipped a trail of gray mist inches from her face, and she realized that she wasn't falling. Anna's finger remained pressed on Emi's trigger; its blue beam hit the concrete floor beneath her feet. She was standing on another one of those nasty-ass spider holes.

Jack dragged Anna toward him and Emi's beam whipsawed around the basement, revealing a curtain of static mist. The basement was corrupted in more ways than one. She refocused Emi's beam back to the patch of concrete on the basement floor. Under Emi's blue light, a dark hole birthed a thousand-legged electrical monster.

"It's another one of those things," Anna said to Geneva.

"I see it," Geneva said. "I see it."

Anna looked to Jack. "There was one in Geneva's room, too."

Fascinated, Jack reached one arm toward the edge of the magnetic hair ball. His hand, tinged blue under Emi's beam, went straight through several twitching gray hairs like they were a hologram.

He turned to Geneva. "EMFs?"

Geneva was ashen-faced. "They must be. That's what Emi was designed to pick up. Is there an electrical source under the basement?"

Jack shook his head.

"We discovered a similar anomaly without an apparent electrical source on the wall above my bed."

Saul cleared his throat, and they all swiveled their heads toward him as he backed up in the direction of the stairs.

"I'll leave you all to your new gadget. I'm afraid I have another appointment."

That was his reaction? *I have another appointment.* Anna's bullshit detector went off. Shouldn't Saul be having a fit that two of his "properties" faced this troubling affliction? It was like he wasn't even surprised.

Anna took a couple quick steps toward the stairs, blocking Saul's exit.

"You *were* at the office last night."

"You know," Saul said, tapping a finger on the side of his head. "That's right! Silly me. I did stop by to make sure the water and gas were on. Apologies all around. Now, excuse me."

Anna didn't budge, watching Saul's eyes dart around the room. The same eyes that had seemed to follow her, Dor and Freddy from freshly-seeded lawns as they pedaled down New Bloomtown streets.

"Get out of my way." Saul glowered at her, lunging forward. Surprised, Anna staggered backward, her finger still glued to the trigger. Emi's blue beam landed on Saul, and he brought his hands up to shield his eyes. Jagged bolts of gray lightning shot out of his fingers and a thick static mist swirled around his hands.

"He's doing it!" Anna said, her headache squeezing her skull with fresh vigor.

"Turn it off," Saul pleaded from behind his freakish hands.

Anna kept the beam on him.

"Now we know who's making those EMF holes."

Saul's voice turned soft. "Please turn it off."

"What did you do to our *house*?" Anna yelled, as Geneva and Jack took a step toward her and away from Saul.

"Turn it off, and I'll tell you."

"And Geneva's room?" Anna kept the blue beam on him. "How many times did you sneak into the office to make that thing on her wall?" She looked at Geneva. "Now we know why the EMF readings were so high."

Saul spoke with a childlike cadence. "Please stop. It will hurt me."

Perfect. Anna *wanted* him hurt.

Jack put a hand on her arm.

"Anna, enough."

Reluctantly, she released Emi's trigger.

"The light from the machine," Jack said. "It will…harm you?

Saul looked at them with hollow eyes. "No. *It* will hurt me…when it comes back."

Geneva stepped forward.

"I think we need to boil some tea and have a talk upstairs," she said. "Jack, let's escort our guest to the kitchen. Anna, get some holy water on this mess and then meet us upstairs."

Jack seemed reluctant to leave Anna's side.

"It's okay, Dad," she said. "We zapped the other one the same way. It'll take three, maybe four ounces, tops. Easy peasy."

As the others climbed the creaky, fly-littered stairs, Anna took the Windex bottle out of her backpack, unscrewed the top and poured holy water onto the floor. She turned Emi back on, directing the blue beam at the wet concrete. The portal was gone. But who knew how many of those festering electromagnetic *holes* were hidden under Jack's hoard? Something small scurried through the junk heap closest to her. Perhaps only the rats knew. They'd created a labyrinth of tunnels through the hoard piles, further destabilizing them. And from the smell of things, those same tunnels had become their burial chambers. *So gross.*

Anna joined the others in the kitchen, sucking in a lungful of the relatively fresh air. She nodded at her father to signify that the deed was done. Jack turned his attention back to Saul, slumped in a kitchen chair. Tears dropped from Saul's cheeks onto his popped collar as he sobbed, his shoulders hunched and shuddering. Given such a pathetic display, it was hard not to feel sorry for him.

Geneva and Jack stood on either side of Saul's chair. Floor space was limited among Jack's growing kitchen hoard. Anna had no choice but to stand directly in front of Saul, who was starkly lit by the hanging lamp above the kitchen table. She'd never seen a man cry except for her father. Wait, that wasn't true. Freddy had cried the night Penelope died. He'd tried to hug her on the lawn and she'd pushed him away, but not before noticing his watery eyes.

Jack put his hand on Saul's shoulder and urged him to explain himself, assuring him that everything was going to be okay. Anna noted her dad's grime-crusted nails; a not-so-white knight he was. Geneva was more reserved, giving Saul a weak smile when he glanced up at her, contrite and guilty.

Geneva plucked a clean hand towel from the hoard under the table and passed it to Saul. He wiped his eyes and blew his nose with a loud honk before placing his hands on the kitchen table. His palms rolled upward in a gesture of openness, or perhaps resignation, but his eyes remained downcast.

"The trouble started many years ago," Saul said. "It was 1986 and I was a kid, thirteen years old. Me and my two buddies, Lance Hickey and Sammy Mulligan, met up at this old, abandoned shack that we'd discovered in the woods behind the ACME. We usually hung out there and played Dungeons and Dragons. But that Saturday, Lance brought a Ouija board he found in his older brother's closet, and the three of us ending up sitting on the rotten wood floor, each with a finger on the pointer."

Anna and Jack exchanged a knowing look. They'd heard many stories with similar beginnings from some of Jack's most miserable clients. More often than not, spirit boards led to no good.

"It was all a big joke at first, all of us pushing the pointer to spell out curse words and such. Then Lance decided I should ask it a question. He was pretty much the head honcho of our threesome, but I didn't let him push me around. So, to kind of get his goat, I asked, 'Does Megan's carpet match her drapes?' The story around the neighborhood was that Megan McNally let Lance get to third base. Lance pushed the pointer to YES, and me and Sammy made a big deal of oohing and ahhing."

Jack cleared his throat, glancing at Anna.

"It was Sammy's turn," Saul said, "and he asked the board if Ernie Halstead, this kid in our class, was a homo. Sammy was always wondering about the sexual status of other boys, paranoid that any homos might be around. So, I said, 'Why, you wanna french him?' Sammy's face got red and he punched me in the shoulder. Last I heard, he moved to Reno with his boyfriend and opened a pet store."

Saul looked up then, a smile playing at the corner of his lips.

"Go on," Jack said, stone-faced.

"Anyway, Lance told us to put our fingers back on the pointer. He asked another question about Megan McNally. I won't repeat it. It was pretty vile."

"Thanks for that," Jack said.

"Nothing was happening, and Sammy and I wanted to quit and play D&D, but Lance got the hard look in his eye that he had when he was real serious about something. He told me to say I'd sell my soul to the devil if it talked to us. I said no way. Lance started chanting, 'Chick-en-shit, chick-en-shit!' Sammy joined in. He was such a follower.

"At this point I had to go to the bathroom something fierce, but when I got up, Lance stood in front of the door, and Sammy started laughing in this shrill way that made my insides twist. Lance said, 'C'mon, chickenshit, say you'll sell your soul to the devil,' over and over, until I finally said 'Fine'—my bladder was aching at that point—'I'll say it.' We sat on the floor again, each of us with a finger on the pointer. And then I said it."

Saul banged his fists into his thighs. "I said I'd sell my soul to the devil if it answered a question. I'd do anything now to take that back, because wouldn't you know, as soon as the words came out, the pointer starts shaking. All three of us let go. But then, all on its own, it scrapes across the board and points directly at me. Lance said to put my fingers back on it and, like an idiot, I did. You see…" Saul scanned their faces. "We were all terrified, but excited, too, eager in a strange way, like when you see an accident on the highway."

"Speak for yourself," Anna said under her breath. Jack gave her a sharp look.

Saul bowed his head again. "I put two of my fingers, one from each hand, back on the pointer, and it started moving in smooth circles around the board. I asked what it wanted, and it spelled *H-E-N-R-Y*."

"Who's Henry?" Jack asked.

"*Me*," Saul said. "Henry's my first name. Saul is my middle name. No one but my parents knew that. I tried to release my fingers but I couldn't. My arms were dead weight, glued to the pointer. It was *holding* them there. Then Lance stood up and said Gino's Pizza just got a Pac-Man and he wanted to check it out. There was an ugly lightness in his voice, a cheap mimicking of childhood exuberance. None of us were ever children again after that night, especially me. I begged them not to go, but they did.

"Once I was alone the temperature in that shack dropped so low I could see my breath, and this was late May we're talking about. I still couldn't move my hands, and I…I lost control of my bladder. It was so cold the wet spot on my jeans froze over. So cold I thought I'd freeze to death."

Saul shivered in his seat as if lost in the memory.

"At least it would be over, I thought, but it wasn't. The pointer jerked my arms across the board, spelling out *Y-O-U A-R-E M-I-N-E*, and then my fingers finally released. I stumbled out of the shack and into the woods, too cold to feel the sticker bushes tearing my skin. My mother screamed when I walked in the house, bloodied and urine-soaked, eyes like saucers. But I never told her what happened. I didn't want to make it mad."

A tear rolled down Saul's cheek. "And that night, it was on me."

"Do you want to take a break?" Jack asked him gently.

Saul wiped his eyes. "I'm almost done. That night I awoke before dawn, paralyzed on my bed with something heavy on my chest. I couldn't see it, but I could feel it. It came again and again, night after night, pushing me into the mattress and making a high-pitched buzzing sound in my ear. Over time the buzzing deepened in tone and then broke up into a series of grunting sounds, as if it was trying to form words. In the hours before dawn on my fourteenth birthday, it finally spoke. It said, *Feed me.* And at last I understood what I needed to do. Right then I stopped resisting, forcing my mind to think of other things, forcing my body to relax, inch by inch, starting with my toes. And then, some barrier, some protective force around me, was finally penetrated. *Take it,* I said, and let it feed.

"When it was done, hours passed before I could move again. It fed on my energy whenever it wanted for the next couple of years. I was tired all the time, quit sports, quit seeing friends, became a loner. As time went on I could feel when it fed elsewhere or was sleeping. When it slept I felt nothing. Well, I felt free, I guess, in the way a trapped animal is free when it dreams. Then one day it stopped feeding from me altogether, like it was bored of me. I went to college, got my real estate license, was *happy.*"

Saul picked up the towel again for another round of nose blowing, one that went on for far longer than Anna thought was necessary.

"And now it's back," Saul said, "and it's learned how to use me to feed from others. Using my hands to make portals where people feel the safest, their homes."

Saul exhaled, his face haggard.

Jack knelt down and patted Saul's forearm. "So, you've been creating these EMF abnormalities, these *portals,* as a food source for this friend of yours?"

"My *friend,* Jack?"

"Forgive me."

Anna's hackles went up. Jack was asking this fraud for his forgiveness now?

"Tell me more," Jack said. "Specifics. How do you make them?"

"It did something to my hands when it first came back a few weeks ago. I was half-asleep, but I remember it felt hot—zappy—like when you screw in a lightbulb with the light switch on. Since then, it tells me where to put my hands. I mean, it's not *me* doing it. I'm just the conduit."

"So, it's not inside you?" Jack said. "It's not controlling your body?"

"No," Saul said. "It talks to me, tells me what to do."

"That's good," Jack said. "That's real good."

Saul looked at Jack like he was nuts, but Anna understood her father's reaction. He was glad he didn't have another demon on his hands.

"You called them portals," Anna said. "Portals to where?"

Saul shrugged. "How am I supposed to know?"

"You could ask it," Anna said. "I mean, you said it talked to you, right?"

Saul fingered his collar, about to respond, but Jack butted in. "Saul, do you believe that you sold your soul to the devil?"

Saul nodded. "It will torment me until my dying breath and then take my soul to hell." He choked back a sob. "I would have killed myself years ago, but how could I knowing what I'd face?"

Anna shuddered, thinking about the unknown fate of her mother's soul. Was she too hard on Saul? His life, like her mother's, was shattered by a parasite. But Saul had survived. Maybe that's what bothered Anna the most.

"That's why this thing has power over you," Jack said. "Ouija boards are portals just like the ones you created. Gateways. When you give permission to a negative entity to attach to you, to manipulate you, it will take full advantage. This thing was opportunistic, that's all."

"What are you saying?" Saul said, hope burgeoning on his face. "You don't think it's the devil?"

Anna couldn't contain herself. "Why would *the* devil be spending its time messing with a real estate agent in Bloomtown? Wouldn't it try to start a nuclear war or something?"

Jack glared at her, holding a finger up to his lips. He was always careful about stepping on anyone's belief system. He measured his words carefully.

"Saul, I think that what we're dealing with is more along the lines of an *energy vampire*, an entity—rare, mind you, but documented—that draws power from the energy of living beings. The entity is not a demon, Saul. It's not powerful enough for a full possession. That's the good news. You're going to survive this."

Saul sagged with relief and the two men thumped each other's backs in an awkward hug.

"So, if this entity is feeding *from* these portals. The portals aren't just transmitting EMFs, but sucking *in* energy, too?" Geneva asked.

"Yes," Jack said. "And I'm guessing that the energy this thing feeds on is *pain* energy—guilt, hatred, fear, misery. The portals had astronomically high EMF readings, correct?"

Geneva nodded. "Off the charts."

"I'm sure you're aware that high EMF levels can affect the brain, and therefore people's moods and behaviors?"

"I read some of those testimonials during my research," Geneva said. "Mostly from people suing power and phone companies, lawsuits that went nowhere in the courts."

"Never underestimate the power of lawyers and lobbyists to discredit legitimate claims," Jack said, "especially when there's billions in profits at stake. I can tell you that EMF-related psychosis is very real. I've run into it a few times during paranormal investigations. You see, EMF spikes *can* indicate the presence of a spirit. However, sustained levels of strong electromagnetic fields from manmade sources, like those found near high-voltage wires, can alter brain waves and make people feel uneasy, like they're being watched."

"So, people think there's a ghost in their house when there's not," Anna said.

"Exactly. There are protocols that I follow during investigations to qualify the EMF source," Jack continued. "And with your invention," he said to Geneva, "that job will get a whole heck of a lot easier, but that's not important right now. What I'm getting at is that these portals could be spitting out EMFs that are *designed* to trigger extremely negative emotions, off the charts, as you said."

"And then the portals feed on the negative energy they create," Geneva said quietly, "sucking it back in."

Jack and Geneva locked eyes, the current between them palpable. Two minds in simpatico. Anna squirmed a little, keeping an eye on Saul. He was following the conversation closely.

"Can EMFs cause headaches?" Anna asked, all too aware of the thumper she'd been lugging around in her head.

Jack looked surprised. "You've been having them, too?"

"The last week. Some real doozies."

"Feedback loops…" Geneva murmured, eyes bright. "I think I got it! The portals are a positive feedback loop, just like the closed timeline curves of semiclassical gravity."

Even Jack looked confused. Geneva was going all PhD on them.

Geneva tried to translate. "Physicists encounter a paradox when they analyze time and space as if they are part of a closed system. When vacuums such as wormholes create new particles, the curved timeline of the closed system eventually returns the new particles to their original point of creation, meaning there would now be two particles where before there was only one."

"I think I see what you're saying," Jack said slowly, "but what does this have to do with the portals?"

"I believe they're getting exponentially stronger," Geneva said. "That would explain why certain people in Bloomtown"—Geneva looked pointedly at Jack—"seem to be acting more and more unstable with each passing day. And if we don't stop it, it will only get worse."

Jack beamed at Geneva and Anna felt a bit warm toward her, too. She wasn't sure what Geneva was talking about, but it sounded plausible. The increasingly bizarre events of the past few weeks finally had an explanation, and it wasn't a nasty new breed of Tricksters *or* the solar flares. She couldn't wait to tell Freddy. Yet something nagged at her. A piece of Saul's story didn't add up. If the entity tormenting him was so unwanted, why had he let it back into his life without a fight?

Jack pulled Saul to his feet. "This entity…where is it now?"

"Wandering," Saul said. "I can still feel it a little. Almost like a cord is connecting us." He pointed to the center of his chest. "Feels like a pulling here. I think it must have other hosts in other places—" His voice went flat. "But it will come back, and then it will punish me."

"We'll do what we can for you." Jack turned to Anna. "How much holy water do we have left?"

"A couple jugs, and those were on credit."

Jack looked back at Saul. "You'll tell us where these portals are?"

Saul nodded.

"How many are there?"

"About a dozen. I'll write you a list."

Jack took the Windex bottle of holy water out of Anna's backpack.

"I can spray you down. It will make it very unpleasant for that thing to come near you. Holy water is corrosive to a negative entity."

"No," Saul said, stepping back. "Save it for the portals. It's more important, please—I deserve whatever happens to me."

"You have put people in danger, it's true," Jack said. "But I can't leave you unprotected."

Anna blanched. "But he could have asked for help." She confronted Saul. "Why didn't you?"

"Because," Saul said, his fingers working the top buttons of his crisp, blue shirt. He spread the fabric apart, revealing a spattering of gruesome wounds on his chest. "It hurts me."

Jack and Geneva gasped but Anna was unmoved. Because of Saul, Bloomtown was in shambles and her father was on the verge of losing both his business and his marbles. Yet, as bad as things were, there was reason for hope. The portals could be destroyed, and there was one person she knew who'd be dying to hear all about it.

CHAPTER FIFTEEN

FREDDY

A nna checked Freddy's backyard first. She expected to find him there as she had many times before, peering through his telescope pointed east toward the ocean and the darkest part of the sky. But his telescope sat several feet from where he lay in the grass, gazing at the ribbons of green that rolled above him in a celestial light show. It wasn't until she tapped his shoulder with the tip of her sneaker that he noticed her, his eyes dark caverns in the dim light.

"Anna," he whispered.

"You sleeping out here?"

"Just thinking."

What about? The words were almost off her tongue, but she decided they could wait. Anna knelt beside him. "The Big News of the Day," she said, "is that I found out what's happening and it has nothing to do with the solar flares."

"What's happening where?"

His voice was flat and she couldn't see his face, not the details. It made him look like a stranger, or a ghost.

"In Bloomtown, where else? Let's go inside, and I'll tell you all about it."

For a moment he thought she'd come because the growing distance between them was hurting her, too, but no, that wasn't why at all. Of course it wasn't. Freddy turned his head from the vast cosmos, from his own insignificance, pressing his cheek against the cold soil and focusing on the blades of grass. But he found no comfort there either. All around him nature was in harmony. The stars above him, the grass, the insects and the trees, they belonged, but humans were a mutation. The only way he could ever truly belong was to decay.

When he sat up a new and dreadful weight, cementing in his skull all day, began to fall in painful clumps into his chest, turning his insides heavy and stiff. Who cared about the aurora borealis anyway? It didn't mean anything. A painful buzzing started in his head. Nothing meant anything. Despite Anna's presence, he'd never felt so alone.

"Dude, get *up*," Anna said.

Freddy allowed her to pull him to his feet. The back of his light gray hoodie was dirty and wet. Without a word he climbed the steps of his screened-in back porch, barely holding the door open for Anna before shoving his hands back into his pockets. She followed him inside to the kitchen. Whatever he was sulking about—maybe the door slamming episode at the office?—he was sure to get over it when she told him about the portals.

Freddy's mom, Gloria, was on the phone, her long curly hair tamed in a bun. Gloria winked at Anna and ruffled the mop on Freddy's head as they passed. He clicked his tongue in annoyance before ascending the stairs, two at a time, toward his bedroom. Anna followed, the pain in her head sharpening as the sound of Gloria's chatter faded away.

Anna would have done *anything* to feel her mother's touch again, to hear her voice, but Freddy took all that for granted. She swallowed a strong surge of resentment, knowing that her exposure to the portals could have lingering aftereffects. The portals affecting her and Jack had been extinguished, and so, she hoped, would the fits of rage she now attributed to them. Still, she needed to be careful not to overreact.

Anna closed his bedroom door behind them. Freddy studied her impassively, but Anna was sure that the playful light in his eyes would return soon enough.

"That thing above Geneva's bed," she whispered, moving closer. "It was a portal."

Instead of leaning toward her in his usual posture of coconspirator, Freddy straightened up, increasing the space between them. Did she have bad breath?

He raised an eyebrow. "A portal to where?"

"We're not sure yet. But we know who made it. This real estate agent, you know, the guy with bleached teeth on the for sale signs in people's yards, Saul Gleason?"

Freddy stared back at her blankly.

"You know him, c'mon. The *guy*. His face was plastered in the window of Yo! Yogurt for like, two years, on that dumb flyer."

But Freddy remained nonplussed. "I guess."

Anna had expected him to be excited, to at least *care*. She was talking about portals here, actual *portals* to an unknown world. Freddy had floor-to-ceiling bookshelves lined with books about astronauts and wormholes in space. He still had glow-in-the-dark solar system stickers on his ceiling—stickers that looked greenish and worn under the lamplight.

"Is something up, Freddy? You're not having headaches, are you?"

Her own headache thudded along with the anxious pulse of a growing paranoia. Maybe she should get Emi and do a sweep of Freddy's house. But if Freddy's house was on Saul's list, her Dad would've told her, wouldn't he?

Freddy brushed some dirt from the back of his jeans. "No, Doctor Fagan. The Sunday night blues are a little worse than usual, that's all."

He plunked down in his chair and booted up his dinosaur of a PC. A guitar riff blasted out of his speakers before he turned the volume down.

She spoke without thinking. "Is that the Manarchists?"

Freddy's glare grew icicles. "Shine's cruddy band? You gotta be kidding."

He dismissed her with a swivel of his chair, planting his back to her. Anna sighed and retreated to a corner of Freddy's mattress. This wasn't going well. She debated whether or not she should leave or give him a minute to chill the hell out.

Freddy hoped that Anna's infatuation with Shine would pass like it had with the other idiots she'd crushed on over the years, but this one was sticking. Freddy forgave her a long time ago for not loving him back. But now she pulled farther from him every day, and their friendship, once thought unbreakable, was disintegrating. Except when she wanted something: a ride to school, help at the office, whatever she was doing here now. But it wasn't him she wanted and maybe it never was. It hurt and Freddy was tired of hurting; he wanted a way out. He hit refresh on his keyboard, and there it was. An email popped up in his inbox from the Cosmology Institute in Florida. As he read it, the new heaviness inside him sunk into his legs, pooling at his feet like an anchor meant to drown him.

"Dear Mr. Simms, while we were impressed with your transcripts, you have not been selected to receive this year's Young Physicists Scholarship. We wish you the best of luck with your future endeavors."

The door opened and Gloria popped her head in. "Five hundred and fifty bucks a month. How's that for pocket change?"

Freddy turned around in his chair. "You're supposed to *knock first*, and it doesn't matter anyway."

"Okay. I just thought you'd like to know that the man from the management office—"

Freddy cut his mother off. "I didn't get in."

"Oh, honey." Her features relaxed. "I'm sorry."

"It's *okay*," he said. "But, do you mind? We're studying."

Sluggish and sullen, Freddy wheeled his chair over to the door like it was a monumental effort and pushed it shut. Gloria's shadow remained under the door for several seconds before her footsteps faded down the stairs.

Anna was on the verge of walking out herself, but then a high-pitched yapping erupted from the side of the bed. Penelope's puppies were huddled on a blanket between a laundry basket and the wall, waking, it seemed, from a nap.

"The pups!" Anna dropped to the floor. The puppies charged her, licking her face in a frenzy of tiny tongues, soft paws and warm bellies.

Laughing, she looked at Freddy, but he was glaring at her.

"Did you forget about them?" His upper lip curled in disdain. "You did, didn't you? You didn't even know they were here."

He was right. Anna *had* forgot about them. How could she? They were Penelope's babies.

"It's the portals," she said, flustered, her face hot. "There was one in our basement, too. I've been trying to tell you. We think they're messing with people's heads, literally, messing with their brains."

None of it was coming out right, but Freddy wasn't paying attention anyway. His focus was back on his computer screen. He hunched over his keyboard, the screen's pale light washing over his face.

She left the puppies on the floor and went to Freddy's chair, leaning over his shoulder. "Since portals are boring you, I'm dying to know what has you so fascinated."

"Right here," he said, tapping the screen. He was looking at the website for the Cosmology Institute of Florida. "Do you see my name? Under enrollment status, it no longer says 'Your application is under review.'"

Under Freddy's name was the text "Your application has been processed."

"That's why you're in such a crappy mood?" Anna asked. "Because you didn't get into space school?"

He looked at her like she was being deliberately obtuse.

"As I was saying," Anna said, "Saul, the real estate guy, was supposedly forced to make the portals by this nasty entity he conjured up as a kid."

Freddy sighed. "A Bloomtown real estate agent. Yep, that seems like the exact type of guy to make inter-dimensional portals."

She elbowed him playfully. "Are you, perchance, being a wiseass?"

Ignoring her, Freddy pushed his chair back and walked to his bookshelf with the ponderous movements of a tired old man. He wiped his finger through a layer of dust on the bottom shelf.

A part of him was desperate to shake off the darkness consuming him. It was Anna, after all, the girl he loved, had always loved. But another part of him was furious at her, and himself, the kind of fury that deadened that love, and maybe that was a good thing.

Freddy looked at the tip of his finger, at the remnants of his hair and skin that lined the bookshelf in a fine dust. He was being processed, all right, and one day he'd be reduced to worm food. The thought brought him a strange peace. Nature was never dusty. You never saw dust in the forest.

Anna felt doubly relieved despite Freddy's sour mood. He had a reason to be in a funk, and he wasn't leaving New Jersey.

Yet he clearly wanted to leave her and Dor behind. Freddy appeared utterly *devastated* to be stuck in Bloomtown. She tried to empathize, but instead her jaw tightened.

"Are you checking out on me, is that it?" Anna asked, standing by the door, arms crossed. "Already mentally in Florida, or wherever it is you can't wait to escape to?"

Freddy made a noise as he turned to her. It might have been a laugh, but one choked with bitterness. "You are accusing *me*," he said, "of checking out on *you?*"

There was more venom in his voice then she'd ever heard from him before. She took a step back, putting distance between herself and Freddy's unfamiliar, dull eyes.

"Why are you still here?" he said. "You want my help with your dad's stupid detective work, is that it? Did it ever occur to you, Anna, that I don't care about the problems that your freak of a father digs up? Whatever's wrong with Bloomtown, it's probably his fault. It's probably *your* fault, too. I think you know that, deep down, don't you? That's why you punish yourself and fall for losers like Craig Shine."

Enraged, Anna searched for something to hurt him just as much.

"At least I let myself fall for somebody," she said, her heartbeat thudding in her ears. "I bet you haven't even kissed a girl. I bet *that's* why you want to run away."

"Wrong, dumb ass. But I suppose you think whoring around with Hastings made you an expert. Is that it, Goblin Girl?"

"*Screw you.*" Anna's hand was on his keyboard. She pulled her arm back, wanting to rip it out of the PC, but it was wireless. Undeterred, she threw it at his bookshelf, hitting a globe bookend that crashed to the floor and broke in half. They were breathing hard and staring at each other when Gloria yelled from downstairs.

"What was that?"

"Nothing, Mom!"

There was a glimpse of softness in his eyes—or maybe it was desperation—asking her for forgiveness, and for something more than that.

"Anna."

"Forget it," she said, so unnerved that she flicked the light switch off on her way out of the room, leaving him alone in the darkness.

Freddy went to the window thinking he'd open it and call out to Anna, but his leaden arms were too heavy to perform such a feat. Instead, he watched the aurora borealis twist through the atmosphere, wishing he could float so easily through space. Space was clean. It was as old as time, but always new and never dusty. It would take a human life, all of its greedy wants and needs, and reduce it to an empty husk, to less than nothing. A thought rose up, buoyant, from the great weight inside him. You are nothing.

Anna was right. He wanted to run away and had never kissed a girl. She was gone now and would never come back, not this time, not after what he'd said to her. He was afraid and thought about opening his door and calling for his mom. But he was too old to cry to Mommy like a spineless little shit. What would he say? Help me, Mommy. What's my purpose if not to be with Anna? How pathetic.

Besides, Freddy didn't think his parents believed in a purpose, or a God. Don't put your faith in sky monsters, his father had said once during Passover, at an elaborate Seder at his uncle's house. Then why do we do this? Freddy asked him. It was a ritual, his father said, a tradition important to strengthen bonds between family and community. So, there was no God? His father had shrugged. Who knew? Freddy was disappointed that his father didn't believe, betrayed even, but he was just a stupid kid.

Freddy went to his bed, unable to withstand the burden of his body weight any longer. He stared up at the picture on his wall of him,

Dor and Anna camping in his backyard. He was shorter than Anna then, but his curly hair was spectacularly overgrown, giving him a few extra inches. Freddy watched as his image began to fade. He was disappearing. He looked at his open closet, his eyes drawn to the single tie he owned, dangling from a wire hanger. He'd worn it to a memorial dinner for his great-grandmother, Edie.

Edie had died in a concentration camp in Poland in 1942. Freddy had seen pictures of her before the war. When she smiled, the left side of her mouth drooped a little. Edie used to sew dresses for all the girls in the neighborhood. She'd always wanted a baby girl but only had time to have Freddy's grandfather.

We're the real demons, Freddy thought. There was nothing as horrible as the human race in all of existence. Genocide. Torture. The thing that killed Anna's mother was small potatoes compared to the evil humanity inflicted on itself.

He could hear the puppies playing with their tennis ball. He knew that he should get up and play with them, but his body was too dense. Gravity held him down. He was too busy being processed.

Freddy squeezed his eyes shut, holding them closed as his heart and head pounded. They'd be better off without him, his family, Anna, Doreen, the vicious hateful world. He opened his eyes and saw the tie for what it could be, saw that he could knot it in such a way that it would tighten against the slightest pull of his horrible, crushing body weight. An ugliness inside him jeered. Another way to float! Outside Freddy's window, the aurora borealis slithered across the sky.

PART THREE

ANOTHER MANIC MONDAY

CHAPTER SIXTEEN

A NOT SO SPECIAL EPISODE

W hen Anna came downstairs on Monday morning, freshly primped, Geneva was at the kitchen table studying the list of portals that Saul had scribbled out yesterday. Geneva had insisted on spending the night on the couch in the unlivable living room, too unnerved to sleep in her bedroom back at the office.

"Your dad's upstairs funneling holy water," Geneva said, giving Anna an appreciative once-over.

Anna had put extra effort into her eye makeup that morning, following tips from a beauty magazine: *Curl your lashes and open up those smoky eyes—be mysterious and approachable!* She was wearing her sexiest skinny jeans and a pale pink sweater with a low scoop neck. She couldn't wait to see Craig.

"There's a boy," Geneva said.

Anna blushed as she poured herself a glass of water. Was it that obvious? She rummaged through the cabinet above the sink, trying to find something, anything, that wasn't expired. She came upon a dusty box of granola bars that were only a month past due. Good enough. She joined Geneva at the table.

Geneva rested her chin in her palms and leaned forward. "Freddy?"

"No!"

"He seems like one of the good ones."

Anna bristled. After last night, the last person she wanted to talk about was Freddy. And there it was again, the pounding in her head followed by a dull rage. How would Geneva know anything about "the good ones?" She'd married a cheating jerk. Anna didn't need Geneva telling her about Freddy. The woman was a turf invader.

Anna worked to suppress her cynicism, attributing it to the last vestiges of electromagnetic mist in the air. Once the rest of the portals got a proper holy water dousing, Bloomtown should return to its usual boring, uneventful state. But she would still be Goblin Girl, of course, Daughter of a Freak.

Geneva was peering at her, eyebrows raised, wanting to hear more. Why was she so interested? Did Geneva want Freddy to be her little protégé or something? Anna bit down on her cheek. She was being ridiculous. The woman was only being friendly.

"May I?" Anna asked, and picked up the portal list from the table. Neither Freddy nor Dor's address were noted on it, which was both a relief and disappointment. Freddy's hatefulness toward her last night was likely genuine. She recognized a couple names, but they were no one she was close to. But then again, who *was* she close to besides Freddy and Dor? Correction, besides Dor.

"Speaking of goodies," Anna said. "What happened when you found—what's-his-name, the jerk—hooking up with his student?"

Geneva's mouth tightened.

"I'm sorry," Anna said. "It's none of my business." She dug a nail into her thigh to keep herself under control.

"Don't be silly." Geneva waved her hand, brushing away any need for an apology. "We didn't break it off right away. I gave him a second chance, which, in retrospect, was pretty dumb." Geneva took her elbows off the table and placed them on her lap, out of sight. "He promised that it was over, but it wasn't."

"Well, you're not in jail, so I take it you didn't kill them."

Geneva's laughter fell flat when she saw that Anna was serious.

"I got—" Geneva paused. "I'm *getting* through it. It took some time. My meditation practice helps a lot."

"Is that what you were doing when Freddy and I busted into your room?" An image surfaced in Anna's mind of Geneva meditating on her bed, the air around her somehow brighter than the rest of the room.

Geneva nodded. "It takes a little time to settle into a meditation, but you can start by slowing your breath and observing your thoughts instead of *identifying* with them. In other words, the thoughts are not you. You are what's *observing* them. Does that make sense?"

"Kind of. But is that all there is to it?"

"That's it," Geneva said. "Focus on your breath and let your thoughts move on down the road. A little moon bathing is always good as well, to help you go deeper."

"Moon bathing?" Anna's tone was a bit on the obnoxious side, but she couldn't help it.

"Moon. Bathing." Geneva said each word slowly, as if growing wary of Anna's attitude. "Moonlight is crucial for us girls. It renews our spiritual power, always has."

"How come I didn't know about it, then?"

Geneva laughed dryly. "They won't teach it to you in school," she said, "but it's still there, hidden in the rosebushes, as my mother used to say."

"I'm listening."

"I'll try and summarize it for you," Geneva said. "Once religion and the idea of God became more male-focused and controlled, knowledge of moon bathing, or really anything alluding to the feminine divine, was violently repressed.

Nature and female-based religions were considered a threat to the church's authority and vilified. The wise old holy woman that the village revered became the hideous old hag, the evil witch stirring her cauldron. I'll give you some books if you're interested."

Anna was. It ticked her off that divine women, healers, were persecuted for their power. As Goblin Girl, she could relate. Not that Goblin Girl had any power.

"How does it work, moon bathing?"

"We don't know," Geneva said. "Or maybe we did once and then forgot." She shrugged. "It affects every woman differently, I suppose. For me, it helped calm my mind during meditation, very peaceful, but rejuvenating, too. You should give it a try and find out for yourself. All you need to do is let the light of the moon touch your skin."

They heard Jack trundling down the steps and Anna felt a twinge of disappointment. Geneva had good vibes, and Anna needed some of that mojo right about now. *But she's only being nice to you because she has the hots for your dad*, the evil, pulsating voice of her headache said. *Are you that desperate for a mommy?*

Jack emerged from the path and into the kitchen. He was clean-shaven and wearing his "special occasion" khakis. Anna cringed and looked down at the cleavage peeking through her scoop neck sweater. The two of them were like some kind of sitcom with a fake laugh track spitting out canned hysterics every seven seconds. This was the very special episode of *Harry the Hoarder* where father and daughter both have a crush, but they don't want each other to know, and it creates a big and riotous misunderstanding!

Jack placed the jug of holy water he held on the table. "This should be good for about six portals. Do you have Saul's list?"

Geneva took the list back from Anna. "Got it," she said.

"We're going to make a run to a few churches," he said to Anna, "see if we can score more holy water. I want to cover all twelve portals today, so it'll be a late night. Call my cell if you need me. Keep trying if you don't get through right away. The solar storms are supposed to be going out with quite a bang over the next few days—strongest flares yet by far—so reception will be spotty."

A part of Anna wanted to tag along and help them decimate the portals, but the pull of Craig Shine was more powerful. Besides, maybe with Geneva around, she wouldn't need to babysit her dad anymore.

As soon as Geneva and Jack left, a silence filled the ever-shrinking nooks and crannies in the Fagan house. Anna put her backpack on and maneuvered her way to the entranceway, peering through the Mountain of Mail to the street outside. No Major Tom. Freddy wasn't coming, not after what she'd said to him, or what he'd said to her. He and Dor were probably on their way to school already. Outside, a spattering of freshmen walked by on their way to the bus stop. Anna sighed. She had no choice but to follow them there.

The moment she climbed the steps onto the idling yellow behemoth, she was overcome with the bus smell that she'd managed to avoid since Freddy got his driver's license: body odor, stale lunch meat and hot vinyl. At least there were plenty of open seats. Anna chose one in the back.

Alone now and bouncing over Old Bloomtown potholes, she was hit with a stabbing sense of loss. Anna bit her lip to keep the tears at bay. Damned if she'd mess up her eye makeup after all the effort she put into it. This perma-PMS was exhausting. She and Freddy *would* get past their blowup. It's not like he was dead, for frig's sake. As for Doreen, things would work themselves out between her and her mom. Soon, the air in Bloomtown would clear of any trace of the brain-altering mist, and everyone would revert back to their saner selves.

But why was it so freakin' *quiet* on the bus? Anna looked down the aisle. There were a lot of vacant seats. Half the bus was empty. Weirder still, none of the kids were yelling or even chatting with each other. It was silent except for a hushed murmuring from a nearby row. At least *someone* was making noise. Anna pulled herself up to get a better look. The murmuring was coming from two seats in front of her, on the opposite side of the bus. A red-haired sophomore—Anna didn't know her name—was hugging her knees to her chest and whispering furiously to herself. Behind the sophomore, a sweat-drenched freshman was pulling out his eyebrows, carefully examining each one before placing them on his tongue.

Nauseated, Anna slid back down in her seat, massaging her temples as a fresh pressure thundered in her skull. The stale granola bar in her stomach threatened to make an appearance.

The bus arrived at Bloomtown High, and the urge to hurl became a whisper once she stepped into the fresh air. But once she entered the school, her hackles went up. Neither Freddy nor Doreen were waiting by her locker. Although she told herself that it was no big deal, she'd been hoping to tell Dor about the portals, to make a big joke about it so Dor wouldn't get scared. Instead, Anna grabbed her first-period books, feeling exposed and vulnerable without her friends.

But when she spotted Craig across the hall, thoughts of anyone else vaporized, and a thrill bloomed in the base of her spine. Craig was leaning against the wall by the boy's bathroom, looking down at his phone. His dark hair was tousled in perfect disarray, and his free hand was tinkering with a large chain hanging from a belt loop on his black skinny jeans. There weren't that many kids around and the commons was quiet. He had to know she was looking at him, had to feel it. And then he did look up, his gaze unfocused. She smiled at him, but before she could wave he was already striding away. Had he purposefully ignored her? No. Why would he? She was being paranoid again. Anna walked to first period on shaky legs.

As the day dragged on, she realized that Freddy and Dor weren't avoiding her: they had never shown up at school in the first place. And it wasn't just them. There were too many absentees to play soccer in gym class, so the handful of kids that did come were forced to sit through a gruesome video about drunk driving. The sickest part was that Amanda Chessfield, a normally reserved junior, kept laughing at all the gory parts. Laughing *hysterically*, as in doubled over, couldn't catch her breath, tears running down her face kind of laughing. Amanda didn't stop until the frazzled substitute sent her to Steuben's office.

During lunch Anna sat by herself in the maintenance stairwell behind the girls locker room. She called Doreen and got her voicemail. She texted Craig, *sorry I had to leave our chat the other night. experiencing parental difficulties. how was ur wkend?*

It was hard to focus later in Algebra II. She kept her phone tucked under her sleeve, checking it constantly until the bell finally rang. One more class to go and she could go back home, peel off her ridiculously tight jeans and wash her face. If Craig didn't respond she would text him from the privacy of her room and find out why. Plus, she wanted to be there when Jack and Geneva returned; hearing that every last one of the portals had been spritzed into oblivion might help her relax.

On the way to her locker to grab a biology book, she passed by Sydney and two of her cronies in the commons. The orange-skinned one, Lyric Danner (Queen of the Cheap Fake Tanner), pretended to cough while saying something under her breath directed at Anna. Sydney's throaty laugh rang out, causing heads to turn in their direction.

Anna stopped in her tracks, not turning around but waiting to see if they had the guts to say anything that she could actually hear. It wasn't fair how they got away with bullying whoever they wanted, and she was *sick* of being a target. Anna had never done a single thing to Lyric Danner. She hadn't even laughed when Mackenzie threw a fit in the parking lot last year after Lyric left a body-shaped, orange splotch on her precious car seat. And Sydney—Anna hadn't wronged her either. She had only tried to help.

When they were in the fifth grade, Anna, Dor and Sydney had accepted a ride home from the swim coach. They rode in the backseat with Danny Pickens, who was a high school senior then, an assistant coach in training and a chaperone for the team during out-of-town meets. Pickens had a reputation for dating younger girls on the sly—eighth graders when he was a junior, freshmen now that he was a senior—but they didn't yet know what a dirtbag he was.

Anna and Dor shrank back from Pickens when he asked if one of them could sit on his lap to make more room. But when Pickens pulled Sydney on his lap, she smiled at him, conditioned as she was to be a good girl and not hurt anyone's feelings. The smile remained, even as Anna saw the fear in Sydney's eyes. Danny Pickens was looking out of the car window, as if fascinated by the passing scenery, but his hands were moving under the towel he'd thrown over Sydney's lap.

"Syd, come over here!" Anna said, and Sydney scrambled off Pickens's lap and sat in between Dor and Anna. "We should tell," Anna said after the three of them were dropped off at Sydney's house, and they all agreed. They'd gone into the garage where Sydney's dad was cleaning a leaf blower. Sydney told him what Pickens did to her, and Doreen and Anna had backed her up.

They were sure that Pickens would get in big trouble, but that wasn't what happened at all. "You sat on his lap?" Sydney's father said. His baseball cap was on backward and sweat dotted his forehead. "Why'dya go and do a thing like that?" He wiped his brow and a fat drop of sweat splattered on the leaf blower. "I told your mother not to let you wear those little shorts." He looked at his daughter with hard eyes. "Boys will be boys," he said, then looked down at Dor and Anna. "Now you girls go on home."

Sydney had watched them as they left the garage, looking confused, hurt and ashamed all at once. Things changed after that. Sydney changed. She grew distant, hard. Anna and Dor never said a word to anyone about what happened, not even to each other, feeling that they'd somehow failed Sydney, too. But their presence in that garage that day, in that car, seemed to fester in Sydney, and she'd looked at them ever since with cold, accusing eyes. Anna was sick of it.

"Something on your pea brain?" Anna said, turning around in the hallway to face her once-friend, feeling the rage river flowing.

Sydney stalked over to Anna, her beautiful face a mask of snide fury. "Look at Goblin Girl getting *gangsta*."

Lyric started cackling, stepping to Sydney's side. "Yeah, as in *Scarface*."

"Want a new nick name?" Sydney asked. "How 'bout Frankenskank?"

Damn. Anna had spent so much time on her eye makeup that morning that she forgot to cover her scar. Her fists clenched. She was microseconds away from smacking Sydney right in her perfect face. Her palm actually tingled in anticipation of the after-slap burn.

"All dressed up and no place to go," Lyric sneered, indicating the cleavage exposed by Anna's scoop neck.

"Except maybe a whorehouse!" Sydney yelled, attracting the attention of everyone in the commons who wasn't already watching.

One Mississippi, two Mississippi, three Mississippi. Breathe. Anna restrained herself, knowing that in her current state of mind one slap wouldn't be enough. In fact, while the river raged, she might also decide to go ahead and slam Sydney's head into one of the metal lockers, perhaps several times. Nausea rolled in Anna's gut. She was disgusted by the burst of pleasure the violent fantasy brought her. She took her eyes off of Sydney's smug face and scanned the commons. Was there a portal here, too? There must be, but Bloomtown High wasn't on Saul's list.

Anna forced herself to walk away from Sydney and Lyric, ignoring their parting sneers. Was she being paranoid or was everyone in the hallway gawking at her? Anna picked up her pace, her heart dropping into her churning stomach as she passed a blur of scornful faces. Everyone *was* looking at her, and the worst part—she thought about Craig's snub that morning—was that she might know why.

CHAPTER SEVENTEEN

DENTON'S REVENGE

The bell rang and Anna continued down the hall into Denton's class, sitting in her usual seat. It was finally last period, but things were getting off to a bad start. Denton was smirking at her from behind his desk, which was odd because he'd avoided eye contact with Anna ever since their tiff.

But when Denton stood to address the class, it was clear that quite a few things were *out of the ordinary* about him today. He hadn't shaved and his eyes were puffy and bloodshot, as if he'd been crying for hours or hadn't slept in days. Along with his loafers, blazer and tie, Denton wore plaid pajama bottoms. The cherry on top of this ensemble was his pot belly peeking out from behind his poorly buttoned shirt. A few muffled snickers were heard over the loud scraping of chairs as kids found their seats.

"Okay, time to settle, butts on wood," Denton said in his trying-too-hard-to-be-cool voice. "Not clear on why we have so many absentees. But if you speak with your truant peers, tell them to read chapters six through ten for tomorrow. There will be a quiz. But since so many are out today, let's skip the lecture and watch a video. What do you think, guys?"

The class cheered and Denton basked in the validation he so deeply craved.

"We have a special treat today," Denton said. "A certain young lady—actually, *lady* isn't the appropriate term. Let's just say a certain *female* has made quite a splash on the interwebs with her exhibitionism."

The hushed silence was broken by a spattering of nervous giggles. Anna's limbs turned to concrete. He *couldn't* be talking about her.

"Since this certain female likes to spout off at the mouth, let's allow her the chance to comment on her video after our little screening. Sound good?"

No one said a word. The classroom held its collective breath. Denton looked right at Anna. "So nice that she came in all tarted up today for her big debut."

Anna sank into her seat. This wasn't happening. This couldn't be happening. But it was. A shock wave reverberated through the room. A few kids shifted uncomfortably in their seats, but the general feeling was one of a lurid momentum.

Denton clicked a remote and the flat-screen TV in front of the blackboard came to life, displaying shaky footage of Craig Shine sitting in front of a computer screen. She recognized the dirty green couch and the lewd posters—it was *Izzy's* bedroom. And it was Izzy's voice coming from the TV, loud and distinct because he was holding the camera and standing in such a way that he was an invisible participant in the webcam chat Anna had so naively assumed was private. Izzy zoomed the camera in on the computer screen in front of Craig, and there it was, a live shot of Anna, her hair freshly fluffed, smiling like a goofball.

Anna watched herself do her "sexy" walk toward the webcam, looking thrilled, awkward, and ridiculous.

The classroom tittered with nervous laughter while Anna curled her fingers around the edge of her desk. They wanted her to run out of the room in tears, but she wouldn't. She'd be strong. Anna turned and stared at Izzy in the back row. He was kicked back on two legs of his chair, leaning against the wall, arms crossed.

Their eyes met and the river rage overflowed into thundering rapids. She *would* kill Izzy for this. The rough outline of a plan unfolded. Anna would play it cool for now and not make any threats. That way, when Izzy's body was found, she wouldn't immediately be a suspect. She'd act surprised, never telling anyone what she'd done, not even Dor. When it was over she'd find a way to live with herself.

Izzy paled as if reading her mind and shifted forward in his seat. The front legs of his chair hit the linoleum with a faint thunk.

"She's like a bitch in heat!" Frank's shrill voice erupted from the television. On the screen Izzy pointed the camera at Frank, who was perched like a vulture on the dirty green couch.

"Somebody turn it off!"

The high-pitched voice snapped the class out of its collective, salacious gaze. It was Tanisha Matthews, a designer-clad New Bloomtowner who Anna had never spoken to. She felt a rush of gratitude for Tanisha, but then everyone was pulled back in by Frank's doofus baritone.

"Tell her you love her and shit!" Frank said. He sniffed his fingers, and his hyena laughter ratcheted through the TV.

Izzy swung the viewfinder back to Craig, who was nodding to music that wasn't there, pretending to sing but really saying, "Bro, chill. I got this. She's almost there."

Bile rose in the back of Anna's throat. That's why Craig hadn't wanted the sound on. She was *such* an *idiot*. Izzy zoomed the camera in on the monitor again and there Anna was, lifting her shirt and flashing her black bra. Craig pumped his fists in victory, but down low by his side, so that Anna hadn't seen it on her webcam. "I told you she wants my jock," Craig hissed through his teeth. "You just got owned. Fifty bucks."

"No nipple. No cash," Izzy said from behind the camera. "That was the deal."

"You said tits," Craig said.

177

"I didn't see tits. I saw a bra over some tits. You said you could make her do anything."

"Can you make her kill herself like her mom?" Frank said from the dirty green couch.

There were gasps in the classroom. It was the lowest of all blows.

On the TV in front of the blackboard, Craig laughed through his teeth, and then Anna typed "*brb*" and left her bedroom. From behind the camera Izzy said, "She better come back."

But Anna hadn't come back, thankfully. She'd walked into a different hell when she found Jack in the basement.

Knowing that her television debut was over, Anna allowed herself to breathe again as she watched the shaky footage of Craig snatching the camera from Izzy. Then Izzy's oily face filled the flat-screen.

"What's your beef with Fagan anyway, dude?" Craig asked from behind the camera. "You never got shot down before?"

Izzy stiffened. "I wouldn't touch that skank with Frank's junk." His eyes darkened. "You ever have a messed-up dream? When I see her...it's like looking at a nightmare or something."

"Wus-bag" Craig said, and then Frank's hyena laughter was cut short when the screen went black. Today's lesson in suburban film noir was over.

The exorcism. As expected, Izzy couldn't remember it, but he had retained a fear-response associated with Anna. Good. Let the bastard be scared. Too bad she hadn't recorded a video of Izzy humping and licking his smutty poster. Now *that* would go viral. Anna collected her things from her desk and started for the classroom door, walking leisurely past Denton's desk, keeping her head up. He'd wanted her to crack but no such luck. She'd come up against way worse than him in her life. Denton was small potatoes.

"Nothing to say, Ms. Fagan?" Denton asked, his voice shaking, sweat on his bald head.

Anna ignored him, knowing, as he must have, that soon it would be all over town that he'd shown a video of a student undressing in his classroom. Even the ostrich-like ("boys will be boys!") Bloomtown High faculty couldn't keep their heads in the sand for this one. Denton had just lost his job, or worse.

After entering the hallway, Izzy appeared beside her, pale and nervous.

"Don't get hormonal and do anything stupid," he said. "It was a joke."

This was curious. Why wasn't Izzy relishing his victory? Then it clicked. He'd been driving around his mother's white Camry for at least two years. Izzy was eighteen, a legal adult, and this webcam stunt would surely breach the protective bubble of the student body. In the real world, distributing provocative images of a minor was a giant no-no. A smile bloomed on her face.

"Welcome to the sex offender list, dingleberry—or as your neighbors for the rest of your life will call you, the Creepy Pedo Next Door."

Izzy glowered at her, his eyes draining into his skull.

A handful of curious kids spilled out of the classroom, trailed by Denton. He yelled at them to get back inside, spittle spraying from his mouth, but he was wholly ignored. Realizing he'd lost any semblance of authority, Denton deflated and slunk back into the classroom.

It seemed like every last kid in the growing crowd around Izzy and Anna had their phone out. No one wanted to miss out on the next Goblin Girl spectacle, but Anna wasn't about to provide the dramatic material. She turned to walk away and Izzy's thick fingers dug into her sleeve. Anna struggled to free her arm, but Izzy held tight and her shirt came off her shoulder, exposing her bra strap. Aware of the camera phones aimed at him, Izzy had a new glint in his eye.

"Got the grandma special on today?" He snapped the beige cotton strap with his dry, rough fingers. "Are the black lacy numbers just for Shine?"

He slid his arm around her waist and pulled her to him, enveloping her in a cloud of his body odor and sour breath. There was lust in his eyes and hatred, too. For Izzy, they were one and the same. The crowd closed in, as did the walls of Anna's throat.

"Do anything stupid," Izzy hissed in her ear, "and this"—he nodded at the growing number of recording cell phones—"will never be over for you."

Her jaw clenched. Now Izzy was threatening her. Izzy who'd somehow killed Penelope. Peeps, who fit entirely in Anna's hand when Jack brought her home from the shelter. Whose legs quickly grew so long and gangly that she'd stumble and slide across the kitchen floor racing to her food bowl, sending Jack and Anna into hysterics every time. Peeps, who had saved her puppies before she died, who had suffered at the end.

And then, with Izzy's rancid breath condensing on her cheek, the mere intention to do away with him wasn't enough. The scissors in Anna's makeup bag—touted for the purposes of snipping Doreen's tags or errant eyebrows—could surely be put to more pressing needs, couldn't they? Like stabbing Izzy in the throat? She scanned the rabid crowd, her adrenaline coursing. Maybe she *would* give them a show. Life in jail might be worth it.

Suddenly, Izzy rose up as if standing on his toes, and Anna was free of him. His eyes went wide as he was thrown against the wall next to the boy's bathroom. Craig stood in his wake, flexing his hands as if ready to do more damage.

"Kill him, Shine!" Manny Vasquez, the senior class president, called out from the crowd, his voice wavering, then suddenly booming "Kill him!"

The coppery heat of bloodlust ignited the crowd and Anna was forgotten. A dozen or so kids picked up the chant, "Kill him! Kill him!" Anna recoiled, repelled by the violent hunger of the mob. But hadn't she, only minutes ago, wanted to smash Sydney's head into a locker? Wasn't she just about to stab Izzy in the throat with scissors? Something was *wrong* with her. Something was wrong with all of them.

The chanting crowd grew larger, and kids pushed each other out of the way to get a better view. They were all sick, all *infected*, including her. But they couldn't *all* be affected by only twelve portals, could they? She had to call Jack. Saul must have lied about the number of portals. For all she knew, the school was swimming in portal spew. What else had Saul lied about?

Izzy scrambled to his feet and tried to run, but Craig grabbed him by his T-shirt, twisting the cotton in his fists and lifting Izzy up until they were eye to eye.

Zoey Edelman, captain of the varsity cheerleading team, was perched atop the shoulders of her burly wrestler boyfriend. "Kill him! Kill him!" Zoey screeched while digging her pink nails into her boyfriend's thick neck.

More teachers and kids crept out into the hall, staring at the fight with hungry eyes.

"You said the video was just for you," Craig said slowly, inspecting Izzy's face like he was about to take a bite out of it. "You said you wouldn't show it to anyone."

"C'mon man, get off me," Izzy whimpered. "I thought she'd leave school and I'd be rid of her. She did something to me, put a curse on me or some shit. I barely sleep, and when I do, all I can see is her witch face staring at me, *violating* me, bro."

"Shut up," Craig said, tightening his grip.

Izzy twisted his body in a desperate panic to free himself. He managed to squirm himself loose but left his T-shirt behind in Craig's fists. Bare-chested, Izzy broke into a run, but Craig lunged after him, throwing a savage punch that landed with a solid *thwack* on the back of Izzy's head. Izzy fell hard on the trampled carpet, worn down by countless Uggs, and stumbled to his feet in a dizzy, seesawing sprint down the hall. The crowd moved their phones in unison, following his wobbly trajectory into the commons.

And then the bell rang. As quickly as it had assembled, the crowd scattered, peering at their phones as they posted, texted and emailed the video of Izzy's spectacular beat down.

Craig remained where he was, standing next to Anna. They were suddenly alone in the hallway, but he kept his eyes on something distant, unwilling to face her. He jammed his hands in his pockets, hands that Anna had long dreamed of holding, hands that had balled into fists of victory at her humiliation.

"You must really despise me," Anna said.

"Nah. It's not that serious." Craig shrugged, finally looking at her. "It's hard to explain...I get these headaches." His face crumpled for a second and then grew stony again.

So, he'd been afflicted, too. Craig looked away again, this time at his shoes. Maybe he wanted forgiveness, but forgiveness wasn't an option. There was no forgetting his cold laugh after Frank said, "Can you make her kill herself like her mom?" Yet her betraying heart still swelled a little at the sight of his dark eyes thick with pain.

Anna turned her back on him and walked on hollow legs through the commons toward the large glass exit doors. She was acutely aware of the chasm of empty space that bellowed around her when she stepped into the sun's glare. Doreen and Freddy, at least one of them, had always been close by when she needed them, but not today.

182

She crossed the street and cut through the neighborhood adjacent to the school, cursing when she realized that her phone was dead. She'd always been there for Freddy and Dor, too, hadn't she? But as she crossed a back road to the strip-mall parking lot and passed the graffiti-stained dumpster behind the Yo! Yogurt shop, she had to admit that she'd been laser-focused on herself for a while, even before the portal mess. Maybe Freddy and Dor were done with her, for good this time. Maybe she deserved it.

Anna finally made it home, thirsty and tired. Jack's car wasn't in the driveway, only Geneva's hatchback with the busted fender. Jack had said they'd be out late dousing portals, but Anna still felt abandoned. Once inside, the hoard piles flanking the narrow pathway seemed to have swelled incrementally while she was at school. Jack's Crap grew as steadily as hair. You didn't notice the movement until it hung in your eyes, weighing you down.

Anna went to the kitchen and downed a large glass of cold water before trudging upstairs to her bedroom oasis. She plugged her phone into its charger and called Jack. A hyper-fast busy signal blasted into her ear. She tried Freddy and heard the same thing. Dor was next, and this time Anna was treated to a deafening series of cracks. Perfect. The solar storms were jacking-up cell reception. Anna gritted her teeth. No Jack, no Dor, no Freddy. *No Penelope. No Mom. No Craig.*

A darkness flared insider her—a murderous rage grotesquely out of proportion to the circumstances. Anna sat on her bed, dizzy with hatred and loss. There must be a portal in her room. That stupid list was meaningless. The portals were everywhere, for all she knew. Was anything she felt *real*, or was it all generated by portal spew—and how could she tell the difference? Frustrated, she lay back and pulled the covers over her head, burrowing further under the sheets like a hiding child until finally, gratefully, she fell asleep.

CHAPTER EIGHTEEN

TAKEOFF

The weight of her eyelids kept them closed, but Anna was awake and considering the deep canals the plastic braiding of the lawn chair would leave on the back of her thighs. She should get up, but the sprinkler mist was about to hit her feet again and she was *so* hot. Bone-tired despite her nap, it was if she hadn't slept at all, but instead had walked for miles, year after year, miserable and crazed, through a whole other life. Anna had been dreaming that she lived in an ugly world of supernatural portals, demons, and psychotic real estate agents. Worst of all, her mom was dead, and so was Penelope. What a twisted subconscious she had.

She forced her eyes open and her lids, like magnets, fought to meet each other again. The afternoon sun was fierce and punishing, punctured only by the cool mist from a neighbor's sprinkler that intermittently wafted across her feet. In the middle of the Fagan backyard, Jack wielded a spatula, moving hotdogs off the grill into fluffy buns. He was wearing his plumbing uniform: stained jeans and a blue T-shirt with "The Drain Whisperers" stitched on the back.

Several feet from Jack, Anna's mom sat at a picnic table. She was pointing at the grill, probably critiquing Jack's grilling skills. Jack always said that his wife was a backseat driver and a dinner table chef. Helen looked radiant even with her sundress plastered to her body with sweat and the beginnings of a nasty sunburn splashed across her nose and shoulders. The crystal butterfly pin in her wavy brown hair gleamed in the sunlight, creating a faint halo effect around her head.

Anna's eyes clamped shut again and stayed that way even when she heard Penelope's tail slicing through the air next to her. Penelope nudged Anna's hand with a wet nose and whimpered a plea for her to come and play. She really *should* get up for lunch, Anna thought, but her lawn chair was perfectly situated in the shadow of the house, out of the hot sun. Her eyes fluttered open and, *oh lord*, Doreen and Freddy were there, too, sitting at the picnic table across from her mom. Jack was passing a pitcher of lemonade around, and they all had hotdogs on plates in front of them.

Anna *had* to get up. She was being rude, lounging in the shade and leaving Freddy and Dor alone with her parents in the glaring heat.

"I had this dream," Anna called out, sluggish and croaking. Self-conscious, she stopped talking. It was too silly to mention, and horrible. And the dream was fading now, like dreams do. The epic minutiae, intimately known moments ago, now lost. No one at the picnic table was listening to her anyway. They were all on their feet and swatting at a dozen or so bees circling the hot dogs on the table. The odd, fat bees jerked erratically in the air, bumping into each other as if they were drunk. Peeps had probably poked around a hive and pissed them off. Anna focused on keeping her eyelids open. Next on her agenda was moving.

Penelope gave her hand a final nudge and then darted away past the picnic table to another lawn chair in the back of the yard by the fence, where a blonde woman was reading a magazine under an umbrella. Geneva was wearing a big straw hat and a skimpy flesh-colored bikini. What was Geneva thinking? And in front of Anna's parents?

The first prick of fear pierced Anna's sternum.

Geneva was only a figment of the insane dream she just had. What was a figment of her imagination doing in her backyard? Geneva scratched Penelope's head and then became distracted by several wobbly bees dive-bombing her legs. One of them must have stung her because Geneva squealed and jumped out of her chair. She joined the others around the picnic table, swatting at the clumsy, bloated bees with her rolled-up magazine.

Anna tried to heave herself up but only managed to grip the arm of the lawn chair with one feeble hand. The sprinkler mist on her ankles was like liquid concrete, turning her feet to stone. She wasn't just tired; she was trapped. Her mother began slapping at something in her hair. A bee? No. Her mother's butterfly pin. The metal pin was catching the fierce sun and burning her mother's scalp. Anna tried to yell out, but her mouth refused to open.

The sun's glare off the butterfly pin flared and then burst outward in a blinding flash. The picnic table and everyone around it ignited like a match.

Before Anna could process the scene before her, more bees came, hundreds, then thousands. The plague of bees swarmed the picnic table as if the fire had enraged the parasitic fly larvae inside them. They were the *zombie bees* that Anna learned about in Denton's class.

Freddy took a couple of lurching steps toward Anna. He opened his mouth to scream, but his tongue was covered with bees. His mouth continued to stretch, melting, as flames engulfed his face. Anna couldn't move, but her gag reflex convulsed from the smell of his burning flesh. Penelope fell at Freddy's feet, completely blanketed by bees, her body contorting on the ground. No. Oh *no*. It was the bees inside Penelope, they were moving her corpse.

The thin membrane of Anna's sanity tore open like a popped balloon. The bees were inside her parents. They were inside Dor and Geneva, too, jerking their burning bodies around as their faces melted around their widening screams. Behind her madness, Anna prayed that they were already dead. As they burned, their shadows grew long and thin on the scorched grass, stretching toward, *reaching for*, Anna's lawn chair.

Anna sat up in bed. There was pain in her throat and a horrible sound. She stopped screaming and her tongue stuck to the roof of her mouth. She reached for the glass of water on her nightstand and gulped the rest of it down. As water spilled down the sides of her chin, she registered the uncomfortable weight of her skinny jeans, glued to her with a chilled sweat. *Sweat from the heat of a brutal sun.* It hit her like a cold slap. The bees! The flames! Anna bolted to the window, terrified of what she'd see. But there was no charred picnic table outside, no bee-covered corpses. Her shoulders sagged in relief.

She had slept through the afternoon. Outside the brightness of the full moon muted the green and reddish hues of the aurora borealis and illuminated the burned patch of ground in the backyard. It was the charred remnants of the doghouse, *not* a burned picnic table. There was no picnic table. It was only a dream, a nightmare.

Anna took a shaky breath and the tentacles of panic from the gory dream relaxed their grip. Penelope was gone, her mother was long dead, and she was Goblin Girl. But at least she hadn't lost everyone at once in a gruesome picnic table inferno. Bright side.

But her relief was short-lived. Sitting on the edge of her bed, the emptiness of the house reverberated around her. It was almost ten o'clock, but Jack still wasn't home. She tried to call him. *Crack crack crack.* The solar storms again. *Damn.* She needed to reach her father. If Saul had lied about the portals, who knew what Jack and Geneva were up against?

Anna peeled off her clammy jeans and sweater as police sirens rang out in the distance. It was a reminder that she wasn't the only one suffering in Bloomtown. She threw her clothes at the hamper and missed. Something about the nightmare tugged at her, but she resisted the urge to analyze it, not wanting to revisit the horror of watching her mother die again, even if it wasn't real this time.

She slid off the mattress onto the carpet, hugging her knees, and looked at the framed picture of her mother on the bureau. Helen Fagan had carved the wooden frame from the remnants of a slab of black walnut that she'd made into a tabletop. Anna used to run her fingers over the frame, knowing her mother's hands had molded it.

Anna allowed herself a fraction of hope. Maybe with all the craziness in Bloomtown, her mother's evasive spirit might somehow sense her vulnerability and finally respond. She squeezed her eyes shut. *Please give me a sign that you can hear me.* Anna strained to hear her mother's voice, but there was only the wail of fading sirens.

But when Anna opened her eyes, Helen's eyes had receded into a beady, hooded glare, her tongue slithering out of her mouth, licking at her dry, cracked lips. The photograph had once again transformed into the face of the demon.

Anna closed her eyes again. *No.* This wasn't happening. It wasn't real. The demon was only in Anna's diseased mind. She blinked, and once again the frame held the photograph of Helen Fagan, freckled, carefree, and illuminated by dreams yet to die. Helen Fagan, whose soul was probably still trapped somewhere dark and seething, the tortured plaything of the demon that took her life. And Anna was helpless to do anything about it.

Invaded now by a crushing dread, Anna turned from the picture to her reflection in the full-length mirror. The sight of her exposed flesh triggered a painful ringing in her ears, followed by echoes of Craig's cold laughter on the flat-screen in front of the blackboard. Her thin brown hair looked as dry and brittle as a bundle of twigs. Her face was sallow and unwelcoming, the small bump on her nose as repellant as a festering boil. There she was, sitting on the floor in her underwear and bra, all wrong, and entirely *hideous.*

Anna's head thundered as a dark and horrible shame took fast root, its hot thorny branches burning holes in her chest. How could she have been so stupid? In her pathetic attempt to impress Craig, she'd flashed the whole freakin' school!

Gripped by frenzied loathing, Anna scrambled to her feet and tore through her purse on the desk. The scissors from her makeup case were suddenly in her grip. She turned back to her reflection, sneering at the glass. *You stupid slut. You ugly bitch.* Her hand jerked up and the scissors scratched across her thigh. It was a small relief, but so much more was waiting. Anna's mind waged war against her. It wanted her to keep slicing.

Everyone hates you, Goblin Girl. You're a crappy friend, a horrible daughter. Even Freddy and Dor hate you now. Everyone knows what a skank you are. You actually thought Craig would ever like someone as ugly and disgusting as you? You don't deserve to be alive. You should kill yourself like your mother did. You should throw yourself in front of Shady M's bus. You should slice yourself up into a million pieces. You should set yourself on fire and burn like the witch you are, Goblin Girl. You should suffer before you rot in hell.

Anna dropped the scissors and kicked them under her bed. No. It wasn't real. It wasn't *her.* She looked around her room warily, wishing she had Emi with her so she could scan her room for portals. Her bedroom must be rotten with portal spew. She ripped the white sheet off of her bed and wrapped it around her body, watching with queasy horror as a thin line of red saturated the cotton against her thigh. She'd cut herself. How sick was that? But it wasn't deep. It would scab over.

She opened the window, looking for relief from the likely poisoned air, and a balmy wind blew in. She breathed it in as the large moon illuminated the backyard with the reflected and refined rays of the sun.

As the tide of loathing slowly withdrew, Anna peered up at the faint outlines of the mountains and craters of the moonscape. Freddy used to tell her about the moon when they were kids. They'd watch it through his telescope, checking to see if it looked any smaller. The moon escaped earth's gravity a little every year and would one day be slung out of earth's orbit altogether, making its own way through space. The sun, too, like all stars, would eventually burn out. This event would be the final death knell of the long-scorched earth, leaving behind clouds of stardust that would eventually create new worlds.

It touched something peaceful inside Anna, this inevitable cycle of life, death and rebirth. Maybe it was the warm breeze, or the soft moonlight, but her trembling hands grew still.

Anna left the window open and sat down in front of the mirror again, determined to be brave. Geneva's words from their first day together returned to her. *If you can quiet the chatter in your mind and then look deeply into your own eyes, your soul can leave your body and travel through the astral plane, the first level of Source.*

Anna came from her mother's body. They were linked by blood, history and fate. Helen had the courage to sacrifice her own life to spare her family, and Anna must have the same strength somewhere inside her. She stared into the mirror again. If her mother couldn't come to Anna, Anna would go to her.

"Mom, where are you?"

But only her own puffy eyes stared back. She did not understand the girl in the mirror. She was a mystery, a stranger to herself. Imperfect, sure, but what else? Anna didn't know anymore. She had lost who she was, even before the portals.

The portals only magnified that loss. Maybe this was a chance to find herself again. Although it was uncomfortable, Anna didn't look away from her reflection. Slowly, her discomfort gave way to wonder.

There was wisdom behind her eyes, a knowing. She continued the staring contest with herself until the current of connection became so strong that she couldn't look away from the mirror even if she wanted to. And then the details of the yellow flecks around her pupil—the golden starbursts in the hazel of her irises—suddenly grew sharper in the glass, crystallizing. Every muscle in her body tightened. Something was going to happen.

At first Anna thought she was shaking with fear, and then she was sure that a bee had flown into her mouth. Her jaw clenched instinctually, biting down. She braced for the soft crunch and searing sting that was sure to follow, but her teeth met without resistance. There wasn't a bee, but her teeth continued to rattle as an electric *thrumming* spread throughout her body. Was this another portal attack? Anna wasn't sure, but it was a vastly different sensation from the river rage—a much faster and higher-pitched vibration. She waited with dread for the shaking to slow and deepen, for the waves of hatred and misery to roll through her. But the vibration inside her increased in tempo, intensity and pressure.

It was like being in an airplane right before the wheels lifted off the ground—all that *power*. She was vibrating at a body-numbing, incredibly high rate, but was somehow still at the same time, like a tuning fork. It had been a mistake to try this in her room. What if the mirror gazing had opened her up even more to the destructive power of the portal spew? There was something familiar about it, the growing roar in her ears, but she braced herself and resisted with all her strength. *No.*

The roaring and shaking came to an abrupt stop and Anna tore her eyes from the mirror. What the hell was *that*?

When Geneva told Anna about mirror-gazing, she didn't mention anything about vibrating like a guitar string and feeling like you were about to explode. Maybe Anna had screwed up the process somehow.

Nevertheless, whatever happened had shaken the bad juju right out of her. Anna stood up and stretched her arms over her head. She felt pretty damn good, a huge change from only minutes ago when she'd been on the verge of filleting herself. She shuddered at the dark memory, grateful to feel more like her old self. Anna glanced back at the mirror, avoiding eye contact with her reflection. What would have happened if she hadn't resisted the growing power of those vibrations? Her fear, her preoccupation with the destructive power of the portals, had held her back. Maybe that was why her mother couldn't hear her prayers. It was too damn noisy in Anna's head!

Anna looked to the window, toward the peace she'd felt minutes earlier. *Moon bathing.* Geneva said that it helped her go "deeper" during mediation. And wasn't mediation all about calming the mind? Geneva looked so peaceful when they burst into her bedroom to show her that Emi was working. She was meditating as the portal spew rained over her. Maybe the air around Geneva was brighter than the rest of the room, because only a small amount of portal spew fell onto her skin. Perhaps she'd created a protective *barrier* around herself.

Anna's heart rate picked up a notch. She would try it. Why not? She'd tried everything else to reach her mother; she might as well try moon bathing, too.

With one hand gripping the top of the windowsill and the other holding her sheet, Anna stepped gingerly out onto the roof. The slant wasn't very steep, but if she lost her footing she could tumble off. She shuffled forward a bit, the shingles brittle under her feet, and plopped down awkwardly on her butt. The full moon lit up the yard, even the shadowy spaces by the fence. Izzy the creeper was nowhere in sight. A grim smile crept across

Anna's face. He was probably holed up in his scuzzy room, hiding from Craig and immersed in his twisted perversions. She shimmied down the slant before laying back, her body cocooned in her sheet.

The large moon revealed the cotton ball detail of the drifting clouds and the greens and browns of the pine trees lining the perimeter of the backyard. The tops of the pines were a lot higher than when she and Freddy sat out there years ago playing the what-if game. Anna shifted on her back, trying to relax her neck and shoulders, sore from the constant tension of the last week. She found a comfortable position and allowed her body to relax.

Above her the wind played the pine needles like an instrument. How long had it been since she'd listened to the wind rustling through Old Bloomtown pines? Too long. She'd forgotten how peaceful it was, how mysterious.

But there were other sounds coming from inside her room: the humming of her laptop, the faint buzzing of the lightbulb in her lamp. Anna hadn't realized that her laptop made noise, let alone a lightbulb, but there they were, as distracting as a circling fly. Anna sighed. If she didn't chill out, this moon-bathing thing wouldn't have a chance. The sheet was too cumbersome to lug back inside, so Anna climbed back through the window in her underwear and bra. She quickly powered down her laptop and switched off the lamp.

Once she'd settled back on the roof, there was only the moon, the warm wind and the swaying pines. *Observe your thoughts but don't attach to them*, Geneva had said. *Focus on your breath and not your thoughts; let them move on down the road.* Anna closed her eyes, allowing the moonlight to saturate her skin. Despite her exposure, it felt safe and natural bathing in the gentle rays. She inhaled deeply, letting her belly expand, then blew the air out slowly. As the wind rustled the pine needles, Anna let her thoughts drift by like the puffy night clouds.

The more she simply watched her thoughts without letting them carry her away, the less power they had over her. Soon, the mind-chatter that she'd always identified as *who she was* began to feel like something else entirely—something desperate, manic and clawing. She tried not to think, tried to just *be*, and then finally stopped trying and relaxed into each moment. Time passed, and there was only her breath and the caress of moonlight on her skin. She was aware of each and every one of the fine hairs on her body as the wind gently tugged on them, sending a pleasant tingle over her skin.

The wind gusts blew stronger and the swaying trees serenaded her. It was a melodic whispering that grew in urgency and then receded in waves. And then, all at once, every nerve ending in her body seemed to extend into the night to meet the reaching branches of the trees, expanding outward in perfect union with the wind and stars.

Anna was experiencing her inherent connection to *everything*, flooded with the awareness that the world was *hers* to explore, and it had been all along. Was this the power they feared, the forgotten knowledge they had tried to crush? She laughed out loud. This power was *impossible* to destroy no matter what they did.

How could she ever have felt anything less than gratitude for her body? Desire welled within her, stronger, purer than ever before. She closed her eyes, wanting to experience every nuance of it without distraction. A face rose in her consciousness. Not Craig. It was Freddy.

Surprised, Anna's eyelids fluttered open, her vision unfocused, and then there it was. There it was *again*. A floating white orb about the size of a basketball. The moon, of course, but it reminded her of something else. The intense vibrations that she'd felt in front of the mirror. Anna had felt them before, years earlier in the haunted cabin in the Poconos, when an orb of light appeared in the center of the room and illuminated the antique poker on the fireplace. And right before the light of Source disappeared, her ten-year-old self had yearned to fly into it as Mary's spirit had, her teeth rattling as her body shook.

Witnessing that light as a child, her soul had recognized it for what it was: an opening, a gateway through the veil, a passage into Source. The vibrations she'd felt in that cabin that day were her soul preparing to leave her body! It was instinctual, perhaps, for a soul to begin to leave the body when witnessing the light of Source. The most natural thing in the world. All she had to do was let it happen. Anna was ready to try mirror gazing again.

She climbed back inside, feeling as sleek and graceful as a cat, and threw the sheet into her hamper. She reached for her lamp then changed her mind, allowing the moonlight to filter unpolluted through the window. Settling down in front of her mirror, what Anna saw before her—the same body, the same face—was now, for the first time in a long time, beautiful to her eyes. Geneva said that moon bathing renewed spiritual power, but Anna felt more than renewed, she felt *supercharged*.

Anna locked eyes with her reflection, and when the shaking returned she didn't brace against it. She heard a faint chattering, distant and undecipherable. She focused on it and it grew louder. *Go back to bed, dumbass. You think your dad's crazy now? What do you think he'll do if something happens to you?*

Before doubt could poison her resolve, an image appeared in the mirror next to Anna's face. It was vibrating at the same rate as Anna and was therefore still amid the blurred surroundings. It was a girl, her hair flowing around her regal face in dark, shiny waves, like the ocean under moonlight. It was Mary, her wounds gone, her eyes full of urgent compassion. The spirit spoke one word before dissipating—the same word Anna spoke to her years earlier.

"*Go.*"

Anna returned to her own gaze in the mirror. Even as the noise and pressure intensified, she stayed calm, although it was uncomfortable. It was like driving down the parkway in Major Tom when Freddy cracked his window. Anna would have to crack her window, too, in order to release the pressure. As the noise and pressure thundered in her ears, Anna relaxed into it, opened up. She vibrated faster and then faster still, until she couldn't stop what was happening even if she wanted to. The plane was going to take off. *Pop.*

CHAPTER NINETEEN

OUT OF BODY

A girl in her underwear sat cross-legged on the carpet, her head hanging down between her slumped shoulders. *Everything* about this girl was fascinating: the way her skin folded in the creases of her bent knees and elbows, her rib cage rising and falling with her breath, the curve of her belly and breasts, the thickening of skin on the soles of her feet, the lines of her limbs, torso, and neck. The blood pulsing through her veins made her fair, almost translucent skin appear marbleized. There was so much to *see*.

It was possible to zoom in on one of the girl's closed eyelids until her eyelashes resembled a network of massive black bridges that curved over a far horizon. But why stop there? Tunneling further down to a cavernous follicle at the base of a single lash, there was a cluster of microscopic mites. They had long, sectioned, eight-legged bodies covered with blue scales. One mite was half submerged inside the follicle, feeding, while the others huddled in the shadow of the giant eyelash, avoiding the moonlight. The mites had a hissing focus on mating and territory. Although their language was alien, their joys, rivalries and fierce protectiveness of their young were palpable. Was it possible to zoom in further onto their armored skin and discover even more layers of life? Where would it end? Was there an end? Ha! It was like the what-if game.

Wait. The what-if game? In a great swoosh of images and sensations, the memories came of her and Freddy as kids, lying on the slant of roof outside her bedroom window. That's right! She had an *identity*. She was Anna Fagan, also known as Goblin Girl. What was she doing staring at a bunch of microscopic mites on someone's eyelash? Her awareness expanded outward in great swaths of rushing space, further and further from the mites to the cluster of giant bridge-like eyelashes, until she once again hovered above the body of the girl. A realization rippled through Anna—the girl on the floor was *her*.

Anna was floating *above* her physical body, yet she still had a body, kind of, made of soft lavender light. She lifted her hand and examined the luminous quality of her "skin." It was blissful, this freedom from her body's cumbersome weight, cravings and aches, liked she'd sloughed off an uncomfortable costume. But why wasn't she freaking out? Instead, she was serene but intensely curious, almost *aggressively* curious—like how she imagined a large, burly man might feel, at ease in every instance, as if fearlessness was a birthright.

From outside came a sharp sound—a burst of excited affection. An unmistakable bark. Penelope!

Anna shot *through* the roof in a blur of dark wood and pink insulation. She hovered high over the tree line, below her a quilt of houses and streets. The pale bulbous tank of a water tower loomed in the east. Anna floated in the air, enveloped by the most beautiful music she'd ever heard. The melodic whispering of the pine needles was now a grand, complex orchestra. The music flowed through her light-body, caressing her. Who knew such a beautiful sound was even possible? And she was part of it, that symphony, a clear note, distinct and essential to the arrangement. She could have stayed there forever, an obedient and content musician. But then another bark caught her attention. That's right! Penelope!

Penelope, in a body of faint purple light, stood in the backyard where her doghouse used to be, her tail slicing through the air. Anna dropped toward the lawn and descended into soil alive with languid worms and roots sucking water from the earth. The sounds and sights were fascinating, but she needed to be *above* ground. *Pop.* She was in a forest of grass. Each blade sparkled with energy and a sound like the gentle chords of a violin, fluid and soothing.

She floated several feet above the lawn just as Peeps jumped into the air to meet her. They blew into each other, intermingling their purple light bodies. Anna felt Penelope's buoyant love for her and the dog's exasperation over Anna's grief. She laughed with relief. She'd been so *silly*. Penelope was fine. Penelope was perfect! They stayed together, playing and cuddling their light bodies, until a squirrel ran down the trunk of a nearby tree. Penelope scampered after it and then darted away in a blur, chasing something unseen through a neighbor's backyard.

Peeps was clearly adept at maneuvering in this astral realm. Anna, however, needed practice. Now the only question was, who would she visit first, Dor or Freddy? She was closer to Dor's, so maybe she should—*Pop.*

Whoa. There were walls around her, a drastic change of light, air and color. She was indoors. Disorientated, Anna spun around, although it was unnecessary. She could see in every direction at once with no body (or eyes) to narrow her field of vision. Anna was in Dor's bedroom. Doreen sat on her bed, a pill bottle in her hands, her eyes swollen from too many tears. Alarm rippled through Anna's light-body. Doreen was *smoldering*. Puffs of smoke rose from her friend's head and chest. Anna hovered in front of Dor's face and called her name, but Dor couldn't see or hear her. *I'm a ghost*, Anna thought. *An earthbound soul outside my body.* She tried to touch Doreen, but Anna's translucent "hand" traveled right through her friend's arm.

A puff of smoke penetrated Anna's light-body, and she was engulfed by despair and hopelessness. It wasn't smoke but *pain* that billowed from her friend. Without a barrier between them, Anna felt the full brunt of Doreen's powerful negative emotions. A part of Anna wanted to pop away from Doreen's suffering but she stayed put, wanting to help but not knowing how. *Dor, what happened?*

A screech came from downstairs. "Reenie!" It was Doreen's mom, Cindy. "Get my pills!"

Doreen yelled toward the open door. "I already gave them to you!"

Pop. Downstairs in Doreen's living room, Cindy's face was scarlet. Veins bulged in her temples and neck as she sank back into the couch. The living room was thick with portal spew. A murky gray mist shot up through the couch and scattered into the air. Anna popped under the couch just as fresh blood seeped from the cushion to the floor; it joined a pool of dried and drying blood in the center of an electromagnetic hair ball underneath the couch. Anna could see portals! As surprising at that was, she kept her focus on Doreen's mom. Cindy was infected in more ways than one. The blood must be oozing from the surgical wound on Cindy's back.

Anna popped out from under the couch and hovered above Cindy. Gray mist shot up through Cindy's body and then rained back down on her like nuclear fallout. The portal mist was harmless to Anna while out of body, but the puffs of rage and pain emanating from Cindy went through her light-body like barbed wire. Anna grit her teeth as the intensity of Cindy's self-loathing washed through her.

"Did you hear what I said? Get the goddamn pills! *All of them*!" Cindy bellowed.

Anna retreated to the corner of the living room, wanting to be far from Cindy and her pain.

"You useless little bitch," Cindy hissed. "I wish I never had you!"

Remorse rippled through Anna. Dor had been dealing with this alone because Anna was too absorbed in her own self-pity to give a damn. She'd always leaned on Dor and given little back, even before the portals. Going out of body was about more than trying to find her mother, Anna could see that now. Her own failings were being revealed.

Doreen walked into the living room from the stairs, her face a ghost of innocence, pain ballooning out of her. She approached the couch and looked down at her mother.

"I won't do it."

"It's over," Cindy said. "There's nothing left for me."

"What about me?" Doreen asked.

"You are your father's problem now."

"I'm going to call somebody," Doreen said, her voice cracking.

"Call them *after*," Cindy said. "You ruined my life. You know that, don't you? You *are* going to do this for me. *This one goddamn thing!*"

Defeated, Doreen walked into the kitchen. Anna followed, watching helplessly as Doreen placed the pill bottle on the countertop, the pain coming off her in a thick fog of energetic sludge. Doreen opened a cabinet, took out a ceramic bowl and masher, and placed them on the counter. She tipped the pill bottle, and three white pills made soft clinks as they fell inside the bowl. The bottle tipped again and four more pills clinked.

No. Anna surrounded Dor with her light-body, wrapped it around and through her friend. *Dor, you gotta wait for me. I'm coming.* But Doreen couldn't hear her. The intensity of Doreen's pain was too heavy for Anna to bear much longer. She concentrated on looking through the clouds of pain to the skin on Doreen's neck. There was a slight crackle, an electrical charge, coming from Doreen's skin. Anna drew from it, inhaling it with her light-body, and then she screamed, *IT'S ME, IT'S ANNA. HOLD ON, DOR, I'M COMING.*

Doreen jumped back from the counter, slapping at herself as if she'd walked through a cobweb. The bowl fell off the counter, cracking in two, and white pills scattered across the floor. Anna rose to the ceiling, exhausted from her efforts. Doreen ran out of the kitchen and up the stairs, ignoring her mother's vicious barbs. Her bedroom door slammed.

Anna floated near the refrigerator, gathering her strength. She'd made contact with Doreen, scared the bejeezus out of her in the process; but her friend had snapped out of her dark trance, safe for the moment.

To do any more for Dor and Cindy, Anna needed to get back inside her own body. As soon as she did, she'd go to Freddy's, and the two of them would—*pop.*

Freddy slept in his bed. Anna had popped into his bedroom without meaning to. This out-of-body thing really took some getting used to. She drifted over him, basking in the moon rays from his window as they passed through her light-body. She could look at him now without the strange charge between them that had kept their eye contact short over the last year. His hands were clasped on his stomach, rising and falling with his long breaths. His eyes moved back and forth under his closed lids. Freddy was *dreaming.* Anna dropped closer to him and saw gray mist dampening the glow of his skin.

Anna spun, looking for the portal. It was in the back of the closet, a tangle of electromagnetic wires whipping out the vile mist. So there *was* a portal in Freddy's room. The demon must have been there, masquerading as Bloomtown's friendly real estate agent. Damn it. Freddy had said something about his mom renting out his room. Why didn't she pay attention?

Anna scanned the room, searching for more portals. But there was nothing, only Freddy's bookshelves casting long moon shadows on the floor. Frightened, Anna flew to the ceiling. They were only shadows, but they reminded her of something.

The *dream*. The nightmare about everyone she loved burning alive at the picnic table, their shadows stretching toward her as if they were entities unto themselves, desperate to grab her. Anna felt her light-body contract and expand as she made the connection. The dream was her intuition's way of trying to tell her something important, trying to grab her *attention*. Shadows stretching, unnaturally long and skinny. What did it mean?

Of course. A *shadow person* was in the Fagan house on the morning that Saul made an unannounced visit. Anna had spit holy water on it accidentally and it evaporated. Something about that small incident nagged at her. But what was it? She'd think about it. Right now, getting Freddy out of his room and away from the portal was more important. Anna had to wake him up somehow, get inside his head. *Pop.*

An alien landscape lay below her, a pale, spongy earth. Crisscrossing over the strange terrain were narrow scarlet roadways and dark purple superhighways. A new world for her to explore! But wasn't she supposed to be doing something? That's right, she was in Freddy's room. She had been trying to get—*into his head*. Anna was looking at Freddy's brain.

Pop. She hovered over Freddy's sleeping body once more. There had to be another way to reach him. And then she saw it—Freddy's light-body was barely visible, but it was there, a centimeter or two above his physical body in faint lavender. Anna lowered herself toward Freddy, close enough to kiss him. And then without thinking about it, she did kiss him, sinking her lavender light lips into his. The warm sweet thrill of it made her light-body glow brighter as the Freddy Smell filled her ethereal senses. Freddy, where are you? *Pop.*

The main floor of the Bloomtown Shopping Center retreated below her. Anna was riding up an escalator to the second-floor food court. Freddy stood a few grated metal steps ahead of her, his back to her, one hand touching his mouth, wearing his baggy jeans and NASA sweatshirt. Anna walked up the escalator until she was right behind him.

"Exciting dream," she said. "What's next, Target?"

Freddy glanced over his shoulder, his arm falling to his side, and then went back to staring straight ahead. Maybe he couldn't see her? But then his hand went to his hair, smoothing his unruly curls. He saw her.

"Can you hear me?" Anna asked.

"Duh," Freddy said, still not looking at her.

The generic mall music droned on, but the mall itself evaporated along with the merged smell of cinnamon buns, French fries and pizza. They were now riding an unsupported escalator up into the cosmos, surrounded by the black vacuum of endless space sprinkled with the light of countless stars.

"Where are you going?" Anna asked.

Freddy pointed above his head and Anna craned her neck back, following his finger. There was a huge zig-zag crack in the space-fabric of the universe. A brilliant whiteness lay behind it. She gasped, instantly filled with yearning. For a moment Anna was willing to let it all go, Doreen, Freddy, Jack, her mother, *everything* and fly into that light like Mary's spirit had years ago. But instead she said, "I'd miss you."

"You wouldn't even notice." Freddy's voice was full of hurt, old and unacknowledged.

"I don't deserve you, do I? You and Dor."

Freddy was silent.

"Dor's in trouble. It's bad," Anna said.

He finally turned to her, his brow crinkling. "What's wrong with Dor?"

"She needs our help. You have to wake up."

There was a grinding sound of protesting metal as the escalator creaked to a stop and changed direction, heading downward. The cosmos began to waver like a heat mirage around them. Anna looked back up at the crack in the universe, unable to stop the tide of grief. Everyone wants to go home. *Everyone.*

"Do you think that's where my mom is?" Anna asked.

Freddy shrugged. "I can never quite get up there."

But maybe Anna could. She had *popped* into Freddy's dream, hadn't she? This could be it, her chance to find her mother, to travel into the very heart of Source.

"Are you up there?" Her voice echoed up through space. "Mom, where are you?"

Pop.

Anna hovered above a single story house with vibrant, chipping paint. It was dark, but she could see a worn soccer ball in the yard with a logo on it. She dropped toward it and read the lettering. *Federation Mexicana De Futbol.* Anna popped into the house, inside a small bedroom. There were paintings of butterflies on the wall, crude and childlike, but cheerful. A tiny brown dog in the corner of the room jumped up from its bed and bared its teeth at her. Anna was apparently visible to dogs, both living and dead. On the bed, a small body stirred under the sheet.

"Silencio," said the sleepy voice of a child.

Anna knew enough Spanish to understand. *Be quiet.* But the dog kept on yapping as dogs do. The bed covers were ripped down by a girl, about eight years old, with round brown eyes and short dark hair. The girl sat up, clearly annoyed at the unwanted wakeup call, and gave the dog some serious stink eye.

"Silencio!"

The dog's barking dwindled to a chastened whine, and Anna floated over the bed to get a better look at the kid flopping back on her mattress. Within moments, the girl was drifting through the gap between wake and sleep, where the veil between the worlds is thin. The girl's body sagged, her eyelids fluttering shut, and then she looked up at Anna. The child's eyes, strangely familiar, grew large with shock and fear. The girl could *see* Anna's light-body floating above her. But then she tilted her head, her features relaxing, and spoke in perfect English, "Sweet Pea?"

A tsunami of shock rushed out from Anna's light-body. It traveled through the room making the butterfly paintings appear to shimmer and dance. Anna knew those eyes! The girl snuggled back under her sheet, her mouth slack, her eyes shut. Anna, on the other hand, had never been more wide-awake. She now understood why Jack had been unable to contact her mother's spirit, why her mother had never answered Anna's pleas. Her mother wasn't *in* the spirit world. Helen Fagan's spirit had been *reborn*. Her mother wasn't being tortured by the demon who took her life. Helen Fagan was *alive*.

From the center of Anna's immense relief came a piercing regret. She had been blaming Jack all this time, but he was innocent. If only she could go back in time.

Pop.

Anna was home, hovering above her father. He sat at the kitchen table, puffs of exhaustion, stress and grief rising off of him. But his dark hair wasn't speckled with gray and the skin around his eyes was smooth. He was younger than he should be. Anna was in the past. She was a freaking *time traveler.* The wealth of visible floor space was disorientating. Jack's hoarding, which had started almost as soon as Helen died, was still manageable. Her father was sprinkling salt into a bowl of water. Jack was making holy water, his lips moving in prayer, "Wherever this salt falls shall be free from the attacks of malicious entities—"

There was a high-pitched scream. Anna floated after Jack as he rushed out of the kitchen and up the stairs to Anna's bedroom, knowing what she would see. But it was still a shock to be confronted with her younger self sitting up in bed, her

Dora the Explorer pajamas damp with sweat. Anna had nightmares every night for two years after her mother's death, and Jack was there every time she woke up screaming.

All these years, she'd punished him for breaking his promise to contact her mother's spirit. A promise that it was now clear was impossible for him to keep. Yet they had survived, battered and certainly worse for wear, but still together. And now the portals were unraveling what was left of their fragile lives. It wasn't fair after all they had lost. Grief permeated her light-body. Anna let the emotion wash through her. It was just energy, moving. She set her intention on connecting with the larger, wiser part of herself. *Why did this happen to us?*

Pop.

Anna floated near her kitchen ceiling. She'd gone forward in time but hadn't quite reached the present. It was the morning that Saul had stopped by to talk to Jack about opening the new office. She observed herself entering the kitchen and saw Jack introduce her to Saul. She'd never seen the top of her head before. It was odd, like looking at someone else. Anna watched her distracted self accidentally pour a glass of holy water. The shadow person entered the kitchen, and Anna's past-self spit out the holy water, spraying both Saul and the shadow person, who instantly vanished.

"Why is there holy water in the fridge? It tastes weird," she heard herself say.

Saul stood and closed his jacket, quickly hiding the water stains. There was an urgency in Saul's movements that Anna hadn't noticed that morning. It was how he closed his jacket after the holy water hit him; the way his jaw clenched as his fingers fumbled for the buttons. Saul was hiding something. Anna zoomed in on his shirt and saw the dark stains spreading across the wet fabric, saw his flesh pucker and molt through a tiny gap between the buttons.

And then Anna knew. Saul wasn't controlled and tortured by an evil energy vampire. It was the holy water that had caused Saul's chest wounds. It was Saul that was evil, entirely so. Anna zoomed in on Saul's face.

"Where are you now, you lying shit?"

Pop.

It was reading the *Bloomtown Examiner* in its sparse living room, legs crossed, khakis pressed, crisp button-down shirt. It looked right at her, *seeing* her, its skin swimming over an underlying swirling darkness. The Saul-thing bared his teeth in a vile, tongue-flickering grin that Anna hadn't seen in eight years.

"Hello, *maggot*," it said.

And then a loud sucking sound, a horrible wheezing and only blackness.

CHAPTER TWENTY

LANDING

There was a whirl of color and then the heavy weight of bones and flesh gluing her to the carpet. Anna was back in her body, sitting cross-legged in front of her mirror. The wheezing came from the back of her throat as she sucked in air. *Exhale, damn it!* She'd forgotten how to breathe! Anna managed a few shaky breaths and then sprang to her feet only to crumple to her knees, unused to the force of gravity. She stood on her third attempt, threw on jeans and a hoodie, and picked up her phone. It was one o'clock in the morning. She had to get to Doreen. Freddy could back her up. His house was on the way. *Go.*

Anna rushed into the hallway and peeked inside Jack's bedroom. He was curled up and snoring. Relieved, she gently shut his door. Now wasn't the time to tell Jack about Saul—about what Saul *was.*

Her feet barely grazed the steps, but Geneva's white sandals at the bottom of the stairs stopped Anna cold. She peered through the hoard piles in the living room and saw a sliver of blonde hair. Geneva was sleeping on the couch again. Her presence made Anna uneasy in a way that bounced between irritation and hope.

Once outside, Anna broke into a run down Eden Street, dodging toppled over trash cans (hopefully that wasn't Jack's doing) and a car parked askew. A police car sped past with its lights off and distant sirens wailed from the east and west. She got to Freddy's in less than a minute and brazenly reached for the doorknob. *Please let it be open.* It wasn't. Screw it. She rang the doorbell and knocked. Gloria, Freddy's mom, came down the steps in her bathrobe, peering through the tempered glass before opening the door.

"Anna Fagan, what in the—"

"I have to see Freddy."

"It's the middle of the night!"

"Sorry!" Anna darted past Gloria and up the stairs, bursting loudly into Freddy's room. Startled, Freddy sat upright in bed. There in his closet was the portal, still visible but faded. Anna could see portals without Emi. She was still connected to Source.

"You remember?" Anna asked.

Freddy nodded. "Dor needs us." He threw his sneakers on. "Let's go."

They ran down the steps, avoiding Gloria as she wondered aloud just what in the holy *hell* they thought they were doing. The two of them sprinted past several houses on Eden Street and then came to a stop, panting, in front of Doreen's house.

"Why are we here?" Freddy asked.

"It's her mom," Anna said. "She's wounded and there's a portal under her couch."

"Like that thing above Geneva's bed?"

"Yep. I told you about it yesterday, but you were a little... out of it."

He looked away from her. "Anna, I'm sorry—"

"Don't worry about it. There's a portal in your room, too. A big one. The demon must have been there. Was anyone strange in your room?"

"Yeah," Freddy said as they reached Doreen's front door. "Some real estate guy came by to look at it." His eyes narrowed, perhaps remembering what she'd told him about Saul. "Wait. Did you say 'demon'?"

"I'll explain it all later."

The front door was open and they didn't bother knocking. Freddy followed Anna into the darkened living room. It reeked of bedpan and sweat. Cindy was asleep in a sunken mound on the couch. Anna could see the woman's tongue lying thick inside her slack mouth. As Cindy snored, the TV broadcast a hissing, flickering static, giving sound to the portal mist spitting into the air from underneath the couch. The mist was so faint that Anna could barely see it. Freddy, she knew, couldn't see it at all.

"Is that...?" Freddy trailed off. Bloated and filthy, Cindy was almost unrecognizable.

Anna knelt beside the couch and peered underneath. The pool of blood confirmed it. Everything she'd experienced while out of body was real.

"It's her back," Anna said to Freddy. "She's bleeding. Call the paramedics. I'm gonna get Dor."

When Anna entered Doreen's bedroom, her friend was sitting on her bed, hugging her knees.

"You came," Doreen whispered. "I thought I heard you. My...my mom."

Anna put her arms around Doreen. At first unyielding, she slowly leaned into Anna's embrace.

"Freddy's calling for help," Anna said.

It took forty minutes for the ambulance to arrive. Two medics, one tall and broad-shouldered, the other smaller and mustached, wheeled a stretcher into Doreen's living room. Both men had dark circles under their eyes.

Cindy woke up in an ornery mood, snarling at Freddy to quit gawking at her. The medics fired questions at her, but she refused to speak to them, only nodding or shaking her head in response. To free Cindy from the couch, the medics used a pair of shears to cut into the cushion attached to her back. They wheeled her outside on the stretcher, lying on her stomach, a blanket covering the portion of bloody cushion still fused to her skin. Cindy was loaded into the ambulance and Doreen climbed in after her.

Freddy stepped one lanky leg into the back of the ambulance and turned to Anna.

"You coming?"

"I have to go home and check on Jack," she lied.

She couldn't tell him that the demon that caused her mother's death was still in Bloomtown. Freddy would insist on helping and she knew what the demon was capable of. It was too dangerous, and Anna wouldn't put her needs before him, or Dor, again.

She walked back down Eden Street to her house, avoiding shards of glass from broken beer bottles. Once inside, Anna followed the newly dug path to the back of the living room. Curled up and sleeping atop a pile of thrift store sweaters, Geneva looked child-like and vulnerable. Anna wondered if she was doing the right thing by involving her, but there wasn't another option. Jack hadn't fully recovered from the basement fumes, and she wanted to keep Freddy and Dor as far from the demon as possible.

Anna woke Geneva, summoning her to the kitchen so they could talk without their voices carrying up the stairs. They sat at the table.

"It worked," Anna said, wasting no time.

"Anna, slow down. What worked?"

"The mirror gazing. You were right. I left my body, saw Doreen and went to Freddy's. Popped into his dream! And from there I went to Mexico and saw my mom. She's okay! She's a little girl now, but she still loves butterflies and remembers me. But the thing is, *Saul*, I saw him, too. And I know what he is. He's a *demon*, Geneva. The same demon that killed my mother."

212

Geneva gaped at her, her eyes still foggy with sleep.

"You're saying that you had an out-of-body experience, and this somehow led you to find out that Saul is a demon?"

Anna took a deep breath and explained everything again as calmly as possible.

"So," Geneva said, after listening quietly. "You thought about someone, and then you—you just appeared there?"

Anna nodded. "Instantly."

"And this Saul-thing…it's the same entity that…that…"

The words hung in the air. *Killed your mother?*

Anna nodded.

"The story it told about the Ouija board in the shack? Total bull. Saul isn't controlled by some energy-sucking vampire. It's a full demonic possession. Who knows if there's anything left of the *real* Saul. He probably vacated the premises years ago."

"Your dad," Geneva said, her voice tight. "We need to wake him."

"No way."

"I'm not sure I'm comfortable—"

"He's sick, Geneva, from the basement *and* has a head injury. I can't let anything else happen to him."

Geneva exhaled, deflating a little, perhaps relieved that they wouldn't have to tell Jack about what Saul was, at least not now. She was letting Anna have the reins, deferring to her new authority.

"You look exhausted," Geneva said. She pushed her chair back and went to the sink, filling a glass with water that she handed to Anna. Anna tipped it toward her mouth without looking at it. She retched as soon as the liquid hit her throat, gulping another unfortunate mouthful. Anna shot out of her chair and leaned over the sink. Her body ejected the liquid from her nose and mouth as quickly and thoroughly as possible. When there was nothing left to throw up, Anna dry heaved, struggling for breath between each convulsion. Geneva stood beside her, holding her hair back until the jagged waves of nausea passed.

"What did you give me?" Anna asked when she could finally talk.

"Nothing!" Geneva said. "Just water." She picked up Anna's half-empty glass and held it up to the light. "Here, look."

The water in the glass was a murky and dark.

"It's freakin' mud! Can't you see it?"

Geneva was dumbfounded. "See what?"

Anna felt the steam go out of her. Geneva *couldn't* see it. It was plain old water to her.

"I must still be connected to Source," Anna said. "The water, my body rejected it."

She turned the faucet on. The water spilling into the sink was an inky sludge.

"Gross. It's coming out of the faucet like that."

"That water looks dirty to you?" Geneva asked.

"Yes," Anna said, "and worse than that. It's...I don't know, *infected* with something evil."

Feeling woozy, Anna took a can of seltzer out of the fridge and sat back down at the table. The implications of what she'd just witnessed began to dawn on her. Doreen's mom had been surrounded by the empty paper cups. *Take one pill with a full glass of water.* Those were the typical instructions, weren't they? Cindy was consuming a lot of tap water. Plus, she'd been stuck right on top of a portal underneath her couch. A double whammy of bad juju. Could whatever was in the water be as dangerous as the portal spew? A prickly rash of gooseflesh shot down her arms. What if it was worse?

Anna remembered waking from the picnic-inferno nightmare. The first thing she did was drink a glass of water. Soon after she'd spiraled down to the point of cutting herself. If there was a portal in her room she would've seen it upon returning to her body. The *water* she drank must have caused her scissor-wielding meltdown. Something in the water was having the same, and possibly more potent, effect as the portals.

"Geneva, I have to tell you something."

Geneva stopped rinsing puke down the drain with the murky water.

Anna exhaled. *Here we go.*

"I've had some pretty nasty thoughts lately, *violent* ones. There's this kid Izzy at school. We're pretty much mortal enemies at this point. It's a long story. Anyway, yesterday at school, I was thinking about getting rid of him, you know, permanently. Kind of planning it out in my head. And there's this girl, Sydney, who I *fantasized* about hurting. The weird thing is, she's a pain in the ass, but I don't even hate her that much."

The color evaporated from Geneva's cheeks. She sat down next to Anna and cleared her throat, wide awake now.

"Thoughts like that can be a normal way to process stress," Geneva said. "As long as you're not seriously considering acting on any of these fantasies. You're not, right?"

Anna shook her head. After going out of body, the thought of hurting someone made her feel ill.

"But when I got home from school, I drank a glass of water and started having violent thoughts about *myself*, and…I did something."

Geneva stiffened. "Anna, what did you do?"

"I cut myself on my thigh," Anna said. "It wasn't deep."

Geneva had a strange look on her face.

She's judging me, Anna thought. But that wasn't it at all.

Geneva lowered her head. A section of blonde hair fell into her face.

"I have to confess that I've been having similar impulses," she said. "Violent feelings toward my ex and…his student friend. That's why I've been sleeping here. I thought the portal fumes at the office might be behind these urges. But the urges are growing harder to resist. Before I finally fell asleep tonight, I thought about going back to California and attacking him, tearing him apart, really dark stuff. I kept shooting Emi around the living room, looking for portals, but there weren't any. If my ex was anywhere nearby, I'm not sure I could've stopped myself. There was so much hatred inside me. I can still feel it wanting bloody revenge. *Needing* it."

Geneva hesitated. "I sound psychotic."

"It's okay," Anna said. "I get it."

Geneva nodded, relieved, but then the lines on her forehead deepened again. "If the two of us are having these kind of thoughts"—she gestured to the sink—"so is anyone else that consumes this water: drinks it, cooks with it, does their laundry in it, or god forbid *swims* in it. Things could turn much uglier. There could be widespread violence."

"The demon must be behind this," Anna said. "Maximum chaos and misery. That's what demons always want. For us to kill each other, and ourselves."

Geneva nodded, her eyes steely slits.

Anna sipped on the blissfully cold seltzer water, trying not to imagine Geneva ripping anyone's face off. They'd uncovered something significant. But what could they do about it? Scrounge up some holy water, then track down the demon and attempt to douse him with it? That would be exactly what the demon expected them to do.

Geneva drew her hair back from her face.

"The portals may not be the root problem affecting Bloomtown after all," she said. "They could be a symptom of something more treacherous. Like an open sore that suggests an underlying infection, or perhaps a spark that starts a much more powerful engine. Water appears to be the perfect conduit of energy, positive and negative. But what, besides inflicting misery, is the demon *doing* with all this energy?"

"The demon's stronger now than it was," Anna said. "I remember that it couldn't stay inside my mother for longer than a few hours at a time, even when she was too weak to fight. Now it seems to have set up permanent camp inside Saul's body. It must be using the energy as power."

"Yes, but to power *what*?" Geneva tapped the water glass with her nail until it came to her. "Where's the engine? How is it accessing the water supply?"

There was only one answer, and it had been holding court over Bloomtown for as long as Anna could remember. The water tower.

CHAPTER TWENTY-ONE

BAD JUJU

"How much salt does it take to de-spook an entire water tower?" Anna asked as Geneva maneuvered her hatchback through the back roads of Old Bloomtown. Once they turned onto Route 33, the towering pines gave up their sandy roadside sentinel to a strip of behemoth fast food signs. The restaurants were all closed, but the reds and greens of the aurora borealis cast fleeting hues on the golden arches of the McDonald's as they drove past.

"Well, let's see, the average water tower holds 1.5 million gallons of water," Geneva said. "A safe bet is that we need a whole lot of salt."

Anna shivered in the passenger seat. They were totally unprepared for this, but they couldn't wait. Who knew what horrors would unfold overnight if they did? There was also the advantage of surprise. The demon knew its cover was blown and would expect an attack, but it hopefully didn't know that they suspected the water tower was the source of the infection. If the poisoned water was behind the demon's growing power, clearing Bloomtown's water supply—and fast—was their best option. Anna was connected to Source and therefore, in *theory,* should be able to perform the blessing, but she'd never attempted to make holy water before.

They pulled into the parking lot of a 7-Eleven. A bell on the door jingled as they walked inside. Anna spotted the aisle with the familiar blue-wrapped canisters, each adorned with an image of a little girl in a yellow dress. But there were only six left, not even close to enough. They carried three canisters each to the checkout counter.

"Do you have any more salt?" Anna asked the cashier, who didn't bother looking up from her phone. The cashier's tangled hair was pushed back from her face by a pair of glasses. A similar pair of glasses was perched at the end of her nose.

"We got what's out there," the cashier said, still focused on her phone.

"Right," said Anna. "But I was wondering if you might have any more salt somewhere else, maybe in the back?"

The cashier sighed loudly. "Like I said, what's out there is what we got."

Anna glanced at the woman's name tag. "It's just that it's kind of an emergency, Evelyn."

Evelyn looked up then, pushing her glasses back on her nose and assessing Anna with a frothy glare.

"Oh, well in that case, tell you what I'll do," Evelyn said. "I'll quit my scrabble game"—she waved her phone at Anna before placing it behind her on a stack of *Us Weekly* magazines— "leave HockeyDad77 completely in the lurch, and lock up the front door so as not to leave the register unattended. Other customers, they can wait, since we got a little queenie here with a *salt emergency*. Then I'll make my way into the back room and search the inventory. Yep, just start ripping open boxes, tearing the whole place apart if that's what it takes to make sure your every need is met."

Anna's eyes traveled to the large cup of tea that the woman had just about drained. Perhaps the charming Evelyn was affected by the noxious water, or there could be a portal somewhere in the store. Then again, maybe Evelyn was just a jerk.

"Just an FYI," Anna said. "Sarcasm isn't a good look."

"Ain't that a shame. I guess I'll have to drop out of the Miss South Jersey pageant now, and I had my acceptance speech all memorized. Now are you going to buy something, or what? Because loitering ain't allowed."

"We'll take these," Geneva said, gesturing to the canisters on the counter and taking out her wallet. "Please."

Geneva turned to Anna when they got back into the hatchback. "You know," she said, "you can catch more flies with honey."

Anna was baffled. "And why would I want to do that?"

"It's an expression that means showing someone a little kindness gets you a lot further than hostility."

"Oh yeah, I'm sure that little scene was all my fault. It had nothing to do with the shady water special she was drinking."

Geneva raised a brow. "What was it you were saying about sarcasm?"

They both laughed, the brief levity easing their nerves. But they fell silent after pulling back onto the two-lane highway. The water tower loomed eerily in the backdrop of Route 33. The white paint, visible against the dark sky, had taken on the creepy shimmer of the aurora borealis above.

The only other convenience store open past midnight was the WaWa at the gas station. The moment they walked in, it was obvious that the scowling, tattooed skinny guy behind the counter wasn't going to be overly helpful, and there was only one canister of salt sitting on a dusty shelf. Anna hung back, letting Geneva handle it.

"Excuse me, sir," Geneva said, "is it possible that you have any more salt? Maybe you're getting ready to restock your shelves and have some handy? I'm looking to buy as much as possible."

"Try Costco," he said, stone-faced.

"It's not open. Nothing is. You're our last hope unless we want to get on the turnpike, and our need for salt—sounds silly—but it's kind of time-sensitive. So, if you did have any, it would really help us out."

"Lady," he said, smacking his gum. "I make nine dollars an hour, and you want *me* to help *you* out?"

Anna bit the inside of her cheek to keep from chuckling. But the smile on Geneva's face didn't waver as she reached into her purse and took out her wallet.

"How about if this hour," Geneva said, placing a bill on the counter, "you make twenty-nine dollars."

They left the Wawa with a full box of salt canisters still wrapped in plastic. Apparently, some flies didn't like honey after all, but cash was always palatable. They now had a total of eighteen canisters. It would have to do.

• • •

By the time they pulled up to the roped-off gravel road leading to the Bloomtown water tower, the predawn light dimmed the shimmer of the aurora borealis. After Geneva parked the dented hatchback, Anna crouched on the dusty road and poured salt from the canisters directly into her backpack. When her backpack bulged to capacity, they poured the remaining salt into the satchel that held Emi. After securing the salt, they ducked under a rope, ignoring a weathered no trespassing sign. The weight of her backpack pulled on Anna's shoulders as they passed the small pumping station at the base of the tower.

The area of patchy grass surrounding the tower was shrouded in an uneasy stillness. No insects buzzed, no birds sang an early-morning song. Although creepy, the silence had an upside. The pump was off, which meant the tank was full. Anna and Geneva had researched the structure online before they left the house. Water was pumped from a local reservoir up into the tank, and gravity created the water pressure that brought it back down through Bloomtown pipes and faucets. The tower held about a day's worth of water, which was accessed in the mornings when demand was high on the regional water system. Their arrival right before the morning rush was well timed.

Anna counted six steel legs supporting the water tank that loomed a hundred feet above them. A spindly ladder was attached to one leg, extending all the way to the roof of the tank. It was the only way up. Anna craned her neck back. The tower hadn't looked as high from the road. Geneva must have been thinking the same thing. The crease between the woman's eyes was deep enough to stand a quarter in.

"I'll go first," Anna said.

"Wait," Geneva said, taking both of Anna's hands in hers. "Close your eyes."

Anna reluctantly obliged.

"I think it's important that we take a few moments to acknowledge that although what we're about to do may be illegal—well, it *is* illegal—our intentions are for the greater good of this community, and by extension, mother earth as a whole."

Anna rolled her eyes under her closed lids. They really didn't have time for this.

"We good now? Can I open my eyes?"

"Yes," Geneva said. "Just promise me you'll be careful."

"Swear on my life."

Anna gripped the ladder's bottom rung, wincing when rusted metal flakes scratched her sweaty palms. Why would they place the ladder so far from the ground? Her arms protested as she pulled her body up, grabbing for a higher rung, and then another. Her feet flailed, searching for and then finding the bottom rung. Buzzing with adrenaline, her thigh muscles burning, she began to climb, reminding herself that there wasn't a choice. She had to move forward. The demon that killed her mother was trying to destroy everyone she had left, and she couldn't let that happen, not this time.

222

The ladder rattled in Anna's hands as Geneva began her ascent. A thick guilt unfurled in Anna's chest. Because of her, Geneva risked an arrest record, injury or worse.

They scaled the rusty ladder for several minutes, climbing slowly and in sync to keep it from shaking. About halfway up they stopped for a break, both of them breathing hard. Anna used her legs to secure herself to the ladder and wiped her clammy raw palms on her jeans, smearing rusted steel on the denim. She looked down at Geneva.

"Should have worn gloves, huh?"

Not up for chitchat, Geneva nodded, white-knuckling the ladder. They got moving again, both of them focusing on their hand and foot placement and not looking down. There was no wind, which should have been a good thing, but instead the unseasonably muggy air felt heavy, like it was pressing down on them as they climbed.

The ladder finally deposited them at a wraparound catwalk encircling the fattest part of the water tower's bulb. Anna immediately plopped down on the meshed metal of the catwalk's floor. She trembled with relief, but this was not their final destination. Looking up she could see the much smaller catwalk that encircled the very top of the bulb. That's where the hatch was located, usually accessed when the tank was full.

Anna looked out at the twinkling lights of Bloomtown. The corridor of Route 33 was lined with glowing streetlights, while the residential areas were shrouded in darkness. It wasn't much, but it was hers, the only home she'd ever known. Freddy and Dor were down there somewhere, probably drinking awful hospital coffee and waiting to see Dor's mom. Freddy would stay with Dor all night if he needed to, distracting her with dirty jokes.

"We need to keep moving," Geneva said. It took a few more minutes to reach the tiny platform at the pinnacle of the tank.

The bulbous surface was studded with small metal grips that they could place a foot or hand on if needed.

Antennas were bolted to the inner radius of the roof in a spikey, silver crown. They were a good omen. Cell phone companies often leased space on top of water towers to get better reception for their customers. Insulated wires were fed up through the tanks to provide electricity to the cellular antennas. This meant there might be a relatively easy way to access the tank's interior.

Anna squeezed through a gap in the antenna spikes, careful not to touch the metal. They were in luck. The hatch on top of the tower was rusted shut but not padlocked. After a dozen or so attempts, with both of them yanking on the hatch and groaning like juiced-up gym rats, it cracked open. They squatted next to it, shining their flashlights down into the hole. But instead of water, they saw a series of wooden planks—a platform—about six feet down.

"What the hell?" Anna said.

"The workers who installed the antennas probably built that," Geneva said. "I doubt the water ever gets up that high."

"Hold my legs," Anna said, ducking her head down into the hatch before Geneva could refuse.

It was dark inside the tank, oppressive, like there wasn't enough air. Anna fumbled for the flashlight in her back pocket, freezing when she heard a faint splash. *Crack balls!* Did she drop the flashlight? She patted her back pocket. No, it was still there. Anna could scan the top interior of the tank from her position, but the wooden ledge beneath her was blocking her view of the water.

"Help me up," Anna yelled, placing the flashlight between her teeth. Geneva took hold of her outstretched hands and then pulled her up by her backpack straps, maneuvering her out of the hatch and into a sitting position on the roof.

"Thanks," Anna said.

Geneva only nodded, her lips cemented in a tight line. *Demon got your tongue?* A crazed laugh built in Anna's chest, but she resisted it. *Keep it together, Fagan.*

"We have to get down on that ledge," Anna said.

"Oh, hon, I was afraid you were going to say that." Geneva's forehead was peppered with beads of sweat. "It doesn't feel safe. I don't like it."

"But we can't get to the water from here."

Geneva rubbed the crystal on her necklace. Anna braced herself for another speech about mother earth, but instead Geneva turned into a responsible adult at just the wrong time.

"Going up that ladder was one thing, and believe me I wasn't happy about it, but climbing down into this thing? You could fall. You could *drown.* I'd never forgive myself, and your father would kill me."

Anna was running out of patience, not that she had much to begin with.

"He can't kill you if he's already dead, and that *thing* is trying to kill him and everyone else in this town. Pretty soon, the population of Bloomtown is gonna rise from their nightmare-infested slumber and start slurping down more of this water. Who knows how many are on the brink of hurting themselves or someone else?"

Geneva's brow furrowed causing sweat to pool in the crease in her forehead, a drop of which fell onto her tank top, disappearing in the tie-dye pattern. The guilt in Anna's chest sat up and shook its finger. Anna took a softer tone.

"Whatever fear you're feeling," Anna said, "could be coming from this rotten egg we're sitting on. We have to get down there and clear this water."

Anna didn't give Geneva a chance to respond. Gripping the mouth of the open hatch, she dropped down inside the tank and hung, legs swinging, over the wooden platform. She stretched one foot down, testing her weight on the planks.

They didn't budge. The platform was sturdy enough. She let go of the hatch and dropped onto the wooden planks. A tiny creak, a small crack. No big deal. She looked up. Geneva was framed by the circular opening, silhouetted by the faint shimmer of the aurora borealis in the near dawn sky.

You see, Anna was about to say, *easy peasy!* But then the darkness in the tank pressed in on her, squeezing the air from her lungs, and a panic squeezed her chest. This was a horrible mistake. The tank walls were a crypt, a trap that she'd stupidly fallen into.

No. She swallowed it back, steadying her breath. It wasn't *her* fear she was feeling, Anna was almost certain. It was this *place*, dark and full of bad juju.

"You okay, hon?"

"What? Yeah, I'm good," Anna said, hoping Geneva missed the hitch in her voice. "Gonna look around."

She shuffled forward on the ledge using her flashlight to guide her. But the light cut a meager path through the stifling darkness, and all she could see was the wood at her feet. Afraid that she might slip over the unseen edge, Anna placed the flashlight between her teeth and got down on her stomach. She elbow-crawled forward on the wooden planks until she could wrap her fingers around the end of the platform.

A thud and then, even worse, a loud crack, sent Anna's heart racing as Geneva dropped onto the ledge behind her. She shimmied on her stomach next to Anna, adding the glow of her flashlight to the crushing darkness. Anna wanted to hug her but was afraid to move that much. She gave Geneva's hand a quick squeeze. The woman had guts.

Together they peered over the edge of the platform, but the glow of their flashlights was enveloped by the darkness below. Geneva removed her shoulder strap, took Emi out of its satchel, and brought the device to the edge of the platform.

She pointed the machine down into the blackness and pushed the trigger. The tank filled with blue light.

Below them the water was a rolling black lava forming boils that sprayed dark sludge across the tank walls as they burst.

"What's wrong?" Geneva asked. "You okay?"

"Yeah. It's just so *disgusting.*"

"What is?"

Geneva couldn't see what was in the water. She couldn't see the large, oval portal on the back wall of the tank exhaling plumes of dark pain dust that fell into the water and collected on the walls in globs. If the electromagnetic portals were sucking in the pain of Bloomtown, then this was where it ended up. No doubt about it, the water tower was Bad Juju Central.

Instead of feeling victorious, cold despair settled over Anna and her headache took on a punishing rhythm. As the pounding intensified behind her eyes, so did her panic. The tank thrummed with malevolence, and it was squirming its way inside her. Next to her, Geneva was trembling, making Emi's blue beam bounce around the tank, throwing shadows all over the walls.

"I don't feel so good," Geneva said. Her tie-dye was pasted to her chest with sweat. "Is the water...is it bad?"

Anna nodded and wriggled the backpack off her shoulders. She gripped the bottom and let the unzipped top fall forward over the platform's edge. A soft hiss echoed through the tower as the salt hit the water.

She had the salt. She had the water. But for the life of her, Anna couldn't remember what to do next. Who did she think she was, trying to create a ginormous friggin' tankful of holy water?

No, she told herself. She could do this. Only hours ago she was out of body. She'd seen Penelope, had found her mother! Anna took a deep breath and remembered the words of her father—before the hoarding had consumed him, when he could still make holy water. The weight of the backpack diminished as the salt fell, taking with it some of her panic.

"Wherever this salt falls shall be free from the attacks of malicious entities!" Anna shouted, her voice wavering but strong. "Anyplace that it touches will be protected by the powers of Source."

The salt met the water and a loud hiss rose from the depths of the tank. The sound bounced off the walls, surrounding them like applause.

"It's working!" Geneva said.

Anna looked down. A foam was forming on the surface of the water; a dirty color that appeared dark blue under Emi's light but was probably a murky brown. *Please, let the water clear.* But the foam quickly fizzled out and the churning, dark energy saturated the water once more.

"No," Anna said. "It's not."

"Keep going," Geneva said.

Anna opened her mouth and a fresh torture thundered in her head. Wincing, she accidentally let go of the backpack, snatching it with one hand before it fell into the water. Her heart thudded in her chest. Who was she kidding? She couldn't make holy water. Her connection to Source was too weak to cleanse this concentrated cauldron of evil. Inside her the river rage crashed against its levee. She was a fool to think she had a chance.

There was a movement directly beneath them. The planks creaked and Geneva stiffened. Something was attached to the underside of the ledge. It dislodged with a wet squelch and fell into the water. Two floating rows of tiny lights moved in unison through the dark water below them, and then Anna's eyes adjusted.

It was the demon, wearing its Saul costume, floating on its back and grinning up at them, its Chiclet teeth shining in the darkness.

CHAPTER TWENTY-TWO

THE BIG SHOW

"You managed to squirm out of your bone-toilet and find me," the demon said to Anna from the water below. "And now you've found me again. Impressive for your kind, maggot. I always knew you were special."

Anna and Geneva scrambled to their feet, moving to a less vulnerable position on the platform, but now they couldn't see the demon. They inched back to the edge, holding on to each other.

The demon's arms spiraled, whistling a cloyingly familiar tune as it backstroked through the water toward a ladder on the side wall, a ladder that led up to the platform. *Row, row, row your boat, gently down the stream.*

"Let's go," Geneva said in a hoarse whisper.

Anna wanted to bolt for the hatch but couldn't look away from the demon. Her knees clacked together like magnets. On the ladder now, its face twisted up at her.

"No hello for an old friend?" it said. "How rude."

Its deceptively handsome features were still punctuated by a set of garish white choppers, but underneath the costume skin was the same whirling darkness that Anna saw while out of body. The darkness appeared fluid one moment, like an oil slick inside a waterspout, then coalesced into black scribbles that bent and writhed like electricity arcing.

"Come *on*," Geneva said, pulling Anna's arm. Her paralysis broke, and she briefly allowed Geneva to drag her toward the hatch before digging her heels into the planks.

Anna didn't want to run. She wanted answers and then she wanted to kill it.

"What the hell *are* you?" Anna called out. Her voice was steady but seemed to be coming from somewhere else.

A part of her was eight years old and walking into her parent's bedroom to find her mother crouched atop the ceiling fan, her tongue flickering like a lizard. But Anna needed to be in the water tower, *all* of her. She bit down hard on her cheek, hoping the pain would ground her in the present. The demon was on the ladder, out of sight and climbing.

"You'll have knowledge, child," it hissed, "before your death."

The taste of blood remained on her tongue, but Anna scattered again as if blown by a gust of cold wind. Death, yes, first death came and then a funeral. Then the clawing emptiness of the house. A house her father had never stopped filling even as it sat choked and bloated. The demon had ruined them, and it did so with glee.

Geneva screamed that they had to go, *now*, but her words were drowned out by the roar of fire engines and the smell of burning newspapers. The horrible shape of Penelope's body on the lawn. Penelope, who suffered at the end.

No. Anna's jaw clenched as the pounding thundered on in her skull. When she was eight she was powerless, but now, riding the drumming rage inside her, she was strong enough to kill. It was a righteous rage. Revenge. Anna was entitled to it.

But Penelope is okay now. You saw her. The small voice inside her was muted by the snickering of a classroom full of kids, by Frank's voice spitting out of the TV in front of the blackboard. *Can you make her kill herself like her mom?*

"I can taste you, maggot," it said. Its voice rose like fumes between the wooden planks. "Such a large capacity for hate and anger. Much juicier than sniveling Helen."

Anna stepped toward the edge, dragging a protesting Geneva with her. Peering over the side, she saw where the top rung of the ladder met the platform.

"Don't say her name!" Anna called out, her hands curled into fists. She didn't have to wait for the demon. She could climb down and meet it.

Geneva gripped Anna's shoulders, swiveling Anna to face her. "You have to fight the hatred inside you. You're giving it what it *wants*."

Anna pushed Geneva away and turned back to the ladder. The planks shook as Geneva ran toward the hatch. Emi was left on the platform, the trigger compressed, keeping the tank awash in blue light. A loud squeaking was followed by a thump as Geneva pushed the hatch open.

Good. Let her go.

Down below, boils burst from the mud-water, spewing up thick tendrils of concentrated pain that rose and fell around the platform like flames. Bloomtown's misery saturated the air like thick humidity, seeping into Anna's pores. Raw malevolence coursed through her undiluted, filling her with homicidal rage. Anna moaned.

The demon cackled, shooting up onto the platform. It landed on all fours then crawled toward Anna like a bug. Startled, Anna stumbled and fell hard on her butt, sending splinters deep into both palms.

Its button-down shirt and dress pants were impossibly pristine. Water ran off them in thin rivulets instead of absorbing into the fabric. The demon's clothes weren't real, Anna realized. They were as much a part of the Saul costume as its teeth and hair.

"I knew *Helen* much better than you did," it said, turning the ends of its mouth down in mock sadness. "It was such a bore lying in bed all day inside her stinking bone-toilet. I planned to leave her anyway, the day she died. If you hadn't been such a needy little maggot, she would have survived."

It was all her fault. The suspicion that surfaced on quiet nights, when Anna's worst secrets had nowhere to hide, finally spoken aloud. The pain in her skull was a butcher's hammer now, merciless and blunt. Her vision swam as nausea twisted in her gut. She couldn't take much more of the spongy, venomous air.

Anna placed her stinging hands on the platform, pushing herself to her feet. She had to keep it talking and think of a way to kill it, or at least wound it, so she could try the holy water blessing again.

"You said you'd give me knowledge before I died," she said. "Tell me why you came back to Bloomtown."

"Came back?" Its smug laughter ricocheted around the tank. "I never left you, maggot! I traveled a great distance for this feast, and I wasn't about to leave before the main course."

It ran a finger along the tank wall, collecting a clump of pain mud.

"Oh, the rare succulence of a food source unaccustomed to assaults on their magnetic field. Look at the density it yields."

Its eyes stayed on Anna as it sucked greedily on a finger, relishing her disgust. She looked around, hoping to spot a piece of wood, anything that she could use as a weapon. There was only Emi, about five feet away on the platform. But that was her only light source. She needed to think of something else, to keep it talking.

"You came all the way here just to make the portals?"

It flickered its tongue. "I can make portals anywhere."

"Then why here?"

It picked its teeth with a fingernail, consuming its find.

"My kind has evolved past the need for bone-toilets," it said. "We are consciousness disembodied, so advanced that we can invade creatures of flesh and experience the tactile world through their senses. Any interference with lower life forms is strictly forbidden, but some of us are not satisfied to simply observe, we like to *play*. Some of us have even learned to replicate the flesh we inhabit. But to do that we need fuel. And there is no more potent a fuel than the hatred, fear and agony of sentient beings. Even without your star's cooperation, the portal inflow provided enough sustenance for me to maintain poor Saul's bone-toilet. His suffering was *delicious*, but he succumbed years ago. I slipped right into his shiny shoes, and from there the homes of my choosing."

Your star's cooperation. The pain in Anna's hands distracted her from the hammering in her skull, keeping her present, helping her think. *The solar flares.* The worse the sun storms raged, the more Bloomtown was self-destructing. She had sensed the connection but hadn't trusted her gut. It was there in the dream as well. The picnic table inferno, sparked by the blazing sun.

"The sun storms," Anna said. "That's why you're here."

It clapped its hands. "Bravo, maggot. Once the flares began, I drew upon their awesome power to supercharge the electric fields battering your primitive brains through the portals. The resulting abundance of human misery is funneled here for me to gorge upon, while the surplus is recycled back into the population through your drinking water. Very *green* of me, don't you agree?"

"But the flares began a week ago. You killed my mother..." The rage again, cutting off her air. "Eight years ago," she spit the words out. "There weren't any flares."

It grinned, sniffing the air, and took a step closer to her.

"Eight years is nothing, ignorant one. It took many more years of travel to make this pit stop. It can be difficult, even for me, to predict solar occurrences with perfect accuracy, so I had some time to *kill*."

Anna felt the warm, sticky wetness of blood on her palms. The demon waited for her reaction, wanting her rage, but also, Anna realized, to *impress* her.

She peered around the tank, feigning confusion and fearful reverence, stalling for time. "Since the storms began, you've channeled pain energy here through the portals?"

The platform creaked as it took another step toward her.

"Do you still not understand? This water is an energetic *sewer*. One that you fill your doughy bellies with, increasing your suffering tenfold, which in turn further increases the potency of the portal in-flow. You are the power source." It spread its arms over the dark water and puffed out its chest. "And this is the bomb. Hours from now the storms will end. But before that, I'll have the pleasure of watching the vermin of this town rip each other apart like the feral beasts they are. It will be my long awaited dessert. I'll leave this rock with more power than any of my kind has ever amassed and make those that exiled me suffer for all eternity."

So it *was* a demon in one sense of the word. A fallen angel of sorts, ruled by its raging ego, banished after breaking the rules of its advanced community and now an exile seeking vengeance and power.

Jack taught her that the best way to battle spirits was to tap into their belief systems. But the demon seemed to believe in nothing but itself. It took another step toward her, close enough that she could see dark wads of pain mud in between its teeth.

The demon was going to kill her, drown her in the hateful seas below, sucking in her fear as she died. But first it wanted her to know how superior it was. Her heart banging in her chest, Anna retreated another step and felt the tank wall on her back.

Jack's words from Izzy's exorcism came back to her. *If we get him to show off, it'll wear him out.*

"Sounds like your kind are very evolved. Where do you fit in with the gang?"

The demon's eyes narrowed. "Make sense, maggot."

"I mean, you chose to prey on us lowly amoebas for years? Where's the victory in that? No wonder they got rid of you. You're a coward, like a bully that picks on the youngest, smallest kids it can find."

It closed the distance between them with one long stride. Inches from her face, it reeked of electrocuted flesh. It took everything Anna had not to bolt for the hatch.

"What you think you see," it said, "is the quantum slice that I reduce myself to so your ape eyes can take me in. You have no idea what I can do."

Anna waved her hand in front of her face, dispersing its foul breath.

"Let's see you then."

"You cannot *see* me."

"So what, you're an alien?"

"To you, I'm a god."

"Prove it!" Her words ricocheted sharply off the tank walls.

It spat in Anna's face. Cold clumps of pain mud slid down her cheeks. Glaring at her, it moved back to the center of the platform. The demon's mouth dropped open and Anna braced herself for another pelting. But its mouth kept opening, stretching until the skin on its Saul face was reduced to a featureless band of flesh surrounding a gaping black hole. The hole emitted metallic scratching sounds that made Anna's teeth hurt. She pressed her back into the tank wall, covering her ears. This was it. The Big Show.

The dark cavity of the demon's face continued to stretch, curving back on itself, dissolving away its costume flesh from the inside out. What was left was a rolling, dark distortion made of slow moving waves—a rippling black river of energy hanging horizontal in the air. On the crest of one wave came a booming pulse of sound, thick with a thumping harmonic like a bass-heavy car radio, *boom, boom, boom.*

Anna felt the sound as much as she heard it, in her head, her diaphragm and the base of her spine. Her teeth ached like she'd fallen asleep with turbo bleaching strips in her night guard. If there was anything in her stomach, it would have shown itself in a spectacular way.

With every *boom* came a surge of static energy followed by bursts of color and gelatinous flesh. *Boom, boom, boom.* The demon sprouted into a skinny old man wearing Bermuda shorts and a green sweatshirt that said "#1 Grandpa."

Boom, boom, boom and the flesh was changing again, forming into a young girl. She was wearing a private school uniform and had braided hair and skinny legs

I like to play, it had said, *to learn.* How many people had it possessed and killed? How many families had it destroyed? Bile burned the back of Anna's throat as the little girl's arms stretched into gray tentacles that shot up and suctioned to the ceiling. The demon swung its girl body off of the platform and hung from the ceiling.

Boom, boom, boom. The girl body spread apart, ripping in some places, stitching itself together in others, morphing into something like a huge gray jellyfish but with a wide mouth that held several rows of shark like teeth. Eyes were forming along the tentacles and across the gray folds of its body, *hundreds* of blinking black eyes, moving independently of each other.

Anna's hand went to her own eyes, peeking at the horror through her fingers while her bladder threatened to empty. It wasn't too late. She could run to the hatch while the demon was occupied with its theatrics. Her legs tightened, ready to bolt, but something inside her resisted.

This jellyfish thing had once been invaded by the demon. It was a life from another world, probably tortured to death, and now the demon wore its likeness like a trophy fur.

Anna dropped her hands and saw that there were scars on a section of its gray flesh concentrated in a splash pattern. She recognized them as the wounds she'd inflicted on the demon's Saul body when she accidentally spit holy on its chest. No matter how much the demon fed, no matter what it morphed into, the wounds of Source were permanent. But what did it matter if they weren't enough to hurt it? She felt defeated.

"If it's this powerful," Anna wondered aloud, "why doesn't it just kill me?"

"Because it wants you to worship it."

It was Jack's voice and he sounded *pissed*.

Anna swung around. Geneva was back on the platform, and damn it, she'd brought Jack.

"Trouble doesn't even begin to describe the crap storm you're in for sneaking out," Jack said to Anna, his temple vein popping. He yanked a spray bottle of holy water from inside his jacket.

The demon detached its tentacles from the ceiling with a wet *pop* and shot into the water. There was a frenzied splashing and then a smacking sound. It was in the water under the ledge, out of sight and lapping at the walls.

Anna gestured to the spray bottle. "That won't be enough." She took a breath. "It's *the* demon, Dad."

Jack looked at Geneva. "What's she talking about?"

"She didn't want me to tell you," Geneva said, her voice wavering.

"Tell me what?"

"There is no demon controlling Saul," Anna said. "There is no Saul. The demon, Dad, it's *still here*. It's the demon that killed Mom."

Pain dust funneled into Jack's nose and mouth as he inhaled. His lips moved, but the *what?* died in his mouth. His eyes receded into his head and his face contorted into a mask of hate, the evil in the tank already inside him.

The planks creaked as something heavy and wet slapped against the bottom of the platform. The demon's voice rose through the wood.

"You wanted her dead, didn't you, Jacky boy? That's why she stopped fighting."

Its cackling filled the tank as Jack's face darkened. The demon slithered over the platform's edge and stood, facing them, wearing its Saul costume.

"You wanted Helen to stop breathing her ragged breath on the back of your neck every night," it said. "And when she did, you took your first deep breath in months." It clucked its tongue. "Tsk, tsk, tsk."

Jack charged and the demon opened its arms to receive him. Jack rammed into it, punching the open spray bottle into the demon's chest. They joined in a freakish embrace and tumbled together off the ledge, hitting the water with a giant splash. A murky foam rose in the water but quickly settled. Jack popped up, retching.

"Get out of the water!" Anna screamed.

"The ladder!" Geneva shouted, pointing toward the side wall near the edge of the platform.

As Jack swam toward the ladder, two tentacles shot out of the foam and stuck to the ceiling. The demon swung itself out of the water, shaking the foam from its flesh, wearing its Saul face but with tentacles instead of arms.

There were patches on its tentacles so thin that spider webs of green veins were visible; the connective tissue either not fully formed or failing. Anna felt a rush of pleasure. Jack's holy water did some damage.

The demon suctioned itself across the ceiling and plucked Jack from the foam with a pickled tentacle, tossing him through the air.

"Leave him alone!" Anna screamed.

Jack hit the tank wall hard, falling back into the water. He popped up and locked eyes with Anna, mouthing the word *run*. The last traces of foam hissed away in the water, and the dark pain lava reclaimed its dominance. The demon shot back into the liquid depths, immersing its wounds, and emerged seconds later to bare its teeth at Anna, hissing like a snake.

"Little girls, jellyfish and old men!" Anna shouted. "Is that supposed to impress me? Come up here and get *me*, you coward." Her nails dug into her wounded palms.

The demon licked it lips, eyes half closed in twisted ecstasy.

"But the water is so lovely. Won't you join me for a little dip, wash off some of that stink?"

Anna's fingers twitched as the rage energy in the tank pressed into her ears. She wanted to hurl herself onto the demon and tear at it. There were so many little wounds to claw.

Geneva touched Anna's arm. "You have to be calm to connect to Source, right? For the cleansing to work?"

Yeah, no shit. With her heart and head pounding in unison, the concept of calm felt like a pipe dream. Anna struggled to control her breath, pushing back against the tide of rage inside her. Yet, despite their predicament, Geneva appeared remarkably unruffled. Was Geneva somehow more immune to the malevolence in the tank?

Whatever connection Anna had to Source was almost gone. She could still see the dark churning of Bloomtown's pain energy in the water, but it was like the after burn from a camera flash, disjointed and spotty.

Jack struggled to climb the ladder, stunned from slamming into the wall.

"Is there any salt left in your backpack?" Geneva asked.

Anna shook her head.

"We still have some in Emi's bag," Geneva said, holding out the satchel.

"You do it. You say the blessing."

"But, Anna, I don't know the blessing."

"Say one of your speeches, ad lib, whatever, just *hurry.*"

Reluctant acceptance moved over Geneva's face. She readied the satchel, squatting at the edge of the platform. The demon was floating in the water, sniffing at the air. And then it spoke.

"He thought of the girl whenever he was with you. It was the only way he could stomach your touch." The demon clicked its tongue in false pity. "That was the two of you, wasn't it, Geneva? Him aching for her so *desperately* and you too stupid to see the truth."

Rattled, Geneva fell onto one knee, crying out in pain. So much for her immunity. Anna reached out to steady her, feeling the scientist shaking under her grasp.

"She came to him when you were in class," it said. "Did you know that? It got him all worked up, listening to you get ready to leave, knowing that she'd soon be in his arms and in your bed."

Geneva cursed and tore at the bag's zipper until it ripped open. Anna yanked Geneva back from the edge, taking the satchel from her hands.

"Forget it." She'd put Geneva in enough danger. "This is my fight."

"Anna?" a feminine voice rang out, bouncing around the tank.

The demon was using her mother's voice. Bracing herself, Anna looked down at the water. Helen Fagan was treading water and wearing the blue and white striped oversized T-shirt that she used to sleep in.

"How could you leave me with this thing?" it asked Anna. "It's dark all the time and so cold." The demon broke into a sob just like her mother used to, lips trembling, chin crumpled. Anna felt herself scattering again, felt her knees start to buckle.

"Helen?" It was Jack's voice. Then louder and exuberant. "Helen!"

The demon turned toward him.

"Did you ever love me, Jack?" it said. "Because I'm begging you, *help me*."

"What's Jack doing?" Geneva asked.

Anna dropped to her belly. Gripping the edge of the platform, she peered down at the ladder.

Damnit. "He's going back down," Anna said. Back toward the venomous water. A crazed joy punctuated the raw longing on his face, and Anna couldn't help but be swept up by the same delusional hope. Helen Fagan had come back to them.

"That thing is not your mother, Anna." Geneva said. "It's a trap."

But what if it wasn't?

"Look at me," Geneva said, and Anna twisted her head back, pain shooting down her neck. "The demon lies."

Anna nodded, holding tight to the edge of the platform, rooting her body to the wood. *Breathe, Fagan. Don't fly away.*

"Dad!" she screamed.

Her father snapped his head up to look at her.

"That's *not* Mom," Anna said, the rough wood digging into her ribs.

Jack stopped moving down the ladder, his head swiveling between Anna and the thing in the water, confusion clouding his face.

"Please, Jack, it's gone now but it will come back," the mother thing said, struggling to stay afloat. "We have to go now while we still can. Get me out of this water and let's go home, baby." It glanced up at Anna. "She's not well. The demon poisoned her. It's not her fault." The mother thing went under again and emerged seconds later coughing up water.

Jack continued down the ladder, leaning out over the water. *Oh shit.* He was going to jump in. Geneva and Anna yelled at him to stop.

"I need a better look," he called back to them, descending another rung.

Anna had to direct the demon's focus away from Jack.

"Mom!" Anna shouted. But when the thing in the water looked up at her, Anna realized that she'd been wholly unprepared for how the moment would stomp on the reasonable part of her mind—the part that understood full well it wasn't her mother answering her call. Unprepared for how good it felt to have the thing look up at her and say *what is it, honey?* Unprepared for the desperate want to pull her mother to the ladder, to save her this time instead of just watching her die.

And then, from the immediacy of that fantasy, from the possible realization of such fervent hope, some of the lost nuances of Helen Fagan returned to Anna's mind. The way her mother smelled like freshly sanded wood and lilac oil when she came out of the garage. The way she'd pile her hair on top of her head when she worked, sawdust dampening its luster, like a proud goddess sending rains of woodchips down to her subjects. The way Helen's eyes had narrowed when Anna's grandmother sent Anna a pink, plastic vanity for Christmas— one that said "Someday your prince will come!" when a button was pushed. How Helen had Anna write a thank you note before taking the vanity out to the garage and handing her a hammer.

Helen Fagan was a warrior. She'd fought to the very end of her life, doing whatever she could to protect her family. Anna's mother wouldn't be treading water and crying for someone to save her. She'd swim to the goddamn ladder and pull herself out.

A certainty swept through Anna. Her mother wasn't in that water. The demon was. A demon who thrived on lies, on taking the worst of who someone was and making it bloom inside them like a poisonous flower until the poison was all they felt, all they believed they were. And the lie the demon told now was that it still had power over Helen Fagan. It was a lie that had tormented Anna since she was a child, that had embittered her. For that lie was made of hate and blame, and there could be no peace in the Fagan house when it filled the empty spaces, worming its way to the surface no matter how much Jack tried to bury it with his hoard.

"It's not her!" Anna yelled to her father. "It's a trick!"

Anna knew *exactly* where her mother was now. The demon hadn't counted on that. That question had been answered and she was finally free of it.

Something in Anna's voice made Jack believe her. He reversed his climb and headed back up the ladder, struggling with each step.

"I'll pull him up," Geneva said. "The cleansing, don't give up."

Anna reached back for the satchel and then hovered it over the water.

"Wherever this salt falls shall be free—," she turned the bag upside down, but it was empty. *Damn it.* The salt must have fallen out when Geneva ripped it open.

The demon was in the water next to the ladder, struggling to shift. *Boom, boom, boom.* From its Helen torso came two hairy arms as long as tentacles, but with floppy, boneless fingers that flapped against the ladder instead of sticking to it.

Anna continued without the salt. "These waters shall be free from the attacks of malicious entities and protected by the powers of Source."

But the words coming from her mouth fell off her tongue, limp and powerless. The blessing was a dud. The demon hoisted itself up the ladder with its long arms, trailing its tongue against the filthy wall as it climbed. Helen's hair grew wildly out of its head along with clumps of schoolgirl braids.

Anna joined Geneva by the ladder to help pull Jack onto the platform. Bitter tears stung her eyes.

"It's over," Anna said. "We have to run."

Jack was inches away from Geneva's outstretched hand.

"Do you trust me, Anna?"

Without Geneva, Anna might never have found her mother's soul.

"I do."

"You connected with Source before, and you can do it again."

Jack was almost in reach when the demon wrapped a hairy arm around his ankle, dragging him down a few rungs before he kicked free. It began lapping at the wall again, feeding. After its vigorous display of power, the demon was tired. And so was Jack. His arms trembled as he pulled himself back up the ladder. Her father's eyes rolled back for a moment, the whites of his eyes blueish under Emi's light. He already had a head injury and was just tossed against a wall. Jack could pass out and be dragged into the cesspool and drowned if Anna didn't do something *now*.

The demon was not all powerful, the wounds on its body attested to that. If it had a belief system outside of its own entitlement, it must include a fear of Source. If Anna could personify that fear—

"My mother lives," she shouted down to it. "You couldn't destroy her spirit. Only Source governs the destiny of souls! You're not strong enough, not even close."

She leaned over the top of the ladder at the platform edge, hoping to look menacing and fearless while doing everything she could to quell the chaos inside her.

"I see your lies, demon, because I am an extension of Source, a *weapon* of Source."

The demon hissed at her from the water, for the moment forgetting about Jack. Anna closed her eyes, trying to strengthen the traces of Source within her, to recreate the sensations she'd felt on the roof outside her bedroom, the calm that allowed her to hush her chattering monkey mind. But with her father in jeopardy and the demon below, that seemed impossible. She needed a shortcut.

Anna concentrated on the last vestiges of Source inside her, silently asking for guidance. An image popped into her head, a memory: driving down the Garden State Parkway with Dor in the back and Freddy steering Major Tom. Freddy had cracked his window causing the air pressure to rise in the jeep as a pulsating wind pushed inside it. Anna had to open her window, too, so the air could move freely.

It was the same memory she thought of before leaving her body—making that connection was the push she needed to open up to Source. But now it was Freddy she was focused on, and Dor in the back—all of them laughing at some joke. Anna had felt safe with them even while hurtling down a highway full of ragey commuters. Could it be there, in moments like that, that Anna could find the peace she needed? If some memories could torment and paralyze her, maybe others could strengthen her connection to Source. She let the memories come.

Anna's parents surprising her on her seventh birthday with a new puppy. Penelope saying hello with a flurry of paws and licks.

Doreen, Freddy, and Anna camping in Freddy's backyard, telling ghost stories and holding hands. Anna feels their small hands in hers, their softness.

Freddy and Anna on the slant of roof outside her bedroom window, playing the what-if game. Not holding hands, older now, sensing the danger in it. What if each person was their own universe?

Or what if each cell in every living thing held a universe of its own? They feel, for a moment, the expansiveness of Source.

The wooden planks began to tremble beneath her. No. It wasn't the platform. It was Anna. She was *vibrating*. Suddenly, a sound, *her* sound—the same sound she heard while out of body—grew stronger inside until she vibrated like a guitar string. It was purifying, shaking away what didn't belong, what wasn't real. Anna didn't brace against it. She let it flow.

And then a crack opened inside her, and Anna was brave and let it widen. Source spilled into her and she felt herself expand, felt herself *everywhere*, a part of something vast and powerful. A simple truth was clear: the demon couldn't destroy Anna's connection to Source. It could only distract her from it, like the manic tornado of her own infected mind. As in Freddy's dream about the tear in the fabric of the universe, Source was always there, waiting for her behind the madness. She locked eyes with the demon and the sneer wilted on its face—now a grotesque mash-up of Helen's features and gray folds of jellyfish skin.

"You're an outcast," Anna said, "like I am. But I have Dor and Freddy. I have my dad."

"You have me too," Geneva said from behind her. "Now, *go*."

Anna sucked in a huge lungful or air, taking perhaps the deepest breath of her life. Feeling Source well up inside her, ready to burst, she dug the tips of her sneakers into the wood and pushed herself off the platform, going airborne. That was when it screamed.

Splash. Anna hit the water arms first, head dipped in a perfect dive. She opened her eyes in the center of a mushroom cloud of energy that expanded in a flash so bright it should have blinded her, but didn't sting her eyes at all. For a microsecond she was aware of the demon in the water. It was collapsing, flesh and energy, wave and particle, imploding into itself, annihilated.

Anna pushed off the bottom of the tank and swam upward, surrounded by clear blue water, taking another huge breath when she broke through the surface. The tank walls sparkled under Emi's blue light, wet and clean from the explosion of purified water. Geneva beamed down at her from the platform edge, Jack standing next to her. He was swollen and drenched, but other than that he looked okay.

Minutes later, the sun cleared the horizon as Geneva, Jack and Anna emerged from the hatch. They were almost to their cars when the pumping station at the base of the tower rumbled to life. Good morning, Bloomtown.

CHAPTER TWENTY-THREE

THE HANGOVER

C oach Pickens was dead. A housecleaner found his body in the shower yesterday morning. The grisly news broke on Ocean County Crime, a website linking to local news in Portersville, Bloomtown, and a handful of other South Jersey towns. "Solar Flares Reach Peak, Then Fizzle Out!" was below the story about Pickens's death; right under that was "Unprecedented Looting Ends in Bloomtown." Anna scrolled down the page until she found the story she hoped nobody would follow up on: "Elderly Resident Claims Hooligans Climbed Water Tower."

Eager to get back to school, Anna didn't have time to fully process Pickens' fate or the general aftermath of the solar flares. She threw on an acceptable outfit, went downstairs to the kitchen and found Jack washing dishes at the sink. Geneva stood next to him holding a dish towel.

"We thought you might want to take another day off," Geneva said, taking a plate from Jack and drying it.

We? Jack and Geneva were now a "we" apparently. The two of them looked awkward as hell, like they were playing house, but it was still kind of cute.

"I changed my mind," Anna said, exhausted but dying to see Dor and Freddy and catch up on the assignments she missed. Instead of going to school yesterday, she spent the day napping and, along with Jack and Geneva, running the taps in the house to flush out any remnants of the poisoned water.

Dor was staying at Freddy's. Cindy was at the hospital in stable condition and expected to be discharged soon. Dor and Freddy skipped school yesterday, too, feeling queasy and exhausted. Freddy's parents had also come down with a nasty "stomach bug," and from his overly-detailed description, it was a veritable smorgasbord of gastrointestinal distress at Casa Simms.

In a series of texts rife with emojis, Anna had told her two friends about the water tower trip and ensuing demise of the demon. She'd also tended to Geneva and Jack who were both sick with night sweats and nausea. Anna felt tired but not ill, as if all the bad juju had been blasted out of her in the explosion of Source energy inside the tank, sparing her a painful detox.

She asked Jack for a ride to school, ignoring the surprise on his face. Anna usually declined his offers to drive her to school because his presence was an unwelcome reminder that she was the daughter of a ghost-busting weirdo.

As soon as Anna got into the car, she noticed that the mess in the backseat had been rearranged in an almost organized manner. The Ouija Queen sat on the dashboard.

"Is the spirit board going back to the client?" she asked.

"Nope, to the office. I'm setting up a new clearing station there."

Anna eyed the Ouija Queen. That bratty little trickster was no doubt still bound to the spirit board inside.

"That'll slide off once we start moving. I'll hold it," Anna said, bringing the Ouija Queen to her lap. Before Jack could protest, she said "Cleaning up a bit, I see."

"Geneva thought it would be a good idea to get started with that first thing this morning."

Any suggestion that he should clean up normally set Jack's teeth on edge. Was it the portal free, fresh water vibe in Bloomtown that made him so agreeable, or the presence of a certain scientist from California?

"You're into her, aren't you?" Anna asked, as Jack pulled out of the driveway.

"Who?"

"Please."

"Geneva is a special woman. But I want you to know that the relationship your mother and I had, well, it's not something that can ever be replaced. Not something that I can easily move on from."

"You can trust me on this one. Mom has moved on."

He raised an eyebrow, but this wasn't the time. She'd tell him the whole story later. Right now she had another agenda. Distracting Jack with small talk, Anna turned to the backseat, finding something small and secure enough for her needs. A small velvet bag that Jack used to hold vials of holy water. Relaxing back into her seat, she curled the velvet bag into one hand and placed the other on top of the Ouija Queen box. The vibrations came seconds later.

The power running through Anna's body had dimmed considerably since the blast of Source energy in the water tank. But it was still there. She felt it inside her purring like a sleeping leopard. She only had to concentrate on her hand to send Source vibrations down into the box. The Trickster, she knew, would now be desperate to get out.

As Jack muttered condemnations of the other drivers navigating Route 33 rush hour, Anna placed the mouth of the velvet bag at the corner of the Ouija Queen box. She lifted the corner lid and closed the mouth of the velvet bag around the small opening.

The bag puffed as a blast of air blew into it. Anna pulled the drawstring, closing it tightly, and then encircled the bag with her hands. She sent another faint jolt of Source vibrations around the outside of the bag to keep the Trickster trapped inside.

Anna had Jack pull up to the curb directly in front of the school, and when a few kids stopped to gawk at them she rolled down her window and spoke loudly.

"Okay, Pops, see you later for the devil-worshipping session at five. You have your shovel, right? Have a good day at the graveyard. Remember, the fresher the better!"

Jack chuckled and the looky-loo kids moved on sheepishly. Anna hopped out of the car and then leaned back in the passenger-side window.

"Thanks for the ride."

"I love you, Sweet Pea," Jack said. "You know that, right?"

Jack didn't know that those were her mother's last words. The memories came: the blaring of a horn, stuck and broken, the smell of Mrs. Flanagan's coat. But Anna didn't resist them, and they passed through her like a rogue cloud on a sunny day.

"You, too," Anna said.

It was just energy in motion. She was still okay, still Anna Fagan, also known as Goblin Girl, and that was good enough for her. Anna walked into Bloomtown High and across the cavernous commons. Craig Shine was leaning against a column in the cafeteria. He waved her over and Anna moved toward him, feeling Source energy humming through her body. Was her supercharged connection to Source permanent? Time would tell.

Craig's eyes flitted about, finally landing on her face.

"Izzy got expelled," he said, "for uploading that video from a school computer."

"Yeah, I know," Anna said. "A detective called my house yesterday and talked to my father. Principal Steuben, too."

"Oh shit. I hope you didn't get in trouble."

"Why would I get in trouble?"

He stared back at her stupidly.

"If things are cool with us," he said, fidgeting with the silver studs on his leather jacket, "Mom's out of town and we're gonna play a set in the basement. You could come over tonight. That is…if things are cool."

"I don't hate you if that's what you're asking."

Craig put his hands in his pockets and then took them out again. He was the nervous one now. Anna thought about what it might be like, listening to awful Manarchists music in a stuffy basement. She'd had it up to here with basements, but still she said, "Yeah, I'll come."

Craig said he'd text her his address, which Anna already knew by heart—she'd made Freddy and Dor drive by his house a couple times over the summer—but she kept that to herself.

"Did you hear about Pickens?" Craig asked. "They think he had a heart attack."

"Bummer," she said, without much sincerity, then spotted Dor and Freddy standing by her locker. She said goodbye to Craig and half-ran across the commons, giving them both a hug, breathing in the Freddy smell and Doreen's abundance of citrusy perfume.

"Are you *sniffing* us?" Freddy asked, amused.

Anna shrugged and turned to Dor. "Any updates on Cindy?"

"She'll be home in a couple days," Dor said. "The wound in her back is still infected, but they're pumping her full of antibiotics. She won't stop apologizing, but I keep telling her it wasn't her fault."

Dor's eyes glistened and Anna hugged her again.

"What did Shine want?" Freddy asked stiffly.

"He's got cojones trying to talk to you after what he pulled," Dor said.

"Not to worry," Anna told them. "I'm handling it. You know, I was thinking tonight's a great night for a space gaze. The aurora borealis is finally gone and we could get a good look at the stars."

Freddy twisted his mouth like he was mulling it over. "I'll have to check my schedule."

"You do that. I'll be over around nine. So, anyways"— Anna linked arms with her friends—"I was thinking. You two want to go into the family business with me? How about we start our own branch, maybe score a reality show. We could call ourselves the Paranormal Investigative Society—P.I.S. Thoughts?"

"Piss?" Freddy sounded dubious.

"Hmm," Anna said, rubbing her chin. "It may need a little work."

"It's got potential, though!" Doreen said, blushing with excitement.

They walked down the hallway, turned a corner and ran right into Sydney, who was leaning against the old wood-shop door and tapping on her phone. Her Disney-princess eyes flared at the sight of them. Anna wondered if she'd heard about Pickens.

"Hey, slut," Sydney said halfheartedly to Anna. "Flash anyone lately?"

"It was just a bra, Syd," Anna said, facing her beautiful once-friend and whipping up her shirt. Anna had the "grandma special" on again today, but screw it. It was comfy. "Get over it."

Sydney stared, her expression unreadable. Freddy and Dor erupted with laughter.

"Yeah, Syd," Doreen said, giggling so much that she could hardly get the words out. "It's just a bra."

And with that, Doreen lifted her sweater and flashed *her* bra at Sydney, inadvertently exposing the two sweat-sucker pads that she'd attached to her under-sleeves.

Sydney furrowed her brow, confused.

And then Freddy did something incredible. He reached out, ripped the sweat-suckers from Doreen's shirt and turned his back.

"Yeah, Syd," he said, turning back around and lifting his sweatshirt. The sweat-suckers were strategically placed on his bare chest, sticky-side down. It was a maxi-pad bra. "Get over it already!"

The three of them laughed harder than they had in a while, maybe ever, holding on to each other while intermittently gasping for air. And then Sydney actually did seem to get over something—perhaps that echo chamber inside her that whispered *boys will be boys* until her heart had turned to granite. Maybe since they clearly had no shame, some of Sydney's shame, too, was released like a cloud of noxious gas. Instead of pointing her cell at them or calling for one of her cronies, Sydney rolled her eyes, suppressing the beginnings of a smile, and stalked off.

• • •

Craig's New Bloomtown basement was furnished with all the latest accessories his parents' guilt could buy. But despite the plush carpeting, super-sized TV and game consoles, it still smelled like mold. Craig had been bellowing the same verse for several minutes, spraying spit all over his microphone as his band thrashed away behind him.

Cattle people in the schools
Cattle people in the cubes
Cattle people in my head
Cattle people should be dead
Die cattle people! Die!

Feedback from his microphone screeched in Anna's ears as the "song" finally ended—she'd sat through seven of them in total—but she remained blissfully headache free. In fact, her head felt oddly buoyant atop her neck after all the skull crushers she'd endured over the last nine days. Craig hopped off the makeshift stage the band had thrown together and sauntered over to Anna. She said she needed some air and he followed her outside to his front yard.

"Heard Denton got fired," he said.

"I figured. There was a sub today."

"The one with the big fake tits?"

Groan. What did she ever see in this clown? "I guess. She wasn't feeling so well, though. She puked in the garbage can half way through class and excused herself. Probably had the flu that's going around. Did you get it? You look a little rough."

"Nah, just hungover. Nothing contagious." He kicked at something on the ground. "Wanna hang later, just us two?"

"Can't do it," Anna said.

"Still pissed, huh?"

Craig had applied his guy liner with impressive precision, the deep brown of his brooding eyes artfully accentuated. Anna took him in: the studs on his leather jacket, the large chain hanging off his skinnies, the ripped T-shirt exposing sections of his stomach. The whole getup suddenly looked contrived and kind of sad, like a hand-me-down Halloween costume that didn't quite fit. And who was he underneath that costume? Anna had to admit that she had no idea, but she had an inkling he might be devastatingly boring.

"Not so much," she said. "I do have plans, though, so I gotta get going. Want to hug it out?"

He seemed surprised by her confidence. She normally tittered and swooned in his presence like an aging Belieber with a backstage pass.

"That's cool," he said, and opened his arms.

If Craig wanted to apologize, it wasn't necessary. Anna knew that the portals and poisoned water were behind his wretchedness, at least mostly. But he wasn't getting off scot-free for that webcam stunt. No freakin' way.

Anna went in for the hug, enduring the pokes from various studs and buckles as she slipped the velvet bag into one of the pockets of his leather jacket. It wouldn't take long for the small amount of Source energy that she'd placed on the bag to fade away. And when it was gone, the Trickster would emerge and claim its new target, finding its way into Craig's room, Anna was sure, and devising endless ways to torment him. It wasn't cold-hearted revenge she sought, merely the room-temperature variety.

"Yo, Shine."

It was Izzy. He'd pulled up to the curb in his mom's white Camry. His faced paled at the sight of Anna.

"He's dropping something off," Craig said. "I'll get rid of him."

Craig walked over to Izzy's car, reaching in his back pocket for some cash. Perhaps Izzy had taken over his jailed brother's profession and started selling weed. Anna couldn't be sure. She didn't catch what Izzy handed to Craig because her eyes were locked onto Izzy's face, imagining how the bones of his nose might crunch under her fist. Of course, she'd probably break her hand if she face-punched him for real. But the sudden rage inside her didn't want to be bothered with reality.

She said a quick goodbye to Craig—rattled by the murderous anger churning inside her—and cut through his neighbor's backyard to the back road leading to Old Bloomtown. A block from Eden Street, Anna leaned against a telephone pole and rubbed her eyes. The portals were gone, weren't they? The demon destroyed. She'd watched it die, *felt* it die in that water tank. But even as worry and doubt fluttered through her, she was aware of the cool wind rustling the canopy of pine needles overhead, of her feet rooting her to the earth. Yes, it was still there, the light but steady hum of Source energy running through her. And she didn't have a headache.

Perhaps because she'd repeatedly experienced the intensity of the portal-fueled rage—that evil welling up inside her time and again—it lived inside her now. It was a part of her, just as the Source energy was. She might always have to battle that evil. Maybe everyone in Bloomtown would.

Anna made her way to Freddy's back yard. The silhouettes of her two friends were visible in the waning moonlight, along with the cylindrical shape of Freddy's telescope pointed toward the sky. The puppies were there too. Their wiggly small forms put an instant lump in Anna's throat that made her hesitant to pet them as they nipped and lapped at her ankles. Penelope's spirit remained whole and vital in another realm, but Anna still mourned the dog's loss. Quickly boring of her, the pups ran off to investigate some bushes.

Anna's arrival had interrupted an argument between Dor and Freddy over potential puppy names. They were each keeping a puppy and after greeting Anna finally agreed on Itchy and Scratchy. Their quibbling then shifted to how to best use the star-mapping app on Freddy's phone.

"Why don't we go old school tonight?" Anna suggested, sitting down on the grass. Big mistake. The puppies were on her in an instant, slobbering on her face. Dor and Freddy came to her rescue, lying on either side of Anna and absorbing some of the puppy drool. Itchy and Scratchy moved on to chasing each other around the yard, and the three of them were left to ponder the waning moon and starry sky.

After a few minutes of silence Doreen said, "Kind of creepy knowing what's out there."

"What's down here isn't always that great either," Freddy said.

"What if," Anna said, "there are other people, other friends like us—aliens, I guess—having their own space gaze right at this moment?"

"Statistically speaking," Freddy said, "it's possible there are hundreds of thousands, if not millions, of intelligent life forms in the universe doing exactly that."

Freddy didn't respond with a *what if* of his own. He was sulking a bit, Anna could tell. He'd probably heard about her appearance at Craig's. She turned to Dor.

"Anything new on your mom's homecoming?"

"Tomorrow," Dor said. "A healthcare aide is helping out until she can get around on her own."

Anna felt herself relax. "I predict she'll be in a much better mood." Having Cindy home would make Bloomtown feel close to normal again.

Dor's eyes glowed mischievously.

"Me too. Thanks for all those texts. Freddy also filled me in on the demonic real estate dude's visit to his house...and *the kiss*." Dor made an exaggerated kissing face at the two of them, saying to Anna, "Kinda pervy kissing someone when they're asleep."

Anna's heart raced. The light-body kiss. Freddy had felt it.

"Dor, shut up. You have the biggest mouth," Freddy said.

"Sorry, but I'm *not* shutting up this time. I've been through enough crapola lately, and from now on I'm gonna say what I want whether you like it or not. Now this thing with you two? It's *your* problem, not mine. So you deal with it, because it's annoying. And you know what else? I want shotgun sometimes on the way to school."

"Somebody's getting feisty!" Anna said.

Freddy pumped his fists. "Let's get ready to Reeeenie!"

"He promised nothing would change between us," Dor said to Anna. "That we'd still be together, all of us, no matter what."

"Of course," Anna said, feeling discombobulated. "Duh."

Dor was only worried about their friendship changing. She didn't have a crush on Freddy?

"Well, how was I supposed to know?" Dor said. "You two are either pissed at each other and acting like I don't exist, or there's this weird tension and you're acting like I don't exist. Please go somewhere and make out already. Somewhere far from me preferably, because, yeah, *gross*. I need some time before I can witness that."

Freddy sat up on his elbows.

"Do you hear something?" he asked Anna.

Anna feigned confusion. "From where?"

"This general direction." Freddy gestured toward Doreen.

"Don't be silly," Anna said. "For something to make a noise it must *exist*."

Dor stuck a finger into the air. "Aha! But I must exist, you see, because you"—she pinched Freddy's arm—"spent all night with me in the hospital, and you"—Anna got pinched —"went all super hero and saved me *and* my mom. So I feel pretty good about this friendship, and that whatever happens with you two isn't going to mess it up."

Settling back on the grass, they were quiet for a while. There was a chill in the air and Anna felt the heat from Freddy's face on her cheek. Dor broke the somewhat awkward silence by announcing that she'd decided to only drink bottled water, but wasn't sure now because she heard about a huge blob of discarded water bottles floating in the ocean that was the size of Texas.

"Do you know anything about that?" she asked Freddy, slyly nudging Anna.

As Freddy launched into a monologue about The Great Pacific Garbage Patch, Anna and Dor shared a smirk in the darkness, each knowing that pontificating on the subject would put him at ease. While he explained that the patch wasn't a mass of water bottles, consisting instead of tiny particles of degraded plastic, Anna ran her cold fingers through the grass. She remembered how each blade in her own yard had sparkled with intricate life while she was out of body. There was so much to explore, right there, where she'd always been. Anna just hadn't realized it before. Soon enough, her fingers found Freddy's hand in the grass.

CPSIA information can be obtained
at www.ICGtesting.com
Printed in the USA
LVHW111718120919
630868LV00006B/823/P